W9-CDH-399

French Fried

KYLIE LOGAN

BERKLEY PRIME CRIME
New York

BERKLEY PRIME CRIME
Published by Berkley
An imprint of Penguin Random House LLC
375 Hudson Street, New York, New York 10014

Copyright © 2017 by Connie Laux
Excerpt from *Irish Stewed* copyright © 2016 by Connie Laux
Penguin Random House supports copyright. Copyright fuels creativity, encourages
diverse voices, promotes free speech, and creates a vibrant culture. Thank you for buying
an authorized edition of this book and for complying with copyright laws by not
reproducing, scanning, or distributing any part of it in any form without permission.
You are supporting writers and allowing Penguin Random House to continue to
publish books for every reader.

BERKLEY is a registered trademark and BERKLEY PRIME CRIME and the B colophon
are trademarks of Penguin Random House LLC.

ISBN 9780425274897

First Edition: June 2017

Printed in the United States of America
1   3   5   7   9   10   8   6   4   2

Cover art by Tom Foty
Book design by Kelly Lipovich

This is a work of fiction. Names, characters, places, and incidents either are the product
of the author's imagination or are used fictitiously, and any resemblance to actual persons,
living or dead, business establishments, events, or locales is entirely coincidental.

PUBLISHER'S NOTE: The recipes contained in this book have been created for the
ingredients and techniques indicated. The Publisher is not responsible for your specific
health or allergy needs that may require supervision. Nor is the Publisher responsible for
any adverse reactions you may have to the recipes contained in the book, whether you
follow them as written or modify them to suit your personal dietary needs or tastes.

If you purchased this book without a cover, you should be aware that this book is stolen
property. It was reported as "unsold and destroyed" to the publisher, and neither the author
nor the publisher has received any payment for this "stripped book."

Sedro-Woolley Library
802 Ball Street
Sedro-Woolley WA 98284

June 2017

"A fun and intriguing read . . . cannot wait for the next in this series."
—Open Book Society

"A delightfully entertaining debut to a series that I hope is here to stay."
—Dru's Book Musings

A Gallic Getaway

I left Declan somewhere behind me in the crowd when I inched my way to the curb.

By the time I got there, MacLain's car was already stopped at the grandstand, and the historian—book still raised; his arm must have been getting tired—was just getting out.

"So?" I wound an arm through Rocky's and made sure to keep my voice light. "What do you think? Does he look like the kind of guy who knows everything there is to know about the Statue of Liberty?"

"He looks . . ." When Rocky turned away from the grandstand, her eyes were wide and her face was pale. "He looks . . . exactly . . . he looks exactly like I thought he would look," she said. She untangled her arm from mine and she didn't bother trying to negotiate her way through the crowd. Rocky took off running down the middle of the street, away from the grandstand and the parade and the Statue of Liberty expert, as if her life depended on it.

Berkley Prime Crime titles by Kylie Logan

Ethnic Eats Mysteries

IRISH STEWED
FRENCH FRIED

Button Box Mysteries

BUTTON HOLED
HOT BUTTON
PANIC BUTTON
BUTTONED UP

League of Literary Ladies Mysteries

MAYHEM AT THE ORIENT EXPRESS
A TALE OF TWO BIDDIES
THE LEGEND OF SLEEPY HARLOW
AND THEN THERE WERE NUNS

Chili Cook-off Mysteries

CHILI CON CARNAGE
DEATH BY DEVIL'S BREATH
REVENGE OF THE CHILI QUEENS

*My friend Joan is no longer with us, but I can't help
but think of her when I think about Rocky and Rocky's
home in this book.
Joan had the same panache as Rocky, the same love of
place, and the same style.
Yes, she displayed everything she owned! It was one of the
reasons visiting her
was such a treat. Miss you, Joan, our long talks on your
screened porch,
and sharing a glass (or two) of wine!*

Acknowledgments

How often you'll hear an author say that no book is written alone!

It's true. In spite of the fact that we sit here in isolation in front of our computers for months and months, there are bound to be other people who help us and influence us every time we write a book.

This time, like always, I'd like to thank them all, especially my agent, Gail Fortune, the folks at Berkley Prime Crime, and the members of the Northeast Ohio chapter of Sisters in Crime. Great people, all, sisters and misters!

A special thanks to Georgia Schuff, who in addition to being the world's best knitting teacher just happens to be my expert on all things to do with Hubbard, Ohio.

Thanks to my brainstorming group, Shelley Costa, Serena Miller, and Emilie Richards, for always being there to listen and to offer advice. And of course to my family, both the people and the fur kids, *merci beaucoup*!

Chapter 1

"**B**one sue war!"

I was putting the last touches on the quiches about to go into the oven, so I didn't turn around when someone bumped through the kitchen door of Sophie's Terminal at the Tracks and called out the greeting.

I didn't need to.

I'd recognize Sophie Charnowski's voice—and her lousy French accent—anywhere.

Then again, I should. It had been six months since I'd left California and arrived in Hubbard, Ohio, to run what I thought was Sophie's white-linen-and-candlelight restaurant while she had knee-replacement surgery. Six months since I found out that the elegant restaurant she'd lied about for years was really a greasy spoon in an old train station that anchored a battered-but-trying-to-gentrify part of town.

Six months since I'd been embroiled as much in murder as I was in cooking.

The thought hit, and a touch like icy fingers squirmed its way up my back. I twitched it aside and called over my shoulder. "*Bonsoir*, Sophie. Any sign of Rocky yet?"

"No! She is nowhere to be seen, yes?" Sophie tried for a French lilt that pinged around the tile and stainless steel kitchen and fell flat. With her usual good humor, she laughed it away and came up behind me so she could stand on tiptoe and peek over my shoulder at the six quiches on the counter.

"Oh, Laurel, they look fabulous!" Sophie breathed in deep. "Think six will be enough?"

I wiped my hands on the white apron looped around my neck. "We've got three more in the fridge and George will pop them in the oven if we need them," I told Sophie at the same time I glanced across the kitchen. George Porter was leaning back against the industrial fridge, his beefy arms crossed over his massive chest, and a scowl on his face that pretty much said all there was to say about what he thought of quiche.

In spite of the scowl—or maybe because of it—I gave him the kind of smile that said I was sure he was on board with my plan.

George didn't smile back.

But then, what did I expect?

The Terminal's longtime cook was a mountain of a man with more tats on his arms than I had fingers and toes, a meat-and-potatoes kind of guy who was as happy as a cholesterol-challenged clam cooking up the fried eggs, fried baloney, fried steak, and fried chicken that for years had been the staples of the Terminal menu. That is, before

I arrived and started introducing healthier dishes and, in a flash of inspiration, featuring ethnic specials.

We'd started with Irish, and that summer had tried Japanese (sushi did not exactly go over big with the Hubbard crowd) and Chinese (popular, but there were plenty of Chinese places in town and I gave up on a menu that seemed to me to be déjà vu all over again). Now, in honor of a town celebration commemorating the anniversary of the dedication of the Statue of Liberty, a gift from France to the people of America, we'd decided to go with the Tricolor flow. French food, but not the fussy kind that's so off-putting to so many people. We were sticking with French country, French bistro. Delicious, accessible, and easy for a man like George to handle. Even if in his heart-of-fried-food hearts, he didn't want to.

I sloughed the thought aside and reminded Sophie, "There are tartines, too."

"Tartines." Her sigh hovered in the ether somewhere between Nirvana and Utopia. In the weeks since we'd started planning our French menu and I'd introduced her to tartines, she'd become something of an addict. And who could blame her?! The knife-and-fork open-faced French sandwiches are delightful.

"We're going to use some of the heirloom tomatoes still coming in from the local farmers," I told Sophie. "We'll put those on some of the tartines along with eggplant. Then for others, we've got ham and Gruyère, and toasted Camembert, walnut, and fig."

"Walnut and fig."

I ignored George when he grunted.

"Now all we need . . ." I glanced at the quiches that looked decidedly naked. "Did Rocky say what time she'd be here with the herbs?"

"I'm late. I know. I'm sorry!"

For the second time in as many minutes, the kitchen door swung open and this time, Raquel Arnaud bumped into the room. Rocky was a friend of Sophie's, but there couldn't be two women who were more different. Sophie was short, plump, and as down-to-earth as her sensible shoes. Her hair was the same silvery color as Rocky's, but while Sophie's was short and shaggy, Rocky's was long and sleek and as glorious as the woman herself.

But then, Rocky had the whole French thing going for her, including just a trace of an accent that hadn't disappeared in spite of the fact that she'd left her native country nearly fifty years earlier.

Rocky was almost as tall as my five-nine, willowy, and as elegant as her clothing. She was a farmer—herbs and specialty vegetables—a woman whose life revolved around the seasons and the weather and the acreage thirty minutes outside of Hubbard where she grew some of the best produce in the state, yet anyone meeting her for the first time would think she'd just stepped out of the house to shop on the Rue de la Paix.

Well, except for that Friday night.

I did a double take.

That evening, graceful and refined Rocky looked . . .

She was wearing the black A-line dress she claimed was a fashion must, but Rocky's hair was uncombed and her lipstick was smudged. Sure, she was running late, and that might account for the slapdash grooming, but nothing I knew about Rocky could explain—

Sneakers?

Before I came to Hubbard, I'd worked as a personal chef in Hollywood. Believe me, I knew fashion trends, fashion faux pas, and plain ol' fashion disasters.

I'd never known Raquel Arnaud to dare something as unfashionable and as downright un-French as to wear tennis shoes outside of the house. Especially ones that looked to be encrusted with a week's worth of garden goo.

"I knew I was running late so I chopped the thyme at home."

Before I could even think of what to say or how to ask Rocky if she'd completely lost her mind, she raced over and put a basket on the countertop beside me. There was a white linen towel thrown over the top of it and when Rocky whisked it away, I forgot all about her smeared lipstick and her tennis shoes.

But then, who can resist the heavenly woody/lemony aroma of fresh thyme?

I took a deep breath and automatically found myself smiling.

"Always has that effect on me, too." Rocky gave me a playful poke in the ribs at the same time she reached around me to sprinkle thyme on the quiches. "I brought griselles, too," she said. "But since you're already done with these, they'll have to wait for tomorrow's quiche."

I stepped back to admire the finished quiches. "Bacon, onion, and Swiss today," I told Rocky. "Pretty traditional, I know, but I thought that might be easiest if we get a crowd after the book signing. Tomorrow after the big parade, we'll mix it up with spinach and the shallots in some of the quiches." I peeked at the French shallots—what Rocky called griselles—and took another deep breath, and I swear, I could still smell the scent of autumn earth that clung to the shallots.

And to Rocky.

Carefully, I took another sniff.

A fragrant cloud of Chanel No. 5 usually enveloped Rocky. That night, she smelled more like wet soil. And red wine. Lots of red wine.

I guess Sophie noticed, too, because behind Rocky's back, she raised her eyebrows and gave me That Look. The one that said I was supposed to ask what the heck was going on.

Before I could, Rocky pulled a bottle of wine out of the basket she'd brought with her.

"We need to have a glass before we head out, eh?" She didn't wait for us to agree, but reached for the corkscrew she'd also brought along and opened the bottle. "You have glasses, George?" she asked, and since we didn't have a liquor license and there weren't any appropriate wineglasses around, he brought over water glasses. Four of them.

Rocky didn't mind sharing. She poured into each of the glasses and she was just about to take a drink when Sophie stopped her.

"What about a toast?" Sophie asked. "We always have a toast."

"Oh." As if this were a new thought, Rocky blinked and stared into her glass.

This time, Sophie augmented That Look with a scrunched-up nose and a tip of her head in Rocky's direction.

I knew a losing cause when I saw one.

I put a hand on Rocky's arm and couldn't help but notice that when I did, she flinched.

"Are you all right?" I asked. "You seem distracted."

She made a face that would have been convincing if I hadn't spent the last few years of my career as the personal chef of Hollywood megastar Meghan Cohan. I knew actors. Good actors. Bad actors. Rocky fell into the latter category.

"I get so flustered when I'm running late." I guess Rocky forgot all about the toast, because she downed her wine. "We should probably get going, huh? We don't want to miss the book signing."

"Imagine, Aurore Brisson here in Hubbard!" It looked as if Sophie knew a losing cause when she saw one, too, because she gave up on the toast, took a quick sip of wine, and set down her glass. She stepped up beside Rocky. "How exciting it must be for you to have a Frenchwoman here in town. And such a famous one! That book of hers—"

"Yesterday's Passion. Yes, yes." Before Sophie could pilot her to the door, Rocky poured another glass of wine and slugged it down. "I'm anxious to read it. I've always been interested in my country's history but really, I don't know all that much about the Middle Ages. The story sounds so . . . so romantic. Knights, ladies, castles—"

"And that gorgeous hunk, Sam Baker, who's going to play the lead role when the book's made into a TV series!" Sophie grinned and leaned closer to Rocky, speaking in a stage whisper I couldn't fail to hear. "Laurel knows him."

Rocky raised her eyebrows.

"Not well," I admitted because it was better than letting anyone know that Sam Baker had once had an affair with Meghan Cohan and had come on to me one morning while I was getting breakfast ready for the two of them down in the kitchen of Meghan's Malibu mansion. "We've met."

"Is he as gorgeous in person as he is in the movies?" Rocky asked.

He was, and I admitted it. Without adding that he was also a little too much into recreational drugs and other men's wives.

"It's only natural that he's playing the lead. Isn't that

right, Laurel?" Sophie asked. "Meghan Cohan herself is producing and directing and starring. She's playing Cecile. The tabloids say they're having an affair, Meghan and Sam." Sophie paused, waiting for me to fill in the blanks. When I didn't, she breezed right on. "Oh, I can't wait to read the book and see the show and see if they stick to the original story. Is that how it works, Laurel? When they make a film or a TV show, do they usually stick to the original story?"

In this case, only if the original story involved late-night fights of epic proportions, accusations thrown back and forth like rocks from a catapult, and a huge and ugly breakup the tabloids had yet to get wind of. No doubt the network had squelched the truth to get as much mileage as they could out of what they were touting as both an on-screen and an offscreen romance.

"Well, I'm buying a copy of the book, that's for sure," Sophie told us. "And I can't wait to get Aurore Brisson's autograph. How clever it was of John and Mike over at the Book Nook to get her here just in time for the Statue of Liberty celebration. She's such a superstar, so young and pretty. I bet there will be a line out the door of the bookstore. Let's get over there fast."

Fast, of course, is a relative word when it comes to Sophie, who always has a patron to stop and say hello to or a neighbor to greet. Then, of course, there was the matter of Sophie's knee. Oh, she didn't move at a snail's pace because of that replacement surgery back in the spring. She'd recovered from that and gone through rehab and all was well. At least for a few weeks. That's when she twisted her knee. While she was on a Mediterranean cruise. On an island. Drinking ouzo and doing the *Zorba the Greek* dance with some hunky fisherman who emailed her regularly now and called her his little baklava and promised to come visit sometime soon.

To say this new injury annoyed me no end makes me look small-minded when, in fact, it makes sense that I'd be irritated. See, I had no intention of staying in Hubbard and I'd told Sophie that from the start. I promised I'd stay only until she felt better and could take over the management of the restaurant herself again.

Only that didn't look like it was going to happen anytime soon.

I held on to my temper along with the thought that this, too, would pass. And when it did . . .

We had just walked out the front door of the Terminal and a brisk autumn breeze ruffled my hair along with the French flag we were flying from a post out front, and I made sure to keep a smile off my face.

Sophie had an uncanny way of reading into my smiles, and for now, what I knew about how long I was staying and where I might be going when I waved adios to the town that time forgot was my business and mine alone.

We fell into step behind the throngs of people milling in front of the bookstore and slowly making themselves into some sort of orderly line, and while Sophie and Rocky chatted about people I didn't know, I had a few minutes to look around. What was now called the Traintown neighborhood had once been at the heart of Hubbard's industrial center. There were railroad tracks that ran along the back side of the restaurant and six times a day, a train still rumbled by and shook the Terminal to its nineteenth-century foundation. Across the tracks was a factory, long shuttered, just one of the many businesses that had gone south/closed their doors/given up the ghost in what had once been a vibrant community.

Fortunately for the people of Hubbard and the small-business people who wanted so desperately to make a go of life there, Traintown took shape from the battered landscape. It was only one street, anchored at one end by the Book Nook and at the other by the Irish store, a charming little gift shop run by Declan Fury, who was even more charming than every last little stuffed leprechaun he kept in stock.

And he knew it.

Automatically I glanced down the street toward the green shamrock that danced above the shop's front door in the autumn breeze. There was no sign of Declan, and while I couldn't say if that was good or bad, I wasn't surprised. Not only was *Yesterday's Passion* the biggest thing to come out of New York publishing since Scarlett lifted her fist to the sky, it was historical romance it all its overblown, trashy, bodice-ripping glory. Traintown fairly gushed estrogen, and no self-respecting guy would be caught dead in the crowd.

We crossed to the other side of the street and the end of the line that snaked out of the bookstore and past Caf-Fiends, our local coffee shop, and all the way over in front of Artisans All, a craft and gift shop with decent merchandise and prices that made this California girl think she'd died and gone to heaven. There we stopped behind three young women wearing medieval attire: long dresses, wimples, and veils. Though I am certainly no historian, I was pretty sure the tattoo on one girl's wrist wasn't exactly authentic to the period.

"Oh, I forgot to give you the CDs of French music!" Rocky passed a hand over her eyes. "Silly me. You'll find them, Laurel." She put a hand on my arm. "In the basket with the herbs. I brought you Piaf and Maurice Chevalier and, of course, Téléphone!" When Sophie looked at her in wonder, Rocky managed a laugh that for a second, erased whatever it was that was bothering her and transformed her into the vivacious Rocky I knew. "Hey, back in the day, they opened for the Stones!"

The doors of the Book Nook swung open and a buzz of feminine excitement filled Traintown as we surged forward and closer to the shop and to Mike and John, who stood on either side of the front door.

The Guys, as they were affectionately known throughout Traintown, were personal as well as business partners. They were middle-aged, both tall and thin, and they both wore wire-rimmed glasses and had receding hairlines. Mike, dressed tonight in a dapper suit, favored herb teas and had been the first in line when we introduced sushi at the Terminal. John, who sported a beret and a red cravat, adored the strong coffee I made for myself (and shared with him when he stopped in). That evening, he had a cup from Caf-Fiends in one hand, and when we finally got close enough, he raised it in greeting.

"Fabulous turnout." Not that he needed me to tell him. I tried to glance over the crowd and into the shop. "And the guest of honor?"

Behind those wire-rimmed glasses, John rolled his eyes. He looked around to make sure no one was paying attention to us when he mouthed the words *prima donna*.

This didn't surprise me in the least. But then, I had previously lived and worked in a place where prima was never prima enough and every last donna thought she was God's gift.

A few minutes later we were in the shop and just a bit after that, directly in front of the table where Aurore Brisson, blond, plump lipped, and curvy, looked very bored and very eager for the harried assistant at her elbow to grab the next book, open it, and slide it in front of her so she could scrawl her signature and move on to the next fan.

"*Bonjour.*" When Rocky greeted her, Aurore glanced up, but only for a moment. "*Bienvenue à* Hubbard!"

The author's smile was tight.

"Next!" the assistant called out.

Rocky stepped aside and Sophie took her place. "So much for trying to be friendly," I said to Rocky, but she was hardly listening. She'd already flipped open the book and stepped to the side. The last I saw of her, she was headed down an aisle between two bookshelves marked CRAFTS and COOKING, her nose in the book.

"I'm afraid it's my fault." Sophie sidestepped her way around the three medieval maidens who were busy trying to find the best angle for selfies that would include Aurore Brisson in the background. "Rocky's worried. She's nervous. You know, about the symposium over at Youngstown State."

It took a moment for the pieces to fall into place in my brain. "The peace symposium? Rocky's speaking at it, I know, but how is that your—"

"I talked her into it." Sophie's shoulders hunched. "She didn't want to do it, and I talked her into accepting the invitation. In fact, I volunteered her when I heard Professor Weinhart was putting together the symposium. I told Rocky I thought it was important for people to hear about her experiences on the front lines of the peace movement back in the '60s and '70s."

Though Rocky had never said a word to me about her hippie days, I'd heard the story from Sophie before. I knew that Rocky had once been involved in a group devoted to ending the Vietnam War. While they were at it, they did their best to spread peace, love, and joy throughout the land. Now, like I always did, I marveled at the very thought. The only thing Rocky Arnaud was radical about these days was the quality of her produce.

"She has so much valuable information, so many interesting experiences with community organizing and lobbying," Sophie said, glancing toward the aisle where Rocky had disappeared. "They were peaceniks, you know. They were sure they could change the world through their message of love and tolerance. Young people need to hear the story these days, and it wouldn't hurt for some of us old-timers to be reminded, too. But ever since she agreed to speak at the symposium, Rocky's been . . ." Sophie crinkled her nose. "Well, when she first heard Aurore Brisson was coming to town, she couldn't wait to get over here and meet her. And last time I talked to her about it, she was just about jumping up and down with excitement about the big parade tomorrow and the talk that Statue of Liberty expert is giving over at the library. But the symposium is getting closer and closer and now tonight . . ."

"She'll be fine," I assured Sophie. "Maybe it's just a case of the jitters."

Sophie cradled her copy of *Yesterday's Passion* to her broad bosom. "Well, I hope so. At least she's excited about reading the book. I mean, she must be, right, because she couldn't wait to open it and get started. That's a good thing, right? Maybe it will take her mind off that symposium and speaking in front of an auditorium full of people."

Another group of people—all clutching the book—moved away from the signing table, and I grabbed Sophie's arm to get her out of the way. But then, the last thing I wanted to do was see her take a fall and end up in rehab again. "Caf-Fiends is serving cookies and coffee," I told her. "Let's get some."

If the crowd hadn't been so heavy, there was no way Sophie would have agreed. See, in her book, Caf-Fiends is an affront to humanity, a place that adulterated coffee with things like whipped cream, sprinkles, and flavored syrups. Then they have the nerve to charge three dollars a cup for it. Back when I first arrived in Hubbard, there had been plenty of tension between Caf-Fiends and the Terminal because the Terminal was losing business to the new coffee shop with its wraps, its fancy sandwiches, and its killer key lime pie. The good news was that these days with the ethnic specialties on our menu and our crowds up, the Terminal and Caf-Fiends were learning to peacefully coexist.

Well, some of us were.

I stepped up to the dessert table and came eye to eye with Myra, the Caf-Fiends waitress who made no secret of the fact that she had her eye on Declan Fury and that she didn't like it one bit when she saw the two of us together. Hey, I wasn't the one who was going to tell her that she had nothing to worry about. Declan and I, we were—

"Coffee?" Myra held out a cup toward Sophie and pretended I didn't exist. "We've got cookies, too. John and Mike had us bring lots of cookies." When she swiveled to look my way, her chestnut-colored ponytail twitched. "Ours are the best."

"I have no doubt," I said, scooping a cookie from the table even though I didn't want one. I chomped into it, turned my back, and made my way over toward the cash register so Sophie could pay for her book. After that, it was all a matter of waiting. Once the crowd of book buyers dwindled, we were told that Aurore Brisson, she of the too-yellow hair and the too-white smile, would be giving a little talk.

I found Sophie one of the last chairs in the shop and stood behind it, waiting for the big moment, and I have to say, once it came, I was a tad underwhelmed.

Aurore, who spoke decent-enough English, didn't have a whole lot to say other than that her book, it was fabulous, and the cable TV series that was about to premiere . . . well, it was nothing short of extraordinaire!

When she was finished singing her own praises, we clapped politely and Mike moved to the front of the room.

"We've only got a few minutes," he said. "But I think . . . I hope . . ." He smiled at the author, who did not smile back. "Ms. Brisson has been gracious enough to say she would answer a few questions."

"Questions? Questions?" Where Rocky came from, I couldn't tell. I knew only that there she was, out of whatever hidey-hole she'd gone into to read, standing at the center of the room with her arms pressed to her sides and her cheeks flaming, and for a moment, I saw a glimpse of the peace crusader she had once been.

Rocky's head was high. Her shoulders were steady. Her voice rang through the shop like the first strident, brilliant chord of Jimi Hendrix's "Star-Spangled Banner."

"I've got a question for you, Aurore Brisson!" Rocky held her copy of *Yesterday's Passion* to the sky and used her other hand to point a finger at the author. "How did you . . . Why did you . . ." Rocky's voice broke and she pulled in a sob. "How can you stand there and let these *mensonges* . . . these lies . . . leave your lips? Why did you steal Marie Daigneau's book?"

Chapter 2

"She was a friend of Rocky's," Sophie told me later that evening. "Marie Daigneau. I remember the name because they wrote to each other for years and Rocky would always tell me what was happening in Marie's life. She died a few years ago and Rocky was so sad. They knew each other back in France. You know, before Rocky came to this country to attend college."

"And Marie Daigneau wrote a book?"

We were back at the Terminal, and Sophie had a carton of rocky road ice cream in one hand and a spoon in the other. She paused just as she was about to dig in and scoop ice cream into the two bowls she'd put on the counter. In Sophie's world, ice cream was the cure for everything from a broken heart to money troubles to friends who spouted crazy accusations at bookstores that left the proprietors red-faced, the guest of honor with her Gallic knickers in a twist, and the crowd in an uproar.

It was all we'd been able to do to get Rocky out of there in one piece.

Ice cream sounded like a good idea to me, too.

"I wish she hadn't insisted on going home." Sophie filled the bowls to overflowing and pushed one toward me. "And I wish she explained herself before she headed out. I'm worried about her."

I was worried, too, and the next afternoon as we shuffled our way through the festive crowd gathering for the parade that would mark the official opening of Hubbard's Statue of Liberty Festival, I was still uneasy.

The good news was that there were plenty of people there in what was charitably called downtown Hubbard, and certainly that provided a distraction. In a small town like this, a parade was as good as any other reason to gather, and the crisp fall afternoon, the dome of blue sky dotted with cottony clouds over our heads, and the trees in their fiery shades of red and gold and orange gave the folks of Hubbard a perfect excuse to get out and join in the fun. The main street through town was closed to traffic, and it teemed with people. Around us, parents herded children and shoppers gathered at the booths set up by local farmers who sold fat orange pumpkins and warm cider. Since the public library was sponsoring the whole event, they had a huge presence, too, and kids ran hither and yon waving paper bookmarks and balloons and greeting costumed characters who I guessed were the stars of various and sundry kids' books.

The bad news . . .

Well, that didn't smack us in the face until Sophie and

I found ourselves a place at the curb between the Taco Bell and the VFW hall, near the grandstand where the parade would end. That's when Rocky joined us.

And that's when I heard the whispered voices all around.

"Drinks, you know." It was a woman's voice, and I didn't dare turn around and see who it belonged to because if I did, there was going to be another incident, and I figured Hubbard could ill afford two melees in less than twenty-four hours. "Wine. Just like they said in that newspaper article they published about her a couple of months ago. She must have been hitting the bottle last night."

"She's wacky. Has been for years." This came from a man who stood on the other side of me, and caution be damned; I turned and glared him into silence.

If Rocky heard any of this swill—if she cared—I really couldn't tell. Like the night before when she faced down Aurore Brisson with fire in her eyes, her cheeks were bright with color and her eyes shone.

"It was hard to find a parking space," Rocky said, and pressed a hand to her heart. "I was afraid I was going to miss it." She craned her neck and bent at the waist, the better to look down the street in the direction the parade would come from. "They haven't started yet?"

I was just about to tell her that it should be soon when we heard the first notes of "Seventy-Six Trombones" from down the street played by the Hubbard High School marching band.

"It's starting!" Rocky clamped a hand on my arm and gave me a squeeze. "Isn't it exciting, Laurel? The parade is starting!"

Start it did, and I endured forty-five minutes of marching bands, smiling beauty queens, and convertibles where politicians and wannabe politicians grinned and waved and tossed candy to the people waiting along the curb.

"Muriel Ross!" When the lady in question waved in our direction, Sophie jumped up and down (I held my breath and waited for her knee to pop again) and waved back. "Such a nice lady. Her family owns the furniture factory, you know." She gave Muriel another wave, just for good measure. "I hear she's going to be running for state senate. She's a customer of ours."

I recognized the slightly older than middle-aged woman with a mane of highlighted hair, the tasteful style of people who have money, and the aplomb of a seasoned politico. "Who's the guy with her?" I asked Sophie.

Her cheeks shot through with pink. "New husband. Haven't you heard? Ben . . ."

When Sophie stumbled over the name, Rocky provided it. "Newcomb," she said. "Not that I've met him, but I've heard about him."

"Oh, haven't we all!" Since the car Muriel and her hubby were riding in was moving like molasses in January, Sophie had another chance to wave. "They met at some la-di-da resort when Muriel was on vacation earlier this year," she told me. "And I hear it was love at first sight. Lucky dog, Muriel! Every woman in Hubbard is green with envy."

Not every. But I could see the appeal, at least for the women in Sophie's age bracket. Ben Newcomb was a man in his sixties with thick, salt-and-pepper hair, a cleft chin, and a nose as straight and as patrician as that of a Roman statue. He had the kind of build that told me he was a runner or a swimmer, and a smile that dazzled nearly as bright as his wife's. When the sun ducked behind a fat, white cloud, then peeped out again, Ben squinted and tipped his head back, drinking it in, laughing, reflecting all that heat and all that light and all that upper-crust Hubbard glory back at the crowd like a fun house mirror designed to show them that they, too, could be as handsome and as virile—if only they were as rich.

I'd barely had a chance to let the thought register when something pinged against the pavement around me. A few somethings, in fact. It wasn't until then that I realized Muriel and Ben were tossing hard candy wrapped in bright red paper.

"Red-hot?"

The question stroked my ear, and I didn't have to turn around to know who'd asked it. But then, the temperature out there on the sidewalk shot up a couple dozen degrees and the sun, pleasantly warm before, suddenly felt as if it were scorching my cheeks. I turned, anyway, only too aware that when I did, I'd find myself face-to-face with— and lips dangerously close to—Declan Fury.

I was never really sure how I managed to smile when Declan was around. I mean, what with feeling as if I needed to struggle to catch my breath. Smile, I did, though, in that oh-so-California way designed to tell him that the San Andreas might shake, rattle, and roll me, but he never would.

"They're not Red Hots," I said, with a look at the candy he dangled in front of me."Those are small and cinnamony. These are—"

"Sweet and tempting." He held one of the wrapped candies so close to my nose, I had to cross my eyes to see it. "Like me."

The *tempting* part was right.

The *sweet* . . . I wasn't so sure. But then, Declan had a

reputation around town, and not just when it came to women. See, while he was technically the manager of Bronntanas, the gift shop everyone simply called the Irish store because they could never remember the real name of it, he was also an attorney. And not just any attorney. In the months since I'd worked at the Terminal and listened to our patrons chat and gossip and discuss all things Hubbard, I'd learned that Declan had one client and one alone—his huge family. Rumor was, his uncle Pat was involved in the local mob and that Declan's role in the family business was to keep each and every one of his relatives far away from trouble and out of jail.

Having grown up in the foster system, I can't say I know a whole lot about families. I can say that having met Declan's father, his mother, his assorted brothers and sisters and in-laws along with a variety of nieces and nephews and cousins . . . well, I can't imagine it was an easy task.

As for the rumors . . . like talk of Rocky's excessive drinking and Rocky being crazy, I wasn't about to believe what I didn't see with my own eyes, and so far, the only thing I'd seen was that Declan was as delicious as any guy I'd ever met, far more interesting than the run-of-the-mill Hubbardite, and twice as tempting as any hard candy in this or any other parade.

And I wasn't going there.

The reason was simple—I had no desire of starting up a relationship with a guy as family centered, reliable, and just plain nice as Declan.

Not when I had no intention of sticking around.

"Hey, it's not the apple in the Garden of Eden!" Declan bumped my nose with the wrapped candy. "Come on, give it a go."

I plucked the candy from his hand and was rewarded with a thousand-watt smile that crinkled the corners of his gray eyes.

"Some parade, huh?"

A fire truck was just passing by, screeching its siren, and I pressed my hands to my ears and waited for the worst of the racket to simmer down.

"Some parade," I said.

For reasons that always escape me, Declan isn't nearly as impressed by my Hollywood background as the rest of the known Hubbard universe. But then, maybe he's caught on to how my career as a personal chef ended badly when Meghan Cohan accused me of leaking information to the media about her teenage son's drug addiction.

Just for the record, I didn't do it.

Just for the record, Meghan wasn't the type who made those sorts of distinctions.

I was out on my True Religion jeans–covered butt, at loose ends. Meghan, no slouch when it comes to knowing the cream of society, the up-and-comers, and the just plain powerful, poisoned the pool of potential employers and that left me no place to go but Sophie's Terminal at the Tracks.

Did I sigh just thinking about it?

I guess so, because Declan's brows rose a smidgen closer to his dark, always tousled hair.

He glanced to where Rocky was watching the parade with rapt attention, then back toward the Taco Bell, and I got the message.

I stepped to the back of the crowd with him.

"Some parade," I said because really, when you're in the middle of Nowhere, USA, watching elementary school kids troop by dressed like little Statues of Liberty, there's really not much else you can say.

Apparently, Declan didn't have that problem. "So is it true?" he asked. "Last night at the bookstore, did Rocky really—"

"Even you?" I propped my fists on my hips. "Can't you just cut the poor woman a break? Obviously, something was bothering her."

"And obviously . . ." Since I guess it wasn't so obvious after all, Declan pinned me with a look. "I wasn't going to criticize. I'm just concerned, that's all."

Of course he was. If there was one thing I'd learned about Declan in my months of working across the street from him, it was that once he made a friend, he took that person under his wing and was just as loyal and just as unwavering and just as gosh-darned stubborn about what he could do for that person as he was when it came to his own family. And just for the record, that was plenty loyal, absolutely unwavering, and as gosh-darned stubborn as any person I'd ever met.

I was a case in point.

See, though I was still grappling with how I felt about him, Declan had decided early on that I was his friend. Just as early, he made it clear that he was all set to take that friendship to the next level. Sexual tension, sexual attraction, and heated exchanges (not the angry kind) aside, he'd helped me solve the murder of a man whose body was found at the Terminal the day I arrived in Ohio.

And none of that friendship or heat mattered, I reminded myself, since I wasn't planning on staying around.

Then again, Declan had also helped me organize our first ethnic food extravaganza (yes, it was Irish food), going so far as to share family recipes and even members of his family, who showed up at the Terminal to entertain the crowds with rollicking Irish folk music.

And that didn't matter, either. I wasn't staying.

I let go a long sigh that was lost in the noise of the police cars that rolled by with their light bars flashing and their sirens whooping.

"Rocky lost it last night," I said, sidestepping a group of teenage guys who walked out of Taco Bell with bags full of food. "She started reading the book and then she started talking about her friend Marie back in France and then . . ." I shrugged inside my denim jacket because I couldn't explain and I didn't understand and it was impossible to put it all into words, anyway. "That's when she accused Aurore Brisson of stealing *Yesterday's Passion*."

From where we were standing, Declan had a perfect view of Sophie and Rocky. Their backs were to us, but I could see that Sophie was waving like mad at the cops as they went by. Rocky was looking farther up the street, toward the kids and the cars and the couple of rudimentary floats that had already passed by.

"That's not like her at all," Declan said.

"And she was wearing sneakers," I added, and to his credit, he didn't ask what the heck that had to do with anything and just took my word for it that it confirmed what he said.

"Sophie says it's because Rocky's speaking at the peace symposium and she's nervous about it," I told Declan. "She might be right."

"Maybe."

It wasn't what he said that—let's face it—was just about

as unrevealing as anything out of the mouth of an attorney could be.

It was the way he said it.

"What?" I asked Declan. "You know something's going on."

"Did I say that?"

I stepped back, my weight against one foot, and refused to look away from him, even when some politician with a better pitching arm than Muriel Ross beaned me with a butterscotch. "You didn't have to say it. Come on, Declan, share. Sophie's worried about Rocky. If you know something's going on—"

"Lawyer-client confidentiality," he said.

Which didn't exactly convince me.

"Rocky's not a client. You don't have any other clients except your family."

He had the nerve to grin. "Sometimes I make an exception."

"So Rocky is your client! And she's having legal problems? That would explain why she's acting so strange."

"It might. If I said she was a client. And if I told you she had legal problems. Which I didn't. Which I couldn't. You know, on account of—"

"Lawyer-client confidentiality."

We finished the sentence together, our voices blending and overlapping with the unmusical notes of a polka band that oompahed by, accordions gleaming in the afternoon sunlight.

Declan was as exasperating as every other lawyer in the world, and my glare should have told him so, but all it did was make him look more smug than ever.

"Well, if you're going to be cryptic, I can't help you. You want to know what happened with Rocky last night, but you're not willing to tell me anything that you know. Rocky caused a scene. That's no secret. Whatever the reason—"

"Let's just hope it doesn't happen again." Declan pointed toward the street, where a champagne-colored convertible was just going by with Aurore Brisson in it, acknowledging the crowd, her arm as stiff as her spine, her hand barely moving.

I knew the exact moment she caught sight of Rocky over there on the curb because Aurore's breath caught and her cheeks puffed. She held her head very high and very steady but she couldn't control her expression nearly fast enough. There it was for all the world to see: the narrowed eyes, the clamped lips, the little tremor that raced along her jawline and caused her to tremble. Rocky may have been talking crazy over at the Book Nook, and she certainly never explained herself, but Aurore Brisson didn't care. Rocky was an embarrassment, an embarrassment who'd taken the spotlight off Aurore Brisson, and she hated Rocky Arnaud for it.

My mind raced and took my imagination along with it and automatically, my gaze pivoted to Rocky. I half expected to see her charge at the French author, and when I saw instead that she was focused on the grandstand that had been erected in the middle of the street fifty yards ahead of where she stood, I let go a shaky breath of relief. The marching band was poised around the grandstand, stepping in place to the beat of "America the Beautiful." The politicians and the wannabe politicians were clambering up the steps of the grandstand, still waving for all they were worth. The elementary kids in so many aluminum foil Statue of Liberty crowns were lined up on either side of the street, ready to welcome the town's guest of honor.

He arrived in a red car decked out with blue and white streamers, a nice-looking middle-aged man with dark hair and a neatly trimmed beard.

"Andrew MacLain," Declan yelled into my ear, because I guess I wasn't supposed to be able to remember. But I did. Anyone who'd seen a Hubbard newspaper in the last month, listened to a Hubbard radio broadcast, or caught the news on the local Youngstown station knew about Andrew MacLain.

Art historian. Museum curator. The expert on the Statue of Liberty. Emphasis on the *the*.

As if he had to prove it, MacLain waved to the crowd with one hand while with the other, he held up the coffee table book about the statue he'd authored in a *hey, look at me, I wrote a book* sort of way.

His car slowed just as it approached where Sophie and Rocky waited, and I watched Rocky swing her gaze from the grandstand to the man who was The Man when it came to the Statue. He'd be the guest of honor at the night's fireworks extravaganza, and the next day MacLain would speak to a standing room only crowd at the library.

Hey, it was Hubbard and there's not all that much to do on Sundays.

Rocky had already bought the book; she'd stopped at the Terminal the afternoon she picked it up at the Book Nook, and I knew she was excited about the talk and the stellar reputation of the man who was giving it. Though she was in the front row, I saw her stand on tiptoe as if that somehow would allow her a better look at Andrew MacLain.

Just as quickly, she settled herself, and again her gaze swiveled to the grandstand, then back again to MacLain.

Sophie whispered something in her ear and Rocky flinched.

Declan was looking where I was looking and he saw what I saw. That was a good thing—it meant I didn't have to explain when I said, "I'd better get over there and see what's going on."

I left Declan somewhere behind me in the crowd when I inched my way to the curb.

By the time I got there, MacLain's car was already stopped at the grandstand and the historian—book still raised, his arm must have been getting tired—was just getting out.

"So?" I wound an arm through Rocky's and made sure to keep my voice light. "What do you think? Does he look like the kind of guy who knows everything there is to know about the Statue of Liberty?"

"He looks . . ." When Rocky turned away from the grandstand, her eyes were wide and her face was pale. "He looks . . . exactly . . . he looks exactly like I thought he would look," she said. She untangled her arm from mine and she didn't bother trying to negotiate her way through the crowd. Rocky took off running down the middle of the street, away from the grandstand and the parade and the Statue of Liberty expert, as if her life depended on it.

Chapter 3

By the time the parade was over and we got back to the Terminal, there was a message waiting for us on voice mail.

"Sophie . . . Laurel . . ." Rocky's voice was tight and high-pitched, as if she couldn't catch her breath. "I'm sorry I ran out on you like that. I just . . ." She cleared her throat. "What with thinking about the Statue of Liberty and history and . . . well, it all just overwhelmed me and I had to get out of there. I hope you understand. I know you do. You two . . ." Her voice caught. "You're good friends and I'm grateful to have you in my life. I'll see you tonight at the fireworks show. I promise! I'll be there . . . how do you say it? With bells on!"

Only she wasn't.

Earlier in the week, we'd told Rocky we'd meet her that night near the entrance to Harding Park, and when she didn't show and over by the baseball fields the mayor launched into the first of the night's speeches, we figured we'd missed her and she'd already settled herself somewhere in the crowd. I set up the folding chair we'd brought along for Sophie and had a look around.

No Rocky. Not anywhere.

But I did bump into Declan.

"You're alone? The family's over there . . ." He tipped his head in the direction of what looked to me to be a sea of folding chairs, blankets, and baby strollers that had been set up near the playground on one end of the park, close enough to where the fireworks would be shot off to give the Fury family ringside seats, and just far enough away to keep the littlest kids from being startled by the noise. When I glanced that way, at least a dozen people waved. Ellen, his mother, always looked just a tad too eager to see me, and I wondered if it was because her youngest child was in his midthirties and she saw his possibilities for love and romance passing him by.

I hated to be the one to tell her that if she was looking for me to be the solution to the problem, she was looking in the wrong place.

Her husband, Malachi, was a big man with a dark, bristling beard and the same sort of flyaway hair that always made Declan look as if he were going someplace in a hurry or just finishing up with something he shouldn't have been doing. Malachi waved, too, but his smile wasn't as open or as accepting as Ellen's.

I wasn't surprised.

Declan was one of a long line of Travellers, those Irish who are sometimes mistakenly thought of as Gypsies, and though he'd told me his family had been what he called *settled* for a couple of generations, there were still countless aunts and uncles and cousins who maintained the age-old lifestyle, hunkering down in one place for the winter, then traveling in the warm months in search of work. There were legends that claimed that the Travellers were descended from Irish bards who'd once roamed the countryside from castle to castle, entertaining lords and ladies with stories and song.

I couldn't say if that was true.

I did know that like those bards of old must have, Declan had a honeyed tongue and a way of telling a story that made me feel as if I'd been hypnotized, hanging on every word. Like the rest of his family (and believe me, there were a lot of them), he was fiercely loyal, implicitly devoted, and faithful to a fault. This branch of the Fury clan may have been settled for sixty years, but old habits die hard and I knew that no matter how welcoming Ellen might be, Malachi was still having a hard time accepting an outsider. Especially one from California.

I'm not complaining. I'd grown up in foster care, and until I was taken in by Sophie's sister, Nina, when I was fourteen, I'd had too many homes to count. Family was not something I understood, or something I felt comfortable with. Declan's family overwhelmed me.

Next to Malachi sat Claire and Bridget, Declan's sisters, and they looked happy enough to see me, as did his brother Brian and his wife, Nora, who were nearby. As for the assorted nieces and nephews who jumped up and down to get my attention and called out things like, "Uncle Declan has a girlfriend," I smiled and waved and turned away as

quickly as I could rather than handle the tsunami of attention. While I was at it, I scanned the chairs set up all around
them.

There was no sign of Rocky.

"The fireworks are going to start in a couple of minutes," Declan said, and just as he did, the mayor stepped
back up to the microphone.

"We've got a bit of a delay," the mayor announced.
"Seems our guest of honor, that Statue of Liberty fellow
you've all been waiting to meet, has gotten a little lost on
the way over here. Let's listen to the high school marching
band . . ." He waved in their direction.

"Well, maybe more than a couple of minutes," Declan
admitted. "You want to come join us?"

"Can't." There was a bite in the chill October breeze,
and I stuffed my hands into the pockets of my boiled wool
jacket and stomped my feet to the tempo of the lively Sousa
march the band played. "Rocky was supposed to meet us
here and we can't find her."

Declan stepped up to my side. "Then I'll help you look."

We checked out each of the refreshment stands and the
table where the ladies from St. Colman's Church sold tickets for a quilt raffle, and when there was still no sign of
Rocky, I checked out the ladies' rooms. While I was at it,
Declan hit one of the refreshments stands and when I found
him again, shaking my head to let him know there was no
sign of Rocky anywhere, he handed me a paper cup filled
with steaming cider.

I breathed in the scent of apples and cinnamon and took
a careful sip.

"It's not like her to say she'll be somewhere and then
not show," I said.

"From what I can tell, everything she's done in the last twenty-four hours isn't like her."

"It's not." I wrapped both my hands around the cup, relishing the warmth when it seeped into my fingers. "The way she went after Aurore Brisson at the book signing and the fact that she left the parade without a word, as if something was biting at her heels."

"And the way she watched the parade."

It was a surprising statement, and when he made it, I glanced Declan's way. He, too, had his hands around his cup and he looked down into it, as if he wanted to think about what he was going to say so he could make sure he got his story straight. "Remember when—"

His words were swallowed up by a sudden silence from the band, a shrill shriek from a microphone, and Andrew MacLain's voice from the loudspeakers around the park.

"Sorry!" I glanced at the main stage just in time to see the Statue of Liberty expert give the crowd a wave. "Let's get the party started here," he yelled, and waved toward the fireworks crew.

When the first rocket screamed into the night sky, both Declan and I looked up to watch. Rocket after rocket raced into the air and burst into sparkling color over our heads.

What with the fireworks blasts and the oohs and aahs and applause from the crowd, Declan had to lean close and when he did, I smelled cinnamon on his breath. "Remember when we were watching the parade," he said. "We were over by the Taco Bell and Sophie and Rocky were there by the street. When Aurore Brisson rode by—"

"Nothing happened," I reminded him, only I had to do it pretty loudly what with all the noise.

Declan nodded. "Exactly. Friday evening, Rocky was

ready to go toe-to-toe with that author. But Saturday afternoon when Rocky saw her—"

"Nothing happened." I caught on to what Declan was saying and wondered why I hadn't made note of it myself. "You'd think Rocky would have had some reaction. At the Book Nook, she was ready to snap Aurore Brisson's head off. You'd expect her to still be angry, or embarrassed."

"But at the parade—"

"She hardly paid any attention to Aurore Brisson at all."

"She wasn't watching the author when she drove by. Rocky's eyes were on the grandstand," Declan said, and when I thought back to everything that had happened earlier that afternoon, I realized he was right.

In between a pyrotechnic burst of golden, sparkly stars and what looked like a blooming chrysanthemum that started out pink and morphed into streams of red and green, I did my best to clear my mind and picture the grandstand at the parade.

"The politicians were up there," I said. "And the beauty queens."

"And the kids in their Statue of Liberty costumes." Declan pointed back in some indeterminate direction, somewhere toward where his family was watching the show. "Caitlyn and Brendan and Jamie were part of that crew. Cute kids. You know, with all the Fury good looks."

The comment merited nothing more than a stiff smile, so that's exactly what I gave him. "The cuteness of your nieces and nephews aside, I can't see that any of that would interest Rocky all that much. Besides, the only thing she talked about for the last few weeks—I mean, other than reading Aurore Brisson's book and welcoming a fellow Frenchwoman to Hubbard—was seeing Andrew MacLain."

"Statue of Liberty expert!" Declan's skeptical *harrumph* said it all. "The guy's a history geek, not exactly a rock star."

"And Rocky said that history was what overwhelmed her at the parade." I filled Declan in on the voice mail message I'd picked up earlier. "The history of the Statue of Liberty?"

He knew it was as unlikely as I did when I asked the question, so to Declan's credit, he didn't answer me.

We watched a few more fireworks burst in the sky above us and I made up my mind.

"I'm going to Rocky's," I said, already starting out. "Sophie's over there." I pointed across the park. "If you could just go find her and let her know—"

"Oh no." He hooked his arm around mine before I could make my getaway. "We'll both tell her because we're both going to Rocky's."

"Really?" I did my best to untangle myself from him and I should have known from the start it was a losing cause. Like his notion of the supreme importance of family and friendship, Declan's mind is impossible to change. "I've been to Rocky's all by myself," I said anyway. "Lots of times. I can find my way there and back."

"She might be sick."

"So I'll call 911."

"She could be hurt."

"So I'll call 911."

"What if she's drunk?"

I bit back what I was tempted to say because like it or not, he could be right. Like it or not, it would explain the crazy way Rocky had been acting.

Like it or not, I knew it was a very real possibility.

I shook my shoulders to get rid of the thought. "Then I'll make her a pot of coffee and make sure she eats something and on my way over there, I'll stop and pick up an ice pack in case she has a headache."

A rocket flew overhead and burst into a blinding flash of blue that added planes and shadows to Declan's already angular face. It was late, and his chin was dusted with dark whiskers.

"I'll help make the coffee," he said, and he slid his hand down my arm and wound his fingers through mine.

He was impossible. And there was no use arguing.

Not even when I saw that Ellen Fury wasn't watching the fireworks. She had her gaze trained on her son and on the woman whose hand he was holding.

And she was smiling to beat the band.

I INSISTED ON driving because I'd been to Rocky's to pick up herbs for the Terminal a dozen times and I knew my way, even in the dark. Besides, I suspected Declan had arrived at Harding Park on his vintage motorcycle and as tempting as it was to think of myself hitched up on the seat behind him, my arms around his waist and my face buried in the folds of his black leather jacket, it was a chilly night, and body heat aside, I didn't relish the thought of getting cold. Or maybe I just didn't like the idea of all the heat we were bound to generate scattering in the October night air.

It was a thirty-minute drive to her farm on a six-acre plot outside of Cortland, a city (I use the word charitably) nestled up against the not so charmingly named Mosquito Reservoir. Cortland is one of those places with one elementary school, one middle school, and one high school to its name and a gazebo in the center of town, and there was little traffic to contend with. Then again, most of the population from miles around was probably in Hubbard for the fireworks festivities.

Most of the population.

But not Rocky.

I guess I sighed because over in the passenger seat, Declan leaned just a little nearer. "She's fine," he said.

I slid him a look. "You said it earlier—she's not acting like herself."

"Which doesn't mean anything's wrong."

"Which might mean it is."

"We'll find out in a couple of minutes."

I'm sure this comment was supposed to comfort me. Instead, it just made the cha-cha rhythm going on inside my rib cage beat a little faster.

At a red light, I drummed my fingers against the steering wheel and told myself to calm down, to think of something—anything—other than that Rocky might be in trouble. Lucky for me, a billboard just outside the local CVS caught my eye. On the ad for the upcoming cable premiere of *Yesterday's Passion*, Meghan Cohan was front and center and looking as gorgeous as ever, but not at all medieval in a gown with a plunging neckline, her lips slick and pouty.

"You miss Hollywood."

I'm not sure how Declan surmised that from my muttering, "I don't miss her." As if to prove it, I gave Meghan's gigantic picture a cross-eyed look when the light changed to green and I drove past.

"But you do miss Hollywood."

"I miss . . ." I stopped to let traffic go by so I could make a left-hand turn. "I miss the lifestyle."

"Ah, the rich and famous!" Declan tipped back his head. "You said they were snobs."

"Not all of them." My response was instantaneous, but even before the words left my lips, I knew they weren't true. Sure, sure, there had to be some good people, some honest people, some real people among the stratosphere of celebrities where Meghan Cohan lived and worked.

In the six years I was her personal chef, I had met precious few.

I twitched away the thought. "I miss the glamour," I told Declan, but truth be told, I wasn't so sure about that, either. Glamour is as glamour does, and what looks so sparkly and glorious from the outside often has a dark underbelly. "Well, I miss the kinds of wonderful, elegant meals I used to make," I told him and myself, and knew that much was the absolute truth.

He shot a smile in my direction. "You can always invite me over for dinner."

I could, but there was the whole matter of entanglement. His family, his friends, his town. Since the first time I'd driven past the WELCOME TO HUBBARD sign, I'd known I wasn't going to stay. And now . . .

I gave Declan a sidelong look. Maybe it was time for him to know—

I'd been so deep in thought, I nearly missed the turnoff to Rocky's farm. I stepped on the brakes a little too hard, smiled an apology at Declan, and turned into the long drive.

From what Sophie had said, Rocky had lived here on the little farm she called Pacifique, or Peaceful, for something like forty years. Over that time, she'd enlarged her garden again and again, experimented with new and different crops, and earned a reputation for quality produce and fair prices. What had started as a simple farmhouse had been transformed by Rocky's imagination and skill into the kind of charming place I'd seen more than once when I rambled the French countryside with Meghan. Sophie never called it Rocky's house or Rocky's farm, but simply Chateau Chic and Shabby. I had to agree with her.

Stone walkways, flowers spilling from pots even at this time of the year, ivy-covered walls.

Pacifique was beguiling without being fussy or pretentious, and it lived up to its name, too, acres and acres of peace and quiet.

Well, except maybe for that night.

The closer we got to the house, the louder the music became.

"Piaf," Declan said, and I recognized "La Vie en Rose" though I couldn't have translated the words if my life depended on it. It was a slow and mournful song, and so full of heartbreak, the words didn't matter.

It was also loud enough to wake the dead.

Declan and I exchanged looks.

"She could be having a party," he suggested.

But when we wound our way up the twisting drive and got close enough to finally see the house, we could also see that there were no cars around, and though every light in the house was lit, there was no indication that there was anyone inside.

I parked my car and cut the engine.

"Maybe I should go in first," Declan said, but I don't think he ever expected that I'd cave. I guess that's why he didn't look surprised when I got out of the car and walked up to the front door at his side.

I knocked and called out, but really, with Piaf singing away about broken hearts and broken promises and broken dreams (well, to me, that's what it sounded like she was singing about), I was pretty sure Rocky couldn't hear me anyway.

I tried the door and it swung open.

"Rocky!" Still out on the stone stoop, I bent forward and peered into the house. There was a hallway at the center of it and off to my left, the dining room with its whitewashed china cabinet, its table with mismatched chairs on three sides and a bench on the other, its funky chandelier, and the birdcage—as empty as it always had been—that sat in the corner. Beyond the dining room was the kitchen. To my right was the room Rocky used as a study and a parlor. It was where she welcomed her friends and where she conducted business with the wise restaurateurs who came looking for her produce. The CD player and the speakers must have been in there because Piaf's voice oozed from the room with its couch upholstered in blue and white ticking, its pots of herbs on the shelf in front of the window, and the circle of comfortable chairs—none of which matched, all of which looked fabulous together—where Rocky talked religion, politics, and farming with anyone who would listen.

"Rocky!" I tried again, and when there was still no answer, I stepped into the parlor.

That's when my breath caught and my heart stopped and my blood ran cold.

I hadn't consciously registered the fact that Declan walked into the room right after me, but I knew he was there. Automatically, I leaned into him, struggling to keep on my feet, and his arms went around my waist, hanging on tight.

Together, we stared at the red wing chair in the corner, at the table next to it where there was an open bottle of red wine and the one empty wineglass tipped on its side next to that bottle.

And at Rocky, who sat in the chair as if she were doing nothing more than waiting for the next friend to visit.

Except that her eyes were blank and staring at the ceiling.

Her mouth was open in a silent O of astonishment.

And her skin was ashen.

Declan and I raced forward to check for a pulse, but somewhere deep inside me, I knew it was a losing cause.

Rocky Arnaud was dead.

Chapter 4

I don't know which of us switched off Piaf, and I really can't say if Declan helped me into a chair or if I helped him. I only know that when the police arrived, it was deathly silent at Pacifique and we were seated on either side of Rocky, like sentinels charged with guarding her. At the first knock, I flinched and brushed tears from my cheeks. At the second, Declan got up and went to the front door.

"Fury! What are you doing here?" Apparently the cop at the door knew Declan, and if I was thinking more clearly, I would have realized that shouldn't have come as a surprise. The cops back in Hubbard certainly knew him. And didn't like him.

Declan made it clear that the feeling was mutual.

Here, the vibes were different. Maybe it was the magic of Pacifique. Or maybe the officer who walked into the room ahead of Declan realized that there is a certain respect we all must pay in situations like the one we found ourselves in, and a certain, special kindness that needs to be shown to those who are left to handle the grief in the wake of a visit from Death.

The cop was a man of forty, maybe, a little shorter than Declan and a bit broader. He had light eyes, honey-colored hair that was a couple of shades darker than mine, and an air of competence that I hardly registered at the time, but was grateful for later. The first thing he did was come up to where I was sitting and bend down so he could look me in the eye.

"Are you all right?" the cop asked.

I couldn't make a sound pass the lump in my throat so I just nodded.

The cop looked over his shoulder. "The medics are right behind me. They'll be here in a minute. If you need anything—"

"I'm fine." I shook away the shock that stole my words. "But Rocky—" I made to get up and go to her, but the cop stopped me, one hand on my arm.

"There's nothing you can do for Rocky," he said. "But maybe Declan . . ." He glanced that way. "Maybe he can take you into the kitchen and you can make a pot of coffee."

I shook my head. "I don't want any coffee."

The cop's eyes shone. "You might not, but I do. It's late, and I think I'm going to be here for a while. If you could handle that for me . . ."

He didn't wait for me to answer; he stepped aside so I could get up, and together, Declan and I went into the kitchen.

I had always liked Rocky's kitchen. Sure, it was small,

but that didn't mean she didn't pack as much French pizzazz into it as she possibly could. The cupboards were whitewashed like that china cabinet in the dining room, the floor was wide oak planks, the walls were covered with the kind of kitschy, whimsical art that always made a visit to Rocky's a treat. There was a Grateful Dead poster on one wall and okay, it wasn't exactly French, but with its vivid blue background, red roses, and grinning skeleton, it had always made me smile. That night, thinking about Rocky staring, unseeing, at the ceiling in the parlor, I turned away from the skeleton and concentrated on a small oil painting of chickens in a farmyard and the framed photograph of Julia Child that hung next to it.

"You know where the coffee's at?" Declan asked.

I couldn't say for sure, but I'd been there plenty of times when Rocky insisted on making a pot of coffee for us to share so I shook myself to reality and searched for her stash of illy beans, and when I found them, I ground them and put a pot on to brew. When it was finished, I loaded a tray with a carafe, cups, sugar, and milk and took it into the parlor, where now three medics were standing around Rocky, speaking in hushed tones to the cop I'd talked to a few minutes before.

He briefly nodded his thanks to me, then turned away to say something to one of the medics, and I went back to the kitchen and started another pot of coffee so Declan and I could have a cup.

That's when I thought of Sophie.

My throat tightened and my eyes filled with tears. "I need to call her," I said. "Sophie needs to know—"

Declan wiggled his cell phone at me. "Already done. She wanted to come out but I told her the police weren't

allowing anyone near the house. And before you tell me
it's not true, I know that. I just didn't want her driving here
in the dark by herself."

It was a good plan and I told him as much while I ground
more beans and a torrent of tears streaked down my cheeks.
When I was finished and our coffee was in cups, I grabbed
a linen towel from the sink and dabbed my cheeks, then
sat down in a chair across from the one Declan had taken
at the table, neither of us knowing where to begin or what
to say.

I sipped my coffee. "You know the cop."

"Yeah." Declan ran a finger around the rim of his cup.
"Tony Russo. He went to school with my brother Riordan.
I've known him for years."

"He likes you."

"You mean he doesn't dislike me, not like Gus Oberlin
back in Hubbard."

"Gus is—"

"An idiot."

"And Tony?"

Even though from where we were sitting, we couldn't
see into the parlor, we could hear the murmur of voices
from in there, and Declan glanced that way. "Tony's good
people."

"I didn't think I'd ever hear you say that about a cop."

"I'm not that hardheaded." Declan drank his coffee.
"I'm more than willing to give credit where credit is due.
In Gus's case, it isn't due."

"And in Tony's?"

"Like I said, good people. He isn't convinced that every
Fury is a criminal and every Traveller who passes through
has felonious thoughts on his mind."

"That's because he knows your family."

"And he isn't an idiot."

There was something wrong about having such a seemingly normal conversation in light of what we'd come to Pacifique and found. I edged back in my chair, putting some distance between myself and the memory, and when I saw that my cup was empty and Declan's was, too, I got up and refilled them.

"You're never going to sleep tonight," he said, even as he loaded his coffee with milk and sugar.

"There's no way I'm going to sleep, anyway. I might as well stay awake with really good coffee in me." As if to prove I didn't care, I slugged down half the coffee in my cup and dared to say the words that had been nibbling at the edges of my mind since we'd walked in and found Rocky.

"Declan, you don't think—"

"Good coffee." I turned toward the doorway and found Tony Russo standing there, his empty cup in one hand. "I'm pretty sure Declan had nothing to do with it, so I figured I'd better thank you, Ms. . . ."

"Inwood. Laurel Inwood."

When I introduced myself, Tony's sandy brows rose a fraction of an inch. "The same Laurel Inwood who's turned Sophie's Terminal at the Tracks into a Hubbard hot spot?"

He was making conversation, trying his darnedest to ease the tension in the room so he could talk to me and Declan and hopefully get some sort of sensible statements out of both of us. I knew his easy manner and light tone were all a come-on, and I didn't care. In fact, I appreciated it.

"I don't know about the Terminal being a hot spot," I told Tony. "But I'm glad the word is spreading. Stop by this

week. We're featuring . . ." The words clogged in my throat
and I coughed to clear them. "We've got a French menu
planned. In fact, Rocky was supposed to bring over some
of her favorite recipes for us to use."

He came all the way into the room, poured himself
another cup of coffee, and sat down at the head of the table.
"What can you tell me?" he asked both of us.

Declan and I exchanged looks, and somehow I knew he
wanted me to take the lead. "Rocky was supposed to meet
us at the fireworks show tonight," I told Tony. "And when
she didn't show, we came to see what was wrong."

He had a notebook and he wrote down a line. "You're
a friend of hers?"

I nodded. "She's actually a friend . . . was a friend . . .
of my aunt Sophie's. Who really isn't my aunt."

Maybe Tony was good people just like Declan said because he didn't seem to find this odd. "That's why you
came looking for her?"

Another nod, and then I realized since he was taking
notes, he couldn't see me. "She said she'd be there, at the
fireworks, and after the way she left the parade so quickly
this afternoon—"

When Tony looked up, I realized we needed to start
from the beginning.

I told him that for weeks, Rocky had talked about little
else except meeting Aurore Brisson and how she couldn't
wait to hear the lecture Andrew MacLain was going to
give at the library. While I was at it, I mentioned that she'd
seemed distracted the night before when she came to the
Terminal, and since he was going to hear it from someone
else if he didn't hear it from me, I even told him about how
she'd made a scene at the Book Nook.

"And the parade?"

Declan filled him in on that part, about how Aurore Brisson's presence didn't even seem to register and about how Rocky ran out before the parade was even over.

"Do you think she had any reason to kill herself?" Tony asked.

I sucked in a breath and for what seemed like a long time, I was so horrified, I couldn't say a word. Finally Declan got up and got me a glass of water and urged me to drink it, and when I did and finished coughing and choking and pounding my chest, I looked at Tony in wonder.

"You can't possibly think—"

"I don't know what to think. Not yet. But I've got to consider all the possibilities."

I thought back to what we'd seen when we arrived. "You're thinking about the bottle of wine that was open on the table near where she was sitting. You think she could have—"

"Like I said, I don't know. We won't know anything for sure until an autopsy has been performed." Tony sat back in his chair. "I'm just wondering if there's any reason you know of that Ms. Arnaud would have wanted to take her own life."

The horror settled so deep inside me, I was certain it would never go away. My voice was flat; my eyes were on Tony. "You're saying she didn't die of natural causes."

"We can't be sure yet," he said.

"Autopsy or no autopsy, you have reason to believe she didn't die of natural causes. You think the wine had poison in it."

To Tony's everlasting credit, he took the comment in

stride. He also managed to keep as straight a poker face as any I'd ever seen.

I could have screamed.

Instead, I gripped the edge of the table until my knuckles were as white as the bones in that Grateful Dead poster. "No way," I said. "No way Rocky would have taken her own life. She left us a voice mail message today. Doesn't that prove it? She said she'd meet us at the fireworks show tonight. She wouldn't have said that if she wasn't planning on being there, and she wouldn't have been planning on being there if she was going to kill herself. And she was excited about the whole French thing going on in Hubbard, about hearing the Statue of Liberty expert speak tomorrow, and even about Aurore Brisson. That is, until she got to the bookstore and met her. But that doesn't mean anything. What matters is that Rocky was excited, that she had plans. That means she either died of natural causes or—"

I couldn't make myself say the words.

As it turned out, I didn't have to. Tony looked from me to Declan. "Is there anyone you know of who would have wanted to see Ms. Arnaud dead?"

Declan scraped a hand through his hair. "She was a nice lady. She sold herbs. There can't be anybody who could possibly—"

"Aurore Brisson wasn't fond of her," I put in. "At the parade . . . well, if looks could kill, Rocky would have been dead on the spot."

"Brisson." Tony wrote down the name. "Seems a little far-fetched, though, don't you think? Ms. Arnaud confronts a total stranger at a bookstore and then the stranger just happens to—"

"Tony?" One of the medics stuck his head into the room. "We're ready to move the body."

He excused himself and went into the parlor.

"It's not happening," I told Declan. "It can't be."

"Hey." He reached across the table and took my hand in his. "They're going to find out it's something normal like a heart attack or a stroke or something. Maybe that's why Rocky was acting so weird. Maybe she wasn't feeling well or maybe she knew something was wrong. Maybe she got bad news from her doctor and just hadn't found a way to tell anybody about it. You'll see." He gave my fingers a squeeze. "That doesn't mean her death isn't sad, but mark my words, it's not criminal."

DECLAN WAS WRONG.

I knew it in my hearts of hearts, but I kept my mouth shut when we got back to Sophie's and sat up all night with her, talking about Rocky, telling stories, and laughing and crying in turn. By the time we were talked out it was nearly dawn, and Declan slept on the couch in the living room while Sophie and I went upstairs and grabbed a bit of sleep before we had to get to the Terminal.

By the time I got up, got showered, and got dressed, Declan was gone, picked up by one of his brothers, and that was fine with me. We'd shared too much the night before—too much shock and too much grief and so much closeness, it made me uneasy—and I was just as glad that I'd be able to spend the day knee-deep in Terminal customers and Terminal problems and not have to share anymore.

I got my wish; the Terminal was packed with Sunday

patrons and our French menu items were a real hit with the crowd.

Earlier in the week, I would have been thrilled. Now, it seemed somehow obscene to celebrate.

"It's not what she would want." I was in the kitchen sprinkling thyme on quiches and sobbing softly when Sophie came in and put an arm around my shoulders. "She wouldn't like to see you crying, Laurel. Rocky would want us to think about her life and celebrate it. She did so much good. With her work with the peace movement and with the food she grew and shared. She wasn't the kind of person who'd want to see us feeling sad."

"She wasn't the kind of person who should have died alone, either," I said. "It's wrong."

"Nobody said life was fair." Sophie reached for the basket Rocky had left at the Terminal on Friday evening and took out the CDs of French music she'd brought us.

"Not Piaf," I said.

Sophie grinned and held up the CD from Téléphone. "I think rock and roll might be just what we need."

Just as I knew she was trying to do, Sophie made me smile, and I went back to working on the quiche and smiled again when the French rockers started in. The music worked its magic on our crowd and by the time I took a break and walked through the restaurant to see how things were going, there were a couple of people dancing.

It *was* the way Rocky would have wanted it, I told myself, and smiled.

My smile lasted only until I turned toward the door and saw Tony Russo outside.

Sophie's Terminal at the Tracks is housed in an old train station, and I zipped through the main dining area, ignoring as I always did (or at least tried to), the mishmash of faux Victorian, things like teddy bears in puffy-sleeved gowns and posters that advertised items like unicycles and mustache wax. In the months I'd been there, I'd been slowly getting rid of as much of the kitsch as I could, but there was still lace everywhere, doilies and rickrack and curtains and bunting. Someday, I promised myself. Someday I'd get rid of it all.

Then again, I wasn't planning on hanging around long enough for someday to come.

I walked through the small waiting area, where a wall of windows gave me a view of the French flag we flew outside, and I opened the front door. "You coming in?" I asked Tony.

He was out of uniform that morning, dressed in khakis and a sweater in a soft shade of bluish gray that matched his eyes. He shrugged. "The sun's shining and it's plenty nice out here. How about you come outside and we talk?"

I looked back over my shoulder into the restaurant to make sure everything was under control and stepped into the morning sunshine.

"I don't have time for breakfast," Tony said. "I need to take my parents to church this morning."

Hubbard was that kind of place. Apparently, Cortland was, too.

"I just wanted you to know . . ." He poked his hands into the pockets of his pants and as casual as he was acting, I couldn't help but feel my stomach bunch and go cold.

"The bottle of wine was poisoned," I said.

Tony shook his head. "I'll admit, that's what I thought we'd find, too. But, no."

I was so relieved, I thought my knees would give way

right then and there. I let go a long breath and collapsed, my back to the sun-drenched front of the Terminal. "I'm so glad!" The instant the words were out of my mouth, I realized how callous they sounded and stood up straight. "That's not what I meant!"

Tony had a nice smile and I realized that while we were at Rocky's the night before, I hadn't seen it. "I know what you mean," he said. "If Ms. Arnaud died of natural causes—"

"It's still sad but not nearly as horrible." As crazy as it seemed, I felt like whooping with joy. Until I stopped and considered what Tony had just said.

"*If* Ms. Arnaud died of natural causes." My voice was hollow. "That's what you said. You said *if.*"

His nod was barely perceptible. "The wine wasn't poisoned," Tony told me. "But there were traces of cyanide in Ms. Arnaud's glass, and you may not know, there's cyanide in a lot of insecticides. She was a farmer, after all. Unless we uncover something that tells us otherwise, right now, we're going with the theory that Raquel Arnaud killed herself."

Chapter 5

It's amazing how fast grief can morph into anger.

And how quickly anger can sink so far deep inside that it turns into stone-cold determination.

Even before Tony said his good-byes and walked away, my mind was made up. I knew there was no way Rocky had killed herself.

I also knew I had no choice but to prove it.

The wheels already spinning inside my head, I whirled and headed back into the Terminal. Right inside the door, I nearly ran over Inez Delgado.

Inez is one of our waitresses, a young woman with curly dark hair, which she had pulled into a ponytail, and big, dark eyes. Automatically, I put a hand out to keep her from falling over.

"Sorry," I said.

"No worries." Inez was dressed in black pants and a

yellow polo shirt with the outline of the Terminal embroidered over the heart, and she gave me a soft smile. "I know what happened. Everybody does. I know you're upset."

She was wrong.

I was so far past upset, there was no place else to go.

Nothing to do but find Rocky's killer.

"I'm just going to go . . ." I poked my thumb over my shoulder toward the Terminal office, a tiny room next to the kitchen. "Receipts and accounts," I said by way of explanation, because it was better than letting Inez know that just like I'd done when a local TV reporter was killed at the Terminal the day I arrived in Hubbard, I was planning to investigate.

Inside the office, I closed the door, blocking out the raucous sounds of Téléphone and the laughter of the people gyrating out on the dance floor. Before I sat down, I grabbed a legal pad. I poised pen over paper, ready to make a list, a plan, ready to plot a strategy that would bring Rocky's killer to justice and give closure to her murder and to her life.

Too bad I didn't know where to begin.

The sound I made was more of a grumble than a sigh, and I plumped back in the uncomfortable old desk chair. While I was at it, I grumbled some more. "Suicide!" I bit the word in half and I swear, if Tony Russo was around, I would have spit it back in his face. "No way." I kicked the desk to emphasize my point and kept right on kicking it, to heck with the toe of my snakeskin ballet flats. "No way, no way, no way!"

I was still kicking for all I was worth when the office door opened a crack and Declan stuck his head inside. "With all the noise going on in here, I figured someone was getting beat up. You okay?"

"Of course I'm okay." To prove it, I stood and raised my chin and I refused to flinch even when my toes protested their recent bad treatment. "It's just that your friend Tony—"

"Yeah, I know. I saw him outside." Declan must have been heading to church, too, and I wasn't surprised. After all, it was Sunday morning and he and his family were loyal attendees at St. Colman's. He was wearing a dark suit that made his eyes look grayer and more intense than ever. His white shirt was blinding and his tie in swirls of mossy green and orange that popped was perfect for the season. He stepped into the office and closed the door behind him. "Taking it out on the office furniture isn't going to change anything."

"I wasn't taking it out on anything, I was thinking."

"Thinking with oomph."

It was more like *ouch* than *oomph*. I shifted my weight from one foot to the other, the better to keep the pain in my toes from reminding me that next time, a little less *oomph* would result in a lot less *ouch*.

"So . . ." The way he said it—so casually—made me realize he knew exactly what was up. "You're thinking, and what you're thinking about is investigating, right?"

I shouldn't have been surprised by the question. After all, Declan had been in on parts of my investigation when the Lance of Justice, that investigative TV reporter, was killed a few months earlier. In fact, Declan and I were together when we found a second victim.

Still, it was one thing sitting alone in an office and thinking about going off and finding a killer.

And another thing to actually admit it to someone who also happened to be a someone who was an attorney.

Tell that to the certainty inside my head that told me that no way, no how, was I going to back down.

"I'm not going to back down." I gave voice to the thought. "I'm not going to let this go. You know and I know that Rocky didn't kill herself."

"If that's true, Tony will find the evidence."

"Not if he's not looking for it!" I threw my hands in the air and did a turn around the room, but since it's a pretty small office to begin with, I didn't have far to go. I found myself right back where I started from, face-to-face with Declan, in no time at all. "I've got to do something," I told him. "I'm not going to stand around and watch the authorities wrap everything up nice and clean and quick. That's not fair. It's not fair to Rocky and, you know what, it's not fair to the creep who killed her, because that person—"

I wasn't trying to be funny, so the spark in Declan's eyes stopped me cold at the same time it made my blood boil.

I guess he knew it because he reached out a hand and took my arm. "I'm not laughing at you."

I yanked my arm out of his reach and crossed my arms over my chest. "It sure looks like you are."

"Well then, I'm sorry."

I backed up a step and turned away. See, here's one of the things I've learned from always being on my own and never having a family and never having to rely on anyone or share with anyone. It's the same thing I've learned about never trusting anyone because every time I'd taken the chance and tried, I'd had my heart ripped out and stepped on.

I wasn't comfortable being on the receiving end of *I'm sorry*.

I didn't know what to say, how to react, what was expected of me.

I couldn't respond so I just turned and stared at Declan.

"I wasn't smiling because I thought you were being funny," he said, and he reached into the breast pocket of his jacket and pulled out a white envelope. "I was smiling because I was thinking about you this morning and I figured this was exactly how you'd react to Rocky's death. In fact, I've got something here that might help."

I eyed the envelope. "Something for me?"

He shook his head and a curl of inky hair fell over his forehead. "Something for Sophie. Is she in the kitchen?"

She was, and there was no way on earth I was letting him go in there with whatever was in that envelope without me.

I beat Declan out of the office and pushed through the kitchen door just a couple of steps ahead of him and we found Sophie sprinkling powdered sugar on three plates of French toast.

"I know. It's not authentic. Not really French." She stepped back to admire her handiwork.

"We can make it a little more French," I told her. I went to the fridge and pulled out a jar of raspberry preserves and spooned some on each plate. "That's how they serve it in France," I said. "They call it *pain perdu*. It means 'lost bread.' In other words, they make it out of the bread that's stale and would otherwise be thrown away." I wouldn't have known any of this if I hadn't been told the story by the housekeeper of Meghan Cohan's French country hideaway. "They always serve a dollop of jam with their *pain perdu*."

Sophie swiped her hands over her white apron. "Told

you she was smart," she said to Declan, and I wondered when they'd been talking about me and why at the same time she rang the little bell that told Inez there was an order for her to pick up.

Declan stepped forward. "Well, I can't say for sure, but Laurel might have a chance to prove how smart she is." He offered the envelope to Sophie.

She didn't take it. Instead, she wiped her hands against her apron again and she looked at that envelope like it was a snake, reared back and ready to bite. "What is it?" she asked.

"I don't know." Again, he poked the envelope in her direction. "It's sealed."

"Well, where did it come from?"

Another poke. "If you opened it, you'd find out," he told Sophie.

She ran her tongue over her lips, took the envelope, and flipped it over, but she didn't open it. Instead, she weighed it in one hand, then glanced up at Declan. "There's something in it. Something heavy. It's from Rocky, isn't it?"

With a look, he urged her to open the envelope and find out.

I got a knife and handed it to Sophie and she slid it under the flap and pulled out a single sheet of paper and two keys. One was certainly a house key. The other, I wasn't so sure about. It was maybe two inches long and very flat.

"The key to a jewelry box?" Sophie asked.

"Maybe the letter will tell you," I suggested.

Sophie drew in a breath. Her lower lip quivering, she unfolded the letter and read it to us. "'Dearest Sophie,'" she said. "'I hope you don't mind and I hope it doesn't mean I've caused you too much trouble or too much work, but

I've made you the executrix of my will. With any luck, neither one of us will care about this for a long time to come, but you know how uncertain life can be. I've left this letter with Declan for when the time is right. He has my will and he'll make sure everything is handled as it should be. He's a good man. Make sure you remind our dear Laurel of that from time to time. Just in case she forgets!'"

Sophie gave me a grin.

I returned it with a grimace and refused to look Declan's way even though I could feel his gaze on me.

She kept reading. "'Here is the key to the back door of Pacifique, just in case you need to get inside. Remember me. Adieu.'"

Sophie sniffled and looked from Declan to me. "Executrix? What does it mean? What do I need to do?"

"You said you weren't her attorney." I stepped between Sophie and Declan before he could answer. "You told me—"

"That I couldn't discuss anything Rocky had told me if she was my client. I never said she was—"

"You never did. But it would have been nice to know," I said.

"It didn't matter. Not until last night. Not until Rocky was dead." The reminder was like a punch in the gut, and I sucked in a breath, but I didn't take it personally. Declan was right.

I pulled in a shaky breath. "So what's the other key for?"

Declan shrugged.

"And what does it mean?" I asked him. "If Sophie can come and go at Pacifique—"

"It means that when the police are done with the house, so as long as Sophie says it's all right, you can go over there and have a look around."

* * *

DECLAN INSISTED ON driving over to Pacifique with me so that I didn't go off poking around (his words, not mine) by myself. He said he'd be back right after church and he'd bring the family along so they could get lunch while we were gone.

The Fury family at the Terminal is a good thing; there are lots of them.

But waiting for Declan to return . . .

Well, I'm the first to admit that patience isn't one of my virtues.

No sooner was he across the street and into the car where Uncle Pat and Aunt Kitty (who owned the beauty salon directly across the street from the Terminal) waited for him then I told Sophie I'd be back in a couple of hours, grabbed those two keys, and took off.

And it was a good thing I got to Pacifique when I did.

If I'd waited for Declan, I might have missed what was happening when I pulled up the long driveway and found a woman with her face pressed up against the front window, peering into the dining room.

She didn't move, not even when I parked the car.

She did, however, jump nearly as high as the top of the dining room window and spin around when I slammed my car door.

"Can I help you?" I asked.

The woman was seventy if she was a day, stick thin, and dressed in jeans with mud caked along the bottom hems, beat-up sneakers, and a neon yellow T-shirt from some-place called Dave's Happy Bar. The outfit was finished off with a maroon cardigan that was longer on one side than the other thanks to the fact that she'd buttoned it cockeyed. Her hair was a mishmash of mouse brown and white streaks and it hung in uncombed clumps over her shoulders. Between all those stringy hanks of hair and the bangs that were so long they covered her eyes, it was just about impossible to see her face.

My car keys in one hand, I stepped closer. "I asked if I could help you."

She swiped a finger under her nose and looked me up and down with a sort of laser-point accuracy that made me squirm in my (recently ill-used) ballet flats. Her voice reminded me of sandpaper scraping across wood. "Maybe it's you, not her."

"Maybe it's me doing what?" I asked her.

"No, no." She wasn't talking to me. She mumbled the words, shook her head, then nodded as if confirming that she knew she was right. "Not her. The other one. Has to be the other one. Has to be her."

"Her who?"

She tipped her head toward the house. "You know. Her. That Frenchy."

It was too soon after Rocky's death to hear her dismissed so flippantly, and I pounded across the space that separated me from the odd little woman so I could return stare for stare. "Rocky's not here right now. Maybe I can help you."

The woman's top lip curled and she spun back around and raced to the other side of the front door and the parlor window. Once again, she pressed her nose to the glass. "I know she's in there. Tell her . . ." A dash to her left and she pounded the front door with her fist. "Tell her Minnie Greenway knows what she did."

Somehow, I managed a smile. How's that for putting my

people skills to work? "I'm sure she'd like to see you, but she can't come outside right now. Like I said, Rocky's not here." This close, I could see that Minnie had a sharp nose, dark eyes, and a mole on her left cheek. Her lips were thin and cracked and caked with what looked like peanut butter and toast crumbs. She stepped back and pointed one bony finger my way. "You're lying. I know. I know she's not going to come outside. On account of what I did to her."

It was hardly a confession, but I couldn't help myself; my stomach went cold. I swallowed hard. "Did you do something?" I asked Minnie. "To Rocky? What did you do? When?"

She squealed her delight, revealing teeth that were jumbled one on top of the other and a gaping hole where a few of them were missing. "You bet I did! I came over here and I—"

"Sorry!"

At the sound of the voice calling from behind me, I jumped and pressed my car keys to my heart. I turned to find a man in khakis and a golf shirt hurrying up the driveway. He was middle height, paunchy, and as bald as a billiard ball, and he was breathing as hard as if he'd just run a marathon.

Huffing and puffing, he stopped next to me and put his hands on his knees. "She was supposed to stay inside," he said, looking at Minnie. "I thought she was inside. I went out to the mailbox by the road to get the Sunday paper and Minnie . . ." His eyes dark with concern, he pressed his lips together. "She promised me she'd stay in the house."

I'd been to Rocky's so many times, I knew there were no close neighbors, but I looked right and left anyway, and the man got the message.

"Over that way," he said, pointing to our left where there was a stand of maples, their leaves a deep, burnished red that sparkled like rubies in the morning light. "We live about a half mile over that way. Greenway Farm. That's what we call it. And Minnie, she promised she'd stay in the house." Once again he looked at the woman who stood near the door, staring at the tips of her sneakers and mumbling to herself. "You promised me, Minnie," the man said, his voice breaking over the words. "You said you were going to stay inside."

"Had to come see her." Dragging her feet, Minnie walked by as if we weren't even there. "Had to see if she liked what I did to her."

It was obvious Minnie wasn't going anywhere fast so the man turned back to me for a moment. "Otis," he said, and extended a hand. "Otis Greenway. I'm sorry if my wife startled you. She sometimes . . ." He glanced over his shoulder to where Minnie shuffled up the drive, sending puffs of dirt around her as she went until pretty soon, she was so lost in the cloud, I could barely see her at all. "Minnie's not well," was all he said before he started after her.

"But . . ." When I spoke, he turned back around. "What was she talking about? She said she did something to Rocky."

Though it was a chilly morning, there was a sheen of sweat on Otis's forehead and he pulled a white handkerchief from his pocket and mopped his brow. "You'll have to excuse Minnie," he said. "She sometimes . . . well, she doesn't always know what she's talking about." He checked the drive again and Minnie's progress. "Tell . . ." He glanced at the house. "Tell Rocky . . . er . . . Miss Arnaud . . . tell her I'm sorry for the inconvenience. Tell her I'll make sure it doesn't happen again."

I watched him catch up to his wife and wind one arm through hers, and together they disappeared around a bend in the driveway.

I didn't need to make a mental note about the encounter. Before I went around to the back of the house and into the barn, I called the Cortland Police Department and left a voice mail message for Tony, telling him all about it. To my everlasting credit, I told him he might want to talk to Minnie Greenway without pointing out that while he was sure Rocky's death was the result of suicide, I'd already found one person—and a pretty crazy one from the looks of things—who admitted she'd done something to hurt Rocky.

Once I ended the call, I pushed open the barn door and stood quietly for a moment, letting my eyes get adjusted to the deep shadows.

Rocky did not now and never had kept animals on her farm. At least that's what I'd heard from Sophie. She used her barn for repotting plants, for starting seeds in the spring, and for storing all her gardening equipment, from hoses to trowels to clippers.

I looked through it all and found exactly what I thought I'd find. Or more precisely what I knew I wouldn't find.

Rocky was a believer in all-natural farming.

There wasn't one container of insecticide to be seen.

This, too, I would mention to Tony Russo, only I didn't bother with another phone call. I wanted to drop this little tidbit on him when I saw him in person and could watch his expression as he realized he'd been dead wrong (poor choice of words) about Rocky's suicide. How could a woman poison herself with cyanide when there was no cyanide to be found on her property?

I kept the thought in mind when I left the barn and went into the house, stepping into the small mudroom outside the kitchen.

It was awfully quiet.

I tossed my cars keys and the back door key on the kitchen table and flinched at the sound of them jingling, but I kept the other key—that small, flat one that had been in the envelope Rocky left for Sophie—in the pocket of my pants.

This early, the sun was just above the trees, and it sent shafts of golden light through the kitchen windows. There were pots of herbs on the windowsill, just like there were in the parlor, and I caught the scent of rosemary and basil and breathed in deep, willing myself to calm down, telling myself that if I was going to discover anything, I could only do it with a clear head.

I'd washed the coffee cups before we'd left the night before and eager for something to do, I grabbed them and the creamer from the dish drainer and put them back where I'd found them, quickly looking through the cupboards while I was at it. Still no sign of anything that might contain cyanide. Done with that, I glanced around, wondering where to begin and what to look for.

I figured the scene of the crime was as good a place as any to start.

I didn't figure on how just walking into the parlor again would make my stomach swoop and my heart pound.

My knees were rubbery and I dropped into the nearest chair and stared at the place across the room where less than twelve hours before, Declan and I had found Rocky dead. The wine bottle was gone and so was the wineglass, and remembering what Tony had told me, that wasn't a surprise. There was gray fingerprinting powder on the table where the bottle and glass had been, and I told myself I'd clean it up before I left, before Sophie came to the house and had to look at it.

Just knowing I had a plan (however insignificant) helped calm me, and I decided that I would start upstairs and look through Rocky's bedroom, the rooms she used as guest rooms, and her office. There might be something—a jewelry box, a diary—that would fit the small key she'd left for Sophie.

My mind made up, I'd just gotten up to go upstairs when I heard the back door creak open.

It was then I remembered that I'd forgotten to lock it behind me.

Chapter 6

Fight or flight?

I knew I didn't have more than a second or two to decide. Whoever had come in through the back door was now in the kitchen; I could hear footsteps on the wooden floor.

I glanced toward the hallway and the front door and wondered if I could make it that far, but the footsteps were getting closer fast and I was pretty sure I couldn't. That's when I looked around for some kind of weapon. With no other options, I grabbed that coffee table book about the Statue of Liberty by Andrew MacLain. Talk about heavy reading!

The book hefted in both hands, I crept closer to the wall, farther from where the person would see me if he—or she—looked into the parlor from the doorway. My back to the framed and autographed picture of Charles de Gaulle, a photo of the Eiffel Tower, and the framed copy of the article about Rocky that had appeared in a local newspaper in the spring, I stationed myself to the right of the doorway and raised the book in both hands, ready to strike.

The moment I heard a movement outside the door, I pounced and after that, the sensory impressions came hard and fast. My gut instinct was to hit and hit hard. But my brain told me the intruder was someone familiar, someone safe, and at the last second, I pulled up and only struck a glancing blow.

Good thing.

"Really?" His arms over his head to protect himself from another assault, Declan scooted past me and to the other side of the parlor and when he was sure he was safe, he rubbed the top of his head and winced. "Did you really think that was going to work?"

I tossed the book down on the nearest chair. "It would have worked perfectly on someone whose head wasn't so hard." I watched him for a moment, grateful I hadn't hit him full force at the same time I hated it that I might have caused him even a little pain. "I'll get you ice," I said, and even though he protested, I scooted into the kitchen, loaded a plastic bag with ice cubes, and wrapped it in a towel. When I got back to the parlor, Declan was sitting where he had been when Tony Russo arrived the night before. I plunked the makeshift ice bag on top of his head.

"Ouch!" He grabbed the bag and repositioned it. "If I've got a concussion, I'll sue. I'm an attorney, remember. I could do it."

I took the seat where I'd been the night before, facing him and next to the chair in which we found Rocky. "If you've got a concussion, it's your own fault," I told him. "Why didn't you yell to me when you came in? And why didn't I hear your motorcycle?" I could see only a small strip of the driveway from where I sat, but I checked it out, anyway.

"I brought Uncle Pat's car. After I dropped him and Kitty and Mom and Dad and a whole passel of nieces and nephews over at the Terminal for lunch. You can thank me anytime. Those kids eat so much, your profits are bound to go through the roof."

"Thank you," I said, but only because I felt I had to. "And the reason you were sneaking around?"

"I wasn't sneaking." Declan removed the ice bag long enough to touch a finger to the top of his head. He made a face and put the ice bag back where it started. "I thought you might be upstairs and I was going to call to you from the bottom of the steps. I only looked in here because . . ." His gaze strayed to that empty chair between us. "I don't know. I was thinking about last night and about Rocky and I just wanted to see the room again. You know, to prove to myself that what happened was real."

"How did you even know I was here at Pacifique?"

"Sophie didn't give it away, if that's what you're thinking," he said. "She didn't have to. I knew you wouldn't wait for me. You should have seen me in church, squirming my way through Father Walsh's sermon. I figured you'd try to do something stupid and—"

"Stupid? You mean like coming up with a suspect in Rocky's murder?"

Declan's dark brows rose a fraction of an inch.

From him, it was the equivalent of a high five, well done, you go, girl!

"Minnie Greenway," I told him. "A neighbor. She practically confessed."

"*Practically* isn't one of those things that stands up in court."

"Well, maybe she will confess once your friend Tony talks to her."

"And did she happen to spill her guts and mention why she killed Rocky?"

"She didn't actually say she did kill Rocky," I said in the interest of full disclosure. "But Minnie did say she did something to Rocky. That's practically the same as a confession, isn't it? Minnie said something about how she knew what Rocky had done and how Rocky couldn't hide from her."

Declan pursed his lips and glanced around. "And where is this deadly neighbor?"

"Her husband came and collected her before I had a chance to get all the details. And just so you know, I mean, in case it's important, I think Minnie might be a little mentally unbalanced. Or maybe a lot mentally unbalanced."

"This just gets better and better." He was about to toss the ice bag on the nearest table, thought better of it, and dropped it on the floor. "Still, it might be worth mentioning to Tony."

I gave him a smile. "Already done."

"Well, you have been busy, haven't you? So . . ." Declan slapped the arms of the chair and stood. "What do we do next?"

It was the same question I'd been asking myself, yet somehow, knowing Declan was there to work through the mystery with me made things seem a little easier to handle. "I guess we look around. Maybe for a date book that would tell us who might have been here with Rocky last night. Or for a diary. You know, because of that little key Rocky gave Sophie."

He didn't look convinced. "I'm thinking safe deposit box," he said.

It made a world of sense.

Grateful for the insight, I asked the next logical question. "Which bank?"

Declan made a face. "That's the thing with safe deposit boxes. They never put the name of the bank on the key. And customers are urged not to keep their keys with any of their bank information. You know, for security reasons."

"Then how do we find out which bank it's from so we can see what's in the box?"

Again, he glanced around the room. "I guess we can start with what's in front of us. We'll look through the house, room by room. There are bound to be bank statements or, like you said, a calendar of some kind. Maybe something will give us some clue as to where the safe deposit box might be and maybe something will help us make sense of what happened here last night."

We started our search there in the parlor which, come to think of it, might not have been the wisest plan in the world. Rocky's parlor was crammed with pictures and furniture and bric-a-brac. The drawers of every bureau were stuffed full with account books and receipts. It was overwhelming.

"Rocky always talked about her home office," I told Declan. I was on my knees finishing with the last of the papers I found in a marble-topped dresser with a pumpkin on top of it and a glittery black cat beside it, Rocky's homage to the upcoming Halloween holiday. "I pictured some room upstairs, something more formal, but something tells me this was her office." I hadn't found anything of interest and I sat back on my heels and sighed. "I don't know about you, but I think we're getting nowhere fast."

Declan had taken a pile of papers from a one-drawer table near the window and sat down with them, and he was just

about at the bottom of it. "Receipts for organic fertilizer, receipts for flower pots, receipts for peat moss and seeds and
the plastic containers she used to package her herbs," he said,
shuffling through the last of the papers. "Nothing here says
murder to me. But there's no sign of cyanide, either, and if
Rocky administered it to herself, you'd think there would be."

Finally, someone was talking sense!

I put everything back where I'd found it and stood. "And
will Sophie have to go through all this?" I asked him. "You
know, as executrix?"

He nodded. "Knowing Sophie, it will take her a while."

"Is that your way of saying we need to keep looking?"

He stood, stretched, and pressed a hand to the small of
his back. Halfway through the pile of papers he'd just been
through, he'd stripped off his suit jacket and rolled up his
sleeves. He looked like a man who was ready to get down
to business. Not to mention handsome and sexy as hell.

I batted the thought away.

After all, I wasn't staying in Hubbard and there was no
use starting something I knew was going to end too soon.

"I'll check the kitchen. You check the dining room," I
said, and I'm pretty sure I managed to make it sound like
a logical plan rather than a tactical retreat from all that
deliciousness. Before he could even begin to suspect, I
dashed into the kitchen and got to work.

I checked the cupboards and the pantry. I even looked
in the dishwasher. The good news is that I didn't find any
papers I needed to look through, so the search went quickly.
I did find a good many wineglasses, including the match
to the one we'd found tipped on the table next to Rocky's
chair the night before. I could tell from the etching and the
thin weight of the glass that it was an antique.

"You know . . ." I took the glass down from the cupboard and twirled the stem in one hand at the same time I walked over to the dining room door. Declan was just about done looking through the china cabinet and he looked up when he heard me. "If Rocky had a guest last night, both these glasses would have been out, don't you think? I mean, you wouldn't have one wineglass out and not another, and if you were going to have two out, you'd use matching glasses, right?"

"Maybe."

It wasn't the ringing endorsement of my reasoning I was looking for.

"What?" I demanded.

When Declan shrugged, his shirt pulled over his broad shoulders. "If there was a person here with Rocky last night . . ." He made sure I understood this was just a hypothesis. "Maybe that person didn't want any wine. Maybe that person did use that matching glass and since he—I'm just calling him he, I'm not saying we know that for sure—since he didn't want anyone to know he was here, he washed the glass and put it away."

So much for brilliant theories.

Declan went right back to work so the face I made at him went to waste. I went back into the kitchen, put the glass where I'd found it, and looked around some more. Unlike the parlor, the kitchen had been pretty simple to search and I was hoping for the same from the other rooms of the house. There was only one piece of furniture I'd yet to check out, a thigh-high wooden cupboard near the back door. It had two doors at the front that swung outward, and eager to finish the kitchen and get upstairs, I opened it. The cupboard was filled with candles. I wasn't surprised. Rocky had been a big proponent of ambience, which always made me wonder why she hadn't talked some sense into Sophie when it came to decorating the Terminal.

I wouldn't have felt I was being thorough if I didn't look through the cupboard so I started with the bottom shelf, where boxes of tea lights were stacked one on top of the other.

Good thing I did.

"Declan!" I guess he heard the urgency in my voice because he came into the kitchen just as I pulled a desk calendar out of the cupboard. "It's a date book," I said, waving it at him. "For this year." The calendar featured pictures of garden plants, was about eight by ten inches big, and spiral bound. It showed a week at a time, spread over two pages, each day marked off by a rectangle.

I took the calendar to the table and sat down and Declan came up behind me and braced his arms on either side of me, the better to see over my shoulder.

I ignored the heat of his body and the scent of his bay rum aftershave (which, I should mention, wasn't easy) and flipped the calendar to the right week, automatically smiling when I saw that Rocky had lived up to her reputation for style and spunk, even when it came to her calendar. I remembered her telling me that she insisted on always writing with a French-made Oldwin fountain pen and she added a flourish to every letter.

"She's got the book signing marked," I said, pointing at Friday. "And this evening's talk at the library by Andrew MacLain. See?" I read what Rocky had written on that day's square. "'Tonight! A chance to hear Andrew speak. Starts at seven, but I'll get there early for a front-row seat!' That should prove to Tony that she couldn't have killed herself," I told Declan. "The fireworks last night, the library talk tonight. Rocky had plans."

"And she's got nothing written on yesterday's date except for the parade in the afternoon and the fireworks in the evening." Declan's voice reflected my own disappointment.

I tapped a finger against the calendar page. "So she wasn't expecting anyone here last night, at least not anyone she'd put on her calendar."

"But what about this?" Declan wasn't even looking at the entry for Saturday. He had a finger on Thursday, where Rocky had written something in teeny little letters.

I squinted and put my nose closer to the calendar, reading Rocky's note. "'It doesn't make sense. I don't understand. Someone in the house last night? Or was I dreaming? Nothing taken, but I swear, I heard—'" The last word was impossible to read because the ink was smeared. My blood ran cold.

"Someone here? In the house?" Yeah, I got it. If it was true, that someone was no longer there. But that didn't keep me from looking into every corner of the kitchen, just to make sure we were alone, that we were safe.

Like I'd been punched in the gut, I sat back in my chair. "No wonder she was distracted Friday when she came to the book signing. She thought a burglar was in the house on Thursday night. She was nervous. And upset. Why didn't she say anything?"

"Why didn't she call the police?" Declan took the chair next to mine, and he knew I was going to ask, so he explained before I could. "If she'd called about a break-in, Tony would have known about it. Rocky's death would have made more sense to him if he had this piece of the puzzle. Still . . ." Thinking, he wrinkled his nose. "Poison doesn't seem like something a burglar would use, does it? I mean, a burglar might shoot someone or knock them over the head. But cyanide in a wineglass? To me, that seems more . . ."

"Personal?" I filled in the blanks for him with the word he refused to say and turned my attention back to the calendar. "Look at the weeks before this week," I told Declan, because he was seated on my left and it was easier for him to turn the pages back to the weeks before Rocky's death. "Let's see what else she has to say."

As it turned out, Rocky said a lot.

The notations started two months earlier.

"Hang-up phone call," the first of them said.

That same note appeared on five other days; Rocky's neat script a little heavier, a little more worried, each time.

"Saw someone on the property," she'd noted just a couple of weeks before the night of the event at the Book Nook. "Maybe just Minnie Greenway. Not sure if I hope it was . . . or wasn't." I poked at the page. "Minnie Greenway! See, I told you she was a suspect."

"Maybe," Declan conceded, but not in a way that made me think he was convinced.

"This is all evidence," I said, and dared him to find an objection, and when he didn't I said, "We need to get this calendar to Tony."

And still, he didn't look convinced. "I'm not trying to be the voice of gloom and doom here," Declan said, the voice of gloom and doom. "But I know cops. Even good ones like Tony. There's always a chance he could say that we wrote those notes there, just to try to disprove his suicide theory."

"But we wouldn't do that."

"I know that. And Tony knows it, too. But I'm just telling you, cops have to be careful and they have to be sure. If they're going to build a case on evidence, they have to know it's rock solid. This isn't going to prove anything to them."

"Unless they're the ones who find it." I snatched up the calendar and put it back exactly where it came from. "If we tell Tony we saw a calendar in the cupboard and pulled it out and when we saw what it was, we put it back right away . . . if we tell him we think it's something he might want to look at . . ."

Declan nodded. "It might work."

"Admit it, it's a brilliant plan."

This, he was not willing to go along with and rather than press it, I asked, "So what do we do next?"

Declan glanced at his phone. "It's after noon. I'll call Tony and let him know we're here and that we found something he might want to look at and that we didn't find any cyanide. Bet he didn't find any cyanide, either, and he's just too stubborn to admit it. Cops." The spin he put on this last word told me exactly what he thought of the law enforcement profession, even when the cop in question was a friend. "Then I don't know about you, but I think I've had it with digging through Rocky's things today. We can always come back another time."

I had to agree. In the meantime, there were plenty of other things to think about: those notes in Rocky's calendar, the key that might belong to a safe deposit box, Minnie Greenway.

And someone in the house just a few nights before.

"Help me check the doors, will you?" I asked Declan, and I didn't even need to explain; he checked the windows, too, and when we were sure everything was locked up good and tight, I peeked into the parlor one more time.

That Statue of Liberty book was on the chair where I'd

dropped it and since it was something Rocky valued, it seemed wrong to leave it there. I picked it up, ready to set it back on the table where I'd found it, but like I said, it was a big book full of color photographs, and heavy. I bobbled the book and when it slipped out of my hands, I made a grab for it right before it hit the floor.

I saved the book from damage but there was nothing I could do about the papers that fluttered out of it and landed all around me.

"Newspaper clippings," I told Declan, making a grab for the first piece of paper. It had been neatly cut not from a local paper, but from the *New York Times*, and was dated a few months earlier. "Andrew MacLain," I said, waving the article and the photograph that accompanied it at Declan. "A profile piece about how he spearheaded the restoration project on the Statue of Liberty." I reached for the next piece of paper. "This one is about MacLain, too."

Some of the articles had landed near Declan and he reached for those that were nearest. "I guess that's no surprise. Rocky was obviously interested in the Statue of Liberty. Except this article . . ." He came up holding it. "This one's dated three years ago, long before that Statue of Liberty book was published."

It was all he said, but to tell the truth, Declan didn't need to say another word. I could just about see the wheels turning inside his head.

"You know something," I said.

He shook himself out of whatever thoughts had frozen him to the spot. "No, I don't know something."

It was such a lawyer thing to say!

"But you suspect something."

"I might, but I can't say—"

"Just like you couldn't say if Rocky was a client or not? Come on, Declan! She's dead, and we both know she was murdered. Doesn't that get rid of attorney-client privilege?"

"She was never a client. I mean, except for her will. She just . . ." Thinking about it, Declan glanced over at that empty chair where Rocky had taken her last breaths. "She came to me four years ago," he said. "But not for legal services. She just wanted advice."

"Four years. Then not about someone prowling her property or breaking into her house."

He shook his head. "She was trying to find someone and she wasn't sure where to begin. She thought because I know the legal system, I might be able to point her in the right direction."

"And did you?"

He looked down at the article in his hands, one from some obscure newspaper in some little town in New York. The headline said something about how native son Andrew MacLain had just been hired to work on the restoration of the famous statue in New York Harbor.

Declan shrugged. "I don't know if I helped her or not. She never said another thing about it after that and though I was tempted, I never asked. I figured if she wanted to talk, she'd talk. Maybe . . ." There were more articles, all of them about MacLain and one by one, he plucked them off the floor and handed them to me. "Maybe I did help her," he said.

I riffled through the articles, everything from a notice from a college publication when MacLain got his Ph.D. to more recent articles about his book, his cross-country speaking tour, his expertise when it came to everything from the cleaning of the statue to how big Lady Liberty's toes are.

"Was she looking for Andrew MacLain?" I asked Declan.

"I don't know. I wish I did. She was . . ." Ever the attorney, Declan searched for the word to describe exactly what he remembered. "She was evasive. I asked her, of course. I told her it would be easier to help if I knew exactly what she was looking for. Who she was looking for. But, well . . . you know Rocky!" He managed to smile at the memory. "She was a great lady, but she could be headstrong and stubborn. She told me flat out that it was none of my business."

"And how long ago did you say this was?"

"About four years."

"Before *Yesterday's Passion* was published. After what happened at the bookstore, do you think she might have been looking for Aurore Brisson?"

His shrug was not the answer I hoped for.

"Then what about Andrew MacLain?" I asked, glancing down at all those articles about the man. "Maybe she was looking for him."

"Maybe."

"And maybe when Rocky left us that voice mail message and said how she was overwhelmed by the past . . ." I wanted so much to have answers, I felt like screaming. "Maybe that message had something to do with one of them. Something to do with this person she was looking for."

He spared me another *maybe*, and for that, I was grateful.

I would have been even more grateful if I could figure out what the heck to do next.

Chapter 7

The way I saw it, I had a few avenues to explore:

There was Aurore Brisson of the too-white smile and the too-plump lips, who stood there at the bookstore with her jaw flapping when Rocky accused her of stealing *Yesterday's Passion* from Marie Daigneau.

There was Marie herself. Sophie remembered Rocky talking about her friend from France, but who was Marie, really? Had she written a book? One that Rocky could have mistaken for *Yesterday's Passion*?

Then, of course, there was Minnie Greenway, she of the questionable personal-grooming habits, the unquestionably unusual mental state, and what sounded like a big-time grudge against Rocky.

And let's not forget Andrew MacLain. Aside from the fact that he was apparently one smart cookie and a nice-enough-looking man, what was it about the scholar that had turned the usually levelheaded Rocky into a fangirl?

Tantalizing possibilities, every one. But my questions didn't end there.

I also had to consider Rocky's date book with its curious entries, along with the safe deposit box key and the fact that Rocky had asked Declan for advice about finding someone who may not have been lost, but was obviously missing from her life.

When it came to investigating, this was all good news. There were lots of people to talk to and that meant lots of possibilities for a break in the case.

From a practical point of view, it was as frustrating as hell. Especially when Sundays are traditionally one of our busiest days at the Terminal and once I returned from Pacifique, I didn't have a moment to myself.

"Tartines!" Sophie waltzed into the kitchen to the rhythm of Maurice Chevalier singing "Thank Heaven for Little Girls" over our sound system and waved a stack of customer orders in the air. "Lots and lots of people want tartines. Can you handle it, George?"

George grumbled, but I knew he'd come through. He always did.

In the meantime, I whipped up a few more quiches, a bittersweet smile on my face when I chopped the griselles Rocky had brought over on Friday night. I got those into the oven and went out front, and since Inez and Misti, our newest waitress, were both busy, I took over the duties behind the cash register so they could concentrate on serving.

Lots of customers and lots of business were all great, but dang, I couldn't help myself; every time I glanced out the front window to where the French Tricolor waved from our flagpole, I thought of Rocky. And every time I thought of Rocky, my breath caught in my throat.

I finally got a break around four o'clock and while Sophie and Inez and Misti invited me to sit down and join them for a cup of coffee in the hopes of recharging their energies before the dinner crowd arrived, I ducked into the office.

Good thing I did. When my phone rang, I was able to take the call in private.

I glanced at the caller ID and took a deep breath to calm my heart and squelch the rat-a-tat rhythm in my voice that might make me sound less professional, less organized, more harried.

"Laurel Inwood," I said when I picked up.

"Ms. Inwood." I knew who it was (hence that rat-a-tat rhythm), but he introduced himself anyway. It was how things were done in the strata of society where he lived and worked. "Fletcher Croft. I'm glad I caught you. I thought perhaps on a Sunday afternoon, you'd be out and about."

In Croft's mind, I'm sure *out and about* was equal to watching a polo match. Or cruising on my yacht. I didn't have the heart to tell him that in my case, it was more like handing out suckers to the kids who came up to the cash register with their parents.

"I'm glad you caught me, too," I told him. "I've been anxious to talk to you."

"And I'm pleased to tell you that Senator Stone is anxious to talk to you. She's narrowed down her search to two candidates. You are one of them. I will admit, she was a little reluctant because of your Hollywood connection, but

I managed to convince her that might actually work in her favor. You're used to the limelight."

"It was hardly shining on me," I reminded him, and toed the line between how much I knew I should disclose and what I thought he wanted to hear. "But I was often there with Ms. Cohan when the paparazzi descended. I can't say I ever got used to it, but there is an art to handling them. Smile, and keep your mouth shut!"

"Yes, yes." He sounded distracted and I heard him shuffle papers. Croft and I had been talking for a couple of months now, and we'd had two face-to-face meetings. (Just for the record, both times I'd told Sophie I was heading to Cleveland for a day of shopping when instead, I was driving to Pittsburgh so I could hop on a plane.) I knew Croft was a tall young man who was prematurely bald. He was also loyal to his employer, thorough, and organized. I pictured him looking over the résumé I had sent in response to the blind job posting I saw on the Internet early that summer. *Prominent family seeks personal chef. Talented, energetic, discreet.*

After all those years with Meghan, who was anything but discreet, and all these months at the Terminal, where energetic might be a requirement, but talented and discreet never entered into the picture, it sounded like heaven.

As did the mansion in Newport.

The penthouse in New York.

The brownstone in Georgetown.

Oh yes, I was talented and I was certainly energetic. I could be plenty discreet, too, as discreet as Senator Katherine Stone and her high-society family needed me to be, especially if it meant leaving Hubbard, Ohio, behind me.

Fletcher Croft cleared his throat. "How does Wednesday

look?" he asked. "Senator Stone has an hour in the morning. In D.C. If you flew in first thing—"

Did I groan?

I guess I did because something stopped Fletcher in his tracks.

I knew it was up to me to fill in the uncomfortable silence. "A friend has died," I told him. "Just last night. I'm not sure yet about the funeral arrangements."

There was another silence on the other end of the phone. Part of me wondered if Croft was trying to think his way through what I'd told him, because folks like him—and Senator Katherine Stone—never took time off from their busy schedules for things like the funerals of friends.

Another part of me wondered if it was even possible for politicians to have friends.

I shook away the thought when Fletcher said, "I'll need to check her availability. I really thought—"

"Yes, I'm interested." Even I knew I sounded a bit too eager, so I forced myself to take a deep breath and play it cool. "I'm very interested. And I'm grateful that the senator is considering me for the job. But I'm sure both you and Senator Stone understand that I've got an obligation here."

I prayed he did understand.

Right before I realized that what Fletcher Croft did—or didn't understand—didn't matter one bit.

What his boss understood would make all the difference in the world.

"Please let the senator know how sorry I am to cause her this inconvenience," I said. "As soon as she has an opening in her schedule—"

"Yes, we'll talk then," Croft said, and without a *goodbye*, he ended the call.

I stared at my phone for a minute or two, torn between calling him back to tell him I'd changed my mind and that of course I could be in Washington on Wednesday, and being angry at myself for caving and considering my obligation to Rocky, Sophie—and Hubbard—before I thought about myself and my own future.

Hadn't I spent a lifetime learning that no one was ever going to look out for me but me?

Didn't I realize that I might be letting a golden opportunity pass me by?

Was I crazy?

I guess I was, because in the end, I didn't call Croft back. I tucked my phone in my pocket, hoped the senator wouldn't hold a funeral against me, and told myself that the dinner crowd would be here before I knew it.

If I was going to get anything done in the way of the investigation, it was now or never.

I set aside my disappointment and got on the Internet to search for Marie Daigneau.

It should come as no surprise that I am no whiz when it comes to computers. I never stayed in one school long enough to develop the background or the skills I needed to understand spreadsheets or word processing or how things like programming work. And even when I had those kinds of classes, I never paid a whole lot of attention. Who would hire a kid like me for a job that demanded brains? Sure, it was a lousy way of thinking, but foster kids can hardly help themselves. A healthy dose of self-esteem doesn't exactly come with the territory.

It should also come as no surprise that I'm plenty determined, not to mention resourceful. As Meghan Cohan's chef, I'd had to pull a culinary rabbit out of a proverbial hat plenty of times, and if nothing else, I'd learned my way around cyberspace. Whether Meghan demanded Styrian pumpkin seed oil or insisted I cook with black truffle oil, whether she had a taste for sea cucumber or would accept nothing less than Persian musk rose syrup to serve chilled to her well-heeled friends, I made it happen with a few clicks of the mouse and Meghan's credit card in hand.

I called on the magic again and got to work, and found nothing at all. Whoever Marie Daigneau was, she led a quiet life that didn't leave an electronic trail, at least not one that was easy to trace.

After fifteen minutes of clicking and grumbling, I was finally rewarded for my efforts and found the one and only mention of Marie Daigneau anywhere on the Web.

Her obituary.

WE WERE BUSY at the Terminal that evening, and I reminded myself over and over that busy meant profits and profits would be good for Sophie, especially once I left for the greener pastures of Newport, New York, and Georgetown.

Yes, I was thinking positively and gearing myself up for when Senator Stone had an opening in her schedule, Croft called me back, and I could plan for what I knew would be the most important job interview of my life.

The thought sent a thrill through my bloodstream all the while I made vanilla crème brûlée in little individual ramekins and gathered the sugar and butter, the orange juice and the orange zest and the Grand Marnier that would go into the crêpe suzettes we were featuring on that evening's menu.

Keeping busy and thinking about my plans for the future was a good thing, I told myself. It kept me from remembering how my heart sank when I learned that Marie Daigneau had been dead for three years. I'd been counting on having a conversation with her, asking her what Rocky could have been talking about when she accused Aurore Brisson. Now that would never happen.

So much for that line of investigation.

Of course I'd been unwilling to throw in the towel so early in the game, so before I came out into the restaurant and got to work again, I came up with a plan B.

Aurore Brisson.

In the hopes of speaking to her before she left town, I'd checked her website, and for the second time that afternoon, I met a brick wall.

That day Aurore Brisson was doing a book signing in Cincinnati. In fact . . . I checked the time on my phone . . . she was no doubt already at the center of a crowd of fawning fans as far on the other side of the state of Ohio as it was possible to get.

I will not report the word I grumbled. I will say that rather than follow a line of investigation that depended on someone else, I decided to rely on my own brain.

And Rocky's date book.

Were the cryptic notes about mysterious phone calls, prowlers, and a burglar we'd seen noted on Rocky's calendar real?

As disturbing as it was to consider, I wanted to believe they were. Otherwise, those rumors I'd heard around town about Rocky—about her drinking and her mercurial personality and her erratic behavior that seemed to surprise no one—might actually be true.

Though Declan and I had left the date book at Pacifique exactly where I'd found it, I didn't need the book to remember at least some of what I'd seen in it. April 19 was the day of the first phone call, a hang-up that had disturbed Rocky so much, she'd made note of it.

"April 19," I mumbled to myself. "What might have possibly happened in Rocky's life that day?"

With nowhere else to look, I went to the city of Hubbard webpage and checked past activities. There had been no town council meetings that day, no big gatherings of any kind, no school bake sales or recycling drives, and nothing in the police blotter more unusual or exciting than a couple of traffic stops.

Just an ordinary day.

A day on which Rocky began receiving harassing phone calls.

"Crêpes for table three!" Misti called out from the order window, and intriguing mystery or not, I shook myself out of my thoughts and got to work. I whipped up the crêpes, made the beurre suzette (the sauce composed of that sugar and butter and orange zest and orange juice), and when I had it all plated, I told George to hit it, and he poured the Grand Marnier over the crêpes.

George Porter is a man of few words and fewer culinary skills.

He looked as pleased as punch when he put a flame to the liqueur and it lit up like the rockets we'd seen over Harding Park the night before.

When Misti carried the crêpes out to the table, I heard the sound of applause from out in the restaurant.

For a few minutes, it was quiet in the kitchen and while he was still pleased enough with himself and the magic he'd created with that drizzle of Grand Marnier, I told George I'd be right back and took the chance of ducking into the office again. Don't ask me what I thought I'd find. Don't even ask me what I thought I was looking for! I knew only that there was something I was missing, something important.

Retracing my steps, I went back to the Hubbard website and from there, clicked on the link that took me to the website of the local newspaper and put in the date, April 19.

And that's when I found it.

"The article about Rocky! The one that talked about her farm!" Yeah, I was talking to myself, but honestly, I was so amazed by the article in front of me on the computer screen, I didn't really care. I remembered reading the article when it was published and thinking that it was a nice feature and because it was so complimentary to her, it was sure to increase her business. I also remembered seeing the article framed and hanging in Rocky's parlor that afternoon.

I sat up and double-clicked to zoom in on the article, and I began to read, and when I was done, I read it again, this time with a pad and pen at hand so I could make a list of every detail mentioned in the story. Truth be told, it was pretty much what I remembered from when I read the story back in the spring, and none of it was very enlightening. During the interview with a reporter name Jane Sczarmak, Rocky talked about how she'd acquired Pacifique years before and how each year, she increased the size of her garden. She talked about what crops she planned to plant this year, how she loved living in the U.S. but how sometimes she still missed France.

The reporter remarked on Rocky's evening ritual—a

trip out into the garden for the last of the day's freshest veggies while a bottle of wine was opened and left to breathe in the parlor, her grandmother's favorite wineglass at hand. There were questions about the upcoming peace symposium that Rocky would be speaking at because she'd been a student at Ohio State University back in the '70s and had been involved in a group that preached tolerance and nonviolence. In light of her French heritage, Rocky even talked about how excited she was about Statue of Liberty week, and there were even a couple of little sidebar stories, one that listed Rocky's recommendations for her favorite French foods and wines, and another of the ten things Rocky claimed every home gardener needed to know.

All commonplace.

All ordinary.

But there was something there in that story that might have made someone—some coward on the other end of the phone who didn't have the nerve to face Rocky and wanted to frighten her instead—sit up and take notice.

I tapped, tapped, tapped my pen against the paper and read over my pathetically small list of hints I'd picked up in the article.

Garden.

Statue of Liberty.

Food, wine, and more garden.

Rocky's habit of having a glass of French wine each night.

I am, of course, not completely dense. I stared at this last entry and I planned to bring it up when next I talked to Tony Russo. To her friends, it was no secret that Rocky had a glass of wine (or two) each evening. But because of the article, the world knew, just as the world knew she drank that wine out of her grandmother's glass.

If I were a betting person, I'd put a million dollars on the fact that the person who killed Rocky was counting on her doing what she did every evening, opening a bottle of wine and going out into the garden. I'd bet that person put the cyanide into her glass while she was outside. Her gardens were extensive and many of them were pretty far from the house. How easy it would have been for someone to come and go undetected!

Before I thought about it too long and my anger got the best of me, I went back to my list.

Pacifique.

France and how much she missed her homeland.

Peace symposium.

I made a note for myself to talk to the Professor Weinhart who the article mentioned was spearheading the "day-long examination of how we view peace, a look back at the origins of the college peace movement of the Vietnam era, and a look forward . . . can there be peace in the world?"

I wasn't so sure about the world, but I knew one thing: there would be no peace for Rocky.

Not until I found her killer.

Chapter 8

Considering I left the Terminal, zipped over to Pacifique, then drove all the way back into Hubbard, I made pretty good time. I arrived at the library just as the woman in charge of programming was introducing Andrew Mac-Lain and letting the crowd know how fortunate the town and its young people were because he'd be spending the entire week visiting classes at the elementary school, the middle school, and the high school.

The main library meeting room was packed, but hey, it pays to have friends in high places. Or at least friends who arrive at popular events before the very last minute.

When he caught my eye, Declan waved me over to the seat he'd saved for me next to his.

"About time," he whispered when I sat down, Rocky's copy of the book about the Statue of Liberty clutched to my chest. "He's about to get started."

"And what are you doing here, anyway?" I asked him in the same hushed tones.

One corner of his mouth pulled into a smile that was less about amusement than it was a comment on how dense I could apparently be. "Same as you. I want to see what's so special about this guy."

What was so special was that Andrew MacLain was a flat-out genius. He was articulate, he was knowledgeable. He had a way of engaging the audience that made each and every one of us feel as if we were sitting across the table from him, sharing a pot of coffee while he regaled us with stories about Lady Liberty.

MacLain threw out facts and figures like a really good pitcher tosses a baseball. Sure, anybody can do it. But not with such finesse. Not in a way that left me and everyone else in the room hanging on every word, making us wonder what we'd hear next and how he'd phrase it and what photographs and drawings and schematics he'd show on the screen behind him to illustrate his points.

Andrew MacLain was the bomb diggity.

"Except Rocky didn't know that," I muttered.

Declan had been listening to MacLain answer a little girl's question about how restoration experts cleaned the statue, and he leaned nearer. "What are you talking about?"

"Look." I pointed at the flyer I'd been given when I walked in the door. It featured a photo of MacLain at the base of the statue and included a brief biography. "It says here that this is his first-ever visit to Ohio," I told Declan. "And . . ."

"And so how did Rocky know how fabulous he is?"

Declan grinned. "Is he? Fabulous?" He stroked his bare chin. "Maybe I need to grow a beard."

"You know what I mean," I said, even though he was a guy and thus, all tied up with his ego, which meant I was pretty sure he didn't. "I just wondered how she became such a huge fan."

Declan shrugged. "She saw him on some TV show. She read the book and enjoyed his writing style. She found a website and—"

"All right. I get it. But that doesn't explain—"

Before I had a chance to explain exactly what it didn't explain—which was Rocky's obsession with Andrew MacLain—Ben Newcomb stood up from his seat directly behind mine. His wife, Muriel, the furniture factory owner and aspiring politician, beamed him a smile and held on to his hand. "I think it's great that you're going to visit the schools here in Hubbard this week," Newcomb said, and really, the way he stood there, all self-possessed and smiling and looking like a million bucks in a pin-striped suit, I couldn't help but think that his wife wasn't the only one in the family capable of schmoozing the electorate.

"Our kids need positive role models," Newcomb went on as if to prove my theory. "They need to know that they can have hopes and dreams and that those dreams can come true if they work hard. Tell us about your childhood. Were you interested in the Statue of Liberty even then?"

"Always," MacLain answered. "I've always had a fascination with the Statue of Liberty, partly because my father, William Scott MacLain, is an engineer, and when I was growing up, he talked about the amazing designs of everything we saw, from office buildings to churches to yes, the Statue of Liberty. I'm an only child." MacLain grinned. "So I got the benefit of his knowledge and his expertise all to myself, all the time."

"William Scott MacLain." The way Declan said it made me think that he'd heard of the man. "Big shot in the world of engineering. Plenty of money."

"Which explains how his kid could go to the best schools and concentrate on the one subject that fascinated him more than any other. He didn't have to worry about making a living."

Before Declan could tell me I sounded as bitter as I knew I did, Ben Newcomb asked a follow-up question. "And you're from a small town in New York?"

MacLain nodded. "Cassadaga, New York. You've probably never heard of it! But just because we lived the small-town dream didn't mean we were unsophisticated. My father traveled the world working on projects for hydro-electric dams. When he returned, he always had wonderful stories to tell."

"I wonder if dear old dad ever visited France," I said, though honestly, I wasn't sure where I was going with the thought. So what if Rocky knew him? So what if she might have met him fifty years before when she was a teenage girl living outside of Paris? That might explain a passing interest in his son, Andrew, but not the full-out kind of fixation we'd seen with all those newspaper clippings, the ones I'd left at Pacifique when I came to MacLain's program.

"Maybe Rocky was just a woman with eclectic tastes," Declan suggested, and when the program ended and he stood up, I did, too. "Maybe she was interested in Mac-Lain the way she was interested in herbs. And wine. And French pastries."

"Except we didn't find a stash of newspaper articles about herbs and wine and French pastries," I reminded him.

"Not yet." With a smile, Declan went to grab us coffee

and cookies provided by the Friends of the Library, and along with many of the people in the crowd, I queued up to have Rocky's copy of MacLain's book signed.

"Great speaker, huh?"

I turned and realized that Ben Newcomb had stepped into line behind me. He had a copy of the book, too, hoisted up under his left arm.

"Interesting man," I said.

"And interesting is always a welcome thing, right? Especially in a place like Hubbard."

I was surprised that a stranger would be so candid, and apparently Newcomb realized it, because he laughed and introduced himself. "You're the young lady from the restaurant, right? I hear you're from Hollywood. I figured you'd appreciate my assessment of small-town life. Me, I'm from a little place called New York City, so you can see how life in Hubbard borders on culture shock for me."

I could. I could also see why the over-sixty crowd found Newcomb so appealing. He had style, he had grace. His tie was Italian silk. His aftershave was expensive and intoxicating.

I may have heard the story, and I was sure it had something to do with his wife, Muriel, but I asked anyway. "So I'm here because of Sophie and the Terminal. How about you? How did you end up in Hubbard?"

He had a broad smile and teeth that were totally straight and blindingly white. I couldn't help but think he must have put his orthodontist's kids through college. "True love! Met Muriel . . ." He glanced across the room to where his wife was chatting up a group of senior citizens. "We were both vacationing and met at a resort in Cozumel and when she explained how her life and her ambitions were here in Hubbard . . ."

Newcomb shrugged. "I didn't care about the advice I got from my head. I listened to my heart. And here I am."

I hadn't listened to my head or my heart when I came to Hubbard, only to the hollow, echoing sound at the bottom of my checkbook, and Sophie's impassioned pleas.

That, of course, was about to change, thanks to Senator Katherine Stone, and thinking about it, I perked right up. But before I had time to savor the sensation, Newcomb lowered his voice.

"So . . ." He leaned close enough to make it clear we were sharing a secret and kept just far enough away so as not to be ill-mannered. "I've heard that there was some excitement around here a few months back, before I got to town. A murder, right? Some TV reporter?"

It was not something I wanted to think about, not so soon after Rocky's death, but Newcomb wasn't ready to let the subject go.

"If my sources are right . . . and they usually are . . . you cracked the case!" he said, his eyes alight with admiration.

"I helped," I admitted, downplaying my role in the Lance of Justice investigation because, let's face it, it sounds a little loony to stand around in a library and talk about how you'd solved a murder—well, okay, two murders—that the cops couldn't. "Just a little."

"So this time . . . this woman who died. This Raquel. Everyone's talking about it," Newcomb said because I guess he thought I was surprised he'd brought it up. "Are you helping out this time, too?"

"The police are sure it was a suicide." How was that for being noncommittal and completely honest all at the same time? I swallowed down the bad taste the words left in my mouth and stuck with a truth I believed in my heart of

Sedro-Woolley Public Library

hearts—even if I wasn't complying with it. "There's really no reason for me to help out."

"Except that you've been talking to the police." There was a gleam in Newcomb's baby blues. "Otherwise, how would you know what they think?"

I gave back as good of a smile as he gave me. "I work at the Terminal, remember. And if there's one thing I'm learning about Hubbard, it's that if you want to hear the latest news or the latest gossip, Sophie's Terminal at the Tracks is the place to be!"

"I'll remember that! And we . . ." Again, he glanced at his wife who was now shaking hands with each and every member of the library staff in turn. "Muriel loves the Terminal. I'm sure she'll bring me over there sometime soon. I hear you're featuring French food. Sounds terrific."

"It is," I assured him. "Some of the recipes we're using were Rocky's . . . er . . . Raquel's," I added, since he might not have realized I was talking about the same woman whose murder he'd just inquired about. "She was a terrific cook."

Apparently, he saw the sheen of tears in my eyes. "And something tells me you were a terrific friend," he said with just the right mix of personal concern and hey-we're-practically-strangers formality.

I could see that Newcomb would be an asset to his wife's political future.

I could also see that it was my turn to get my book signed.

Unlike Aurore Brisson, MacLain did not have an assistant to grab books and open them to the proper page. He handled all the work himself. When I set the book on the table in front of him, he flipped it to the title page, pen poised, then glanced up at me. "Who would you like this signed to?"

"Raquel Arnaud," I said.

And I swear, it wasn't my imagination; he flinched.

Before he could catch his breath, I commented, "She loves your work."

His smile was tight in the center but the corners of it wobbled and as quickly as he could, he scrawled out Rocky's name and signed his own.

I grabbed the book and walked away from the table but don't think I didn't make a mental note of the way MacLain had reacted.

I made a mental note about something else, too.

The way MacLain autographed Rocky's book?

Well, there was nothing odd about that, I suppose. From where I was standing on the other side of the table and reading it upside down, it looked to me like it said, *For the love of Lady Liberty!* But there was something plenty fishy about the fact that he got Raquel Arnaud's name right— without ever asking me how to spell it.

MONDAYS ARE NOT typically our busiest days at the Terminal. Oh sure, the regulars show up, just like they always do, and that Monday like clockwork, Phil Plumline and his buddies, Dale, Stan, and Ruben, were at table three for lunch.

According to what I'd heard from George and Inez, Phil and his buddies hadn't missed a lunch at Sophie's in three years, ever since the factory where they worked shut its doors and they were left with endless, empty hours to fill. These days, they sometimes showed up for dinner on the weekends, too, usually with wives and kids and grandkids in tow. They were nice guys, and except for Stan's wife, Alice, and the woman Dale was dating whose name was either Betty or Debby (Dale was sometimes a little hard to understand, especially when he had a mouthful of food), they were a pretty basic bunch when it came to ordering. In other words, I was pretty sure they weren't going to have tartines for lunch.

In fact, when I zipped by on my way to the front door, Dale called out, "You've got meat loaf on the menu today, don't you, Laurel?"

I could just about hear the thread of fear in his voice. Soon after my arrival at the Terminal and before I discovered the appeal of ethnic foods in a town built by immigrants, I'd tried to change up the menu with the kinds of dishes I loved to eat and learned to cook in sunny California.

The guys still hadn't forgiven me for the lentil and quinoa salad.

Looking back on it, I guess I couldn't blame them. To attract new business (and it had worked!) we'd added ethnic specials and decorations that highlighted whichever country's cuisine we were featuring. But for people like Dale, Phil, Ruben, and Stan, we'd kept the basic menu that had been served at the Terminal since time immemorial—things like fried bologna, meatballs and rice, and yes, meat loaf.

I gave Dale the thumbs-up and was rewarded with a smile.

That is, right before I headed out the front door so I could get back over to Pacifique. Until I finished looking around Rocky's house for anything that even resembled a clue, I wasn't going to be happy. Sophie knew it. The Terminal

closed at five on weekdays, and like I said, we weren't an-
ticipating much of a crowd; she'd given me her blessing to
leave for the day and her permission to look through Rocky's
things.

She hadn't told me she'd alerted Declan to the fact that
I was on my way out.

"What?" He was leaning against the flagpole where the
French Tricolor waved in the early afternoon breeze, and
one look at my face and he stood up tall, his arms crossed
over the rusty-colored sweatshirt he wore with butt-hugging
jeans. "What's that look for?"

He fell into step beside me.

"That," I said.

"And that is . . . ?"

I stopped and turned to him. "You were waiting for me."

A smile inched up the corners of his mouth and made
his eyes spark. "I've been waiting for you all my life."

I somehow managed to control a groan, but I could do
nothing about the rolling of my eyes. "Corny," I told him.

"But true."

It was my turn to cross my arms over my chest. I settled
my weight back against one foot, too, the better to look up
and look him in the eye. "Not true. You told me once that
you only date Irish women."

"And you told me that since you grew up in the foster
system and don't know your biological family, you don't
know what your ethnic background is." The pat he gave
me on the shoulder might have been interpreted as nothing
more than friendly if his hand didn't linger so long. "You're
gorgeous. You're intelligent. You've got determination and
spunk and character. I've decided you must be Irish."

If I knew whether he was kidding, the statement wouldn't

have knocked me so much for a loop. If he knew I knew he wasn't kidding, he would have taken advantage.

I was leaving.

I was going to work for Senator Katherine Stone. Or at least that's what I hoped.

I couldn't afford entanglements. Or regrets. I couldn't risk getting into something I knew it wouldn't be easy to get out of.

And the something I had in mind with Declan would have been very hard to get out of.

I pasted on a smile that probably wasn't completely convincing. "Lucky me. Suddenly Irish. Does this mean I get invited to all your family parties?"

"You're always invited to my family parties. And you're right . . . lucky you. It means I can officially date you now."

I started for my car. "We always seem to be together—doesn't that count as dating?"

"I was thinking less murder investigation, more dinner by candlelight."

When it was with the right guy, I liked dinner by candlelight.

Only I was afraid Declan was a little too right.

I unlocked my car door and looked at him over the hood, where he stood near the passenger door. "Are you coming with me?" I asked him.

"Does that make this a date?"

I unlocked the door for him anyway.

Declan hooked his seat belt and settled back. "So we're going to check out the rest of Rocky's house, eh?"

I waited to give him a sidelong glance until I'd backed out of my parking space and got out onto the street. "You know that. Sophie must have told you. Just like she must have called you and asked you to come along."

"Not really." He scratched a hand behind his ear. "She actually walked over to the shop this morning and told me what you had in mind. No calling involved."

At least he got big points for honesty.

I waited my turn at a four-way stop. "And did she say why she thought it was important for you to be there?"

"Two heads are better than one, remember. And two people will make the searching go faster."

"Only that's not what Sophie said, is it?"

His grin warmed up the small space between us. "You know her well."

"She's easy to know. With Sophie, what you see is what you get."

"I like that in a woman."

It was my turn to grin. "Maybe you should date Sophie."

Declan laughed. "My parents would never approve. Charnowski! She's definitely not Irish!"

We drove in silence for a few minutes before I asked, "So what did she really say? I mean, to get you to come along. Sophie didn't tell you that I needed help searching the house."

"But she did say she didn't like the idea of you being in a house where a murder had recently been committed." Declan's smile settled. "She cares about you, Laurel."

It was true and I knew it. But when I took the time to think about it, I always ended up annoyed. Years of living in the system, and it wasn't that I didn't trust such straight-forward motives, it was just that it was completely impossible for me to understand them.

My answer to the problem was simple—I just didn't think about it, and to prove it, I concentrated on the road ahead.

We arrived at Pacifique just a little while later, but no sooner were we up the long, winding drive than I slammed on the brakes.

"That's her!" I pointed to the front of the house and the woman in the ratty jeans and maroon cardigan who was standing at the door. "That's Minnie Greenway."

When I made to jump out of the car, Declan put a hand on my arm to stop me. "You think she's dangerous?"

"I think she's as nutty as a fruitcake. But I don't care. I want to know what she's doing here." I shook him off, got out of the car, and strode up to the front door. It wasn't until I got there that I realized Minnie had a phone in her hand and a wide (and dare I say it, kooky?) smile on her face.

"What's up, Minnie?"

She chortled. "Calling her." She looked at the phone, not at me, and punched in a series of numbers. "That ought to drive her around the bend! I keep calling. And I let it ring three, four, five times. Then I hang up!" She did just that and laughed her head off. "That ought to teach her a lesson!"

"Teach who?" Declan had followed me up to the front door, but when he asked the question, Minnie barely spared him a look.

"Oh, won't this just get her little French knickers in a twist!" Minnie dialed the number again and from some-where inside the house, I heard the faint ring of Rocky's phone. "Three, four, five . . . six this time!" Again, she disconnected the call and laughed like a loon. "She'll get tired of getting up to answer the phone. She'll get mad."

If Rocky had been there, I actually might have been annoyed. The way it was, I simply felt sorry for Minnie. "Rocky's not home," I told her.

It took her a second to process the information. "What?"

"She's not home," I told Minnie. "That's why we stopped by. You know, to check on the house and pick up the mail and any phone messages she might have."

"Of course she's home!" Minnie dialed again, but this time, she didn't let Rocky's phone ring nearly as long. She hung up, and Minnie's lips folded in on themselves. "That will teach her!" she grumbled, and without another word, a look at the house, or another dialed call, she turned around and walked away.

Declan watched her go. "I see what you mean about her being a little off."

"And a little obsessed with Rocky, too, I think."

Minnie didn't go down the drive, she headed across the front lawn, and we watched until she disappeared into a grove of flaming red maples.

"I don't know," Declan said. "She might be obsessed, but she doesn't exactly strike me as a calculating murderer."

"Maybe not." I fished in my purse for Rocky's key. "But remember those notes on Rocky's calendar. I think we might have just found the source of all those harassing phone calls."

Chapter 9

I knew Tony Russo had stopped over at Pacifique after I called him and told him about the date book; he'd gotten the key from Sophie. From the looks of the house, he hadn't touched another thing. Either that, or he was the world's most orderly cop.

We were upstairs, me and Declan, and I had never been on the second floor of the house and needed to get my bearings.

"Bedrooms that way," I said, pointing down either side of the hallway in front of us from where we stood at the top of the stairway. "Bathroom at the end of the hall, I bet." Then again, the SALLE DE BAIN sign on the door was a dead giveaway. "Where do you want to start?"

Declan stepped around me and peeked into the room nearest to us. "Rocky's bedroom is probably the most logical place," he said. He poked a thumb toward the room he'd just looked into. "That's not it. It's more of a library. Tons of books, an easy chair, a reading lamp."

Tons of books.

And they'd all need to be looked through.

I didn't even realize I'd sighed until Declan put a hand on my arm. "Hey, we don't have to do it all in one day. That's the good thing about Sophie being the executrix. We've got access to the house."

I walked down the hall and looked into the next room. The walls were covered with framed botanical prints, and there were two chairs across from each other and a small table with a stained glass lamp on it over on the far side of the room. In the center of the room was a large table with a chair pulled up to it.

There wasn't a single thing on the table.

"That's weird, don't you think?" I strolled into the room and touched a finger to the table. "Why have a table and not use it?"

"Who says she didn't use it? Maybe Rocky used it all the time. Maybe sometime before she died, she just cleaned up whatever it was she was doing."

I gave Declan a look (head dipped, eyebrows raised, mouth pulled up at one corner) and he got the message.

"Okay. You're right." He joined me inside the room. "If she used it all the time, you'd expect this room to be just like the rest of Rocky's house. And downstairs, things are crammed one on top of the other."

"And this table is as clean as a whistle." Don't ask me what I thought I'd see, but I bent so that I could look at the tabletop in the light that streamed into the room from windows on the opposite wall. "You think the cops have dusted for prints?"

"After that date book you found, I'm sure they did."

"Do you suppose they found anything?"

It was his turn to give me a look. "Tony's a friend, but that doesn't mean he's going to spill the beans to me when it comes to his investigation."

I got it. I really did.

Which didn't mean I believed it.

"So what did he say about the date book?" I asked Declan.

"That he'd look into it."

"And what did he say about Minnie Greenway?"

She was long gone, but he glanced out the window anyway, toward the lawn and the trees and somewhere in the distance, the farm next door where crazy Minnie lived and made harassing phone calls and her husband, Otis, worried about her. "He said people around here know who she is. She's got a reputation."

"For being loony."

"For making threats."

I'd been checking out a hand-colored engraving of a rose, and I spun to face Declan. "And you didn't tell me?"

"I just did."

"She's looking more and more like a suspect to me."

"So, what, you're going to march on over there and arrest her? That's what the police are for, Laurel. They'll get to the bottom of this."

He was right.

I knew he was right.

It bugged the heck out of me.

"So why should we even bother?" I asked him.

"Because if we don't look through what's here, Sophie's going to have to do it, and something tells me that would break Sophie's heart."

Right again.

"And if we find anything that can help Tony out, that's a bonus," he added.

"So we'll look!" But not in that room. Even in the few minutes we'd been in there, I knew that room had no secrets to reveal.

The third room we checked had been turned into a guest room with a four-poster brass bed and a lovely little vanity painted white and highlighted with gold touches. As far as I knew, Rocky didn't have a lot of visitors, but still, the room had a lived-in look, like she sat in there often, maybe toying with the tiny Limoges boxes on the dresser, or arranging and rearranging the French porcelain vase painted with roses and the set of figurines dressed in ruffles and lace that sat on a table near the window.

I breathed in deep and caught the scent of Chanel No. 5 still lingering in the air.

"What happens to it all?" I asked Declan over the ball of emotion that suddenly blocked my throat.

"You mean Rocky's possessions? The house?" He didn't do inscrutable well, but I gave him points for trying. "We'll have to wait and see what the will says."

There was no use debating. He'd only fall back on the ol' attorney-client privilege argument again.

"Will that be after the memorial service?" I asked him.

I had no doubt he'd already heard the details, just like I had no doubt everyone in Hubbard knew them by now. Sophie was hard at work planning Rocky's memorial service. It would be held there at Pacifique, out in the gardens. It was planned for Wednesday.

Like it or not, I had been smart to put off Fletcher Croft and Senator Stone, and now that the service was scheduled,

I wouldn't wait for Croft to call me, I'd call him and find another day for the interview.

"You doing the food?" Declan asked.

He was talking about the memorial service, not Senator Stone, and I nodded and glanced out the nearest window. On this side of the house I could see a sliver of the barn where Rocky did her planting and repotting. "We're having a tent put up over near the barn," I told Declan. "Sophie thought it would be better than having people in and out of the house."

"Smart," he said. "French food?"

"Quiche is easy for a crowd. And there will be salad and fruit. Sophie's closing the Terminal for the day so the entire staff will be here to help. And we'll have French wine, of course! At least enough for a toast. Sophie said she asked you to say a few words."

"She did," he admitted. "I tried to warn her that a few words are never enough for an Irishman, but she wouldn't listen."

"You'll do fine." I knew I was right. If anyone had the gift of blarney, it was Declan. I stepped out of the guest room to go to the only other room left, what must have been Rocky's bedroom. "You coming?" I asked him.

He shook his head and a curl of inky hair fell across his forehead. "A woman's bedroom . . ." He twitched his shoulders. "That's a little personal for me."

I couldn't help but smile. "And you don't get personal in women's bedrooms?"

He stepped nearer. "Depends on the woman."

"You mean it depends on the Irishwoman."

A smile brightened his expression. "Yeah, Irish. Like you."

Trust me when I say that when I turned on my heels and headed into Rocky's bedroom, I made it look oh so casual.

Just inside the door, I stopped and caught my breath and took a look around while I willed the heat out of my cheeks.

Like the rest of the house, the bedroom was a jumble of artwork, framed photographs, and embroidered fabrics. There was a kitschy Eiffel Tower thermometer on the windowsill, a stuffed teddy bear wearing a red, white, and blue scarf on the wing chair nearby. The whole room was done in shades of milky white, light cream, and ivory, and though I am usually a sucker for color, the peacefulness of the room immediately spoke to me.

"Pacifique." I purred the word, and for the first time, I really understood what it was all about. The whole farm was about peace, about quiet. What a shame that a life that had been devoted to serenity had ended so violently.

I shook away the thought and glanced around. Across from me were windows that looked out over the back of the house and the gardens Rocky so loved, and I imagined that every morning, she threw back the curtains that puddled on the hardwood floor and opened the windows and breathed in the scent of soil and herbs and dew-kissed flowers.

Rocky had found her peace here.

Now it was up to me to make sure she also found justice.

The thought burning through my brain, I did a quick turn around the room, from the dresser across from the double bed to the lovely dressing screen of gold-painted wood with lace inserts that was opposite it.

That's when I heard Declan call out, "Hey, Laurel! Come take a look!"

I hurried into the guest room and found him standing in the closet doorway, a hatbox covered in a cheerful floral print in shades of shrimp and green in one hand. The box was open and he reached inside and scooped out a handful of envelopes.

"Letters," he said. "From Marie Daigneau. Some of them look like they go back quite a few years."

I hurried over and took the first stack of letters from him. "Maybe there's some clue," I said, breathless when I opened the first letter. "You know, about what Rocky said. About Aurore Brisson and *Yesterday's Passion* and—"

My words dissolved and my shoulders drooped and I stared at the tiny, crimped writing.

"French," I said. "They're in French. You don't happen to—"

"Not me!" Declan took the letter from my hand and put it back in the envelope it came out of. "Makes sense, two old friends writing to each other. Of course they'd write in French. We'll find someone to translate." He put the letters back in the hatbox and closed it up. "What did you find in the bedroom?"

"I haven't had a chance to find anything yet," I said, and when I left the room I reminded him, "When you're done, don't forget the letters."

Back in Rocky's bedroom I did a look-through of her dresser and of the nightstand next to the bed and found all the usual things: clothing, and souvenir tickets from concerts and plays she'd attended. There was an old note she'd written to herself so she wouldn't forget to buy flower seeds and a gallon of milk and a loaf of bread because—she said in the note—there wasn't time in the middle of planting season to bake a loaf herself.

There was also a stack of letters with a bank logo in the return-address corner of the envelope, and thinking of the safe deposit box key, I kept those out and put them on the bed.

Everything else went back exactly where I found it after I examined it, and, hands on hips, I looked around the room. The dressing screen was against one wall and it didn't look to me like there was any room behind it for much of anything, but I checked that out next, anyway.

"Nothing," I grumbled to myself, seeing that I'd been right; the screen was purely decorative, there wasn't even room in back of it to get dressed or undressed. I stepped forward to get a better grip on the screen and move it back into place and that's when my heart bumped.

"What the—" I stepped to my right, nearer to the wall and at a better angle to see if my eyes were playing tricks on me. They weren't. There was a note stuck not on one of the lace panels, but on the wooden brace that surrounded it. And no wonder. The small, sharp knife that anchored the note to the wood would have ripped right through the fragile lace.

I took another couple of steps, the better to read the words written on the sheet of paper in dark, angry letters.

Leave the past in the past.

WHAT DID IT mean?

And maybe even more important (as Declan pointed out), who had stabbed the knife through the note and left it hanging on Rocky's dressing screen?

I would bet any money it wasn't her. Sure, Rocky had an eclectic style of decorating, and her house was a bit . . .

er . . . jam-packed; she'd never met a bar of French soap or a French photograph or a French antique that she didn't like. But she treasured her possessions. Every single one of them. I could tell because though the house was cluttered, it was clean, and like a museum, each and every thing she owned was put out on display, as if Rocky was dedicated to sharing the beauty with everyone who came to call.

She never would have damaged that lovely dressing screen by jamming a knife into it.

She never would have written a note in which every pen stroke of every letter vibrated with anger and resentment.

Leave the past in the past.

IT DIDN'T MAKE any more sense to me the next day than it had the day I found the note.

"Tony will figure it out," Declan had told me, and I wanted to believe he was right. Tony had the expertise and the forensic backup to check the knife for fingerprints and maybe to even do a little of the kind of *CSI* magic I saw on TV and figure out who could have written the note from the kind of paper that was used, the type of pen, the handwriting.

Still, knowing the experts were on top of things did little to calm the cha-cha in my stomach when I thought of discovering the note.

Had Rocky seen it?

It was certainly well hidden. Yet I couldn't help but picture her casually moving that dressing screen one sunny afternoon, and thinking about how her blood must have run cold when she saw the bold, furious words.

Leave the past in the past.

It was surely a warning, but who delivered the message? And why?

The questions swirled through my head later that afternoon when I drove from Hubbard to Youngstown, the biggest city in the area and home of the university where in just a couple of weeks, Professor Jill Weinhart would be hosting that day-long symposium about peace. Professor Weinhart was teaching a class when I arrived, and I stood in the hallway outside the closed door of the lecture room and wondered as I had so many times over the years, what my life would have been like had I been given the encouragement and the guidance to attend college.

"It would have been like boring," I reminded myself with a smile and a silent prayer of thanks that Nina Charnowski, Sophie's sister, had taken the chance on a kid no one else wanted to take in. Nina had worked at a restaurant and because of her, I'd learned the skills I needed to find a job and move up in the culinary world. In fact, I'd always had a theory that one of the reasons Meghan Cohan hired me in the first place was that I had the background she knew publicists would love: edgy and just a little off-center. By hiring me, Meghan could be viewed as generous, and charitable, and just a little willing to take a walk on the wild side.

Not that I'm complaining. In her own way, Meghan had changed my life every bit as much as Nina had. Every bit as much as Sophie was trying to.

I twitched off the thought just as the door of the classroom popped open and a line of students streamed out. After the last one left, I stuck my head in the room.

"Professor Weinhart? I'm Laurel Inwood."

The professor was a woman of fifty or so with short-cropped hair and big glasses with dark, heavy frames. Though I had chosen tailored pants, a silk blouse, and a tweed blazer for the occasion, she was much more casually dressed in jeans, Toms shoes, and a tie-dyed sweatshirt with a peace symbol on it.

She waved me inside and into one of the desks in the front row, and she finished erasing a time line on the board that showed the progression of the American labor movement, then plopped into the desk next to mine.

"I can't tell you how sorry I was when you called and told me about Rocky," she said, her words as matter-of-fact as the level look she gave me. "That really stinks."

"You liked her."

She pressed her lips together. "I didn't know her well enough to dislike her," she admitted. "But the few times we talked . . . well, I didn't think I was going to like her. Not at first."

It was the kind of thing people don't usually say about the recently deceased, and the way she added a brittle little laugh, I knew Professor Weinhart realized it.

"The first time I talked to her, when I invited her to speak at the symposium, she turned me down flat. No muss, no fuss. Just an instant *no thank you*."

"Did she say why?" I asked.

"She said she knew her friend Sophie had contacted me. She said Sophie was way off base. That there wasn't anything she could tell me that the history books haven't already explored."

"But you didn't buy it."

The professor had to think about this for a moment. "I guess I could have. After all, I didn't know this Sophie person from anyone. When she called . . . you know, that first time when she told me I really should be talking to Rocky . . . she said she'd read about the symposium in the paper and that she had the perfect speaker for me."

I wasn't surprised by any of this. When it came to supporting causes—or people—she felt needed a boost, Sophie was no wallflower. "Did she say why?" I asked the professor.

"She said Rocky had experiences few other people had ever had."

"With the peace movement when she was in college."

The professor nodded. "Only I never got that far with Rocky. Not the first time we talked. Like I said, she cut me off at the knees."

"What made her finally change her mind?"

The professor took a piece of nicotine gum out of her denim purse and popped it in her mouth. She shook her head. "I can't really say. She only said she'd thought about it. That she'd reconsidered. She said she thought it was time to put the past behind her."

Leave the past in the past.

Rocky's words were another variation on the theme of the unsigned note I'd found in her bedroom. "Did she explain?"

"She said all would be made clear at the symposium." The professor made a face. "Don't get the wrong idea. It's not like I was going to let some stranger just show up here and start talking and I had no idea what she was going to talk about. I met with Rocky . . ." She squeezed her eyes shut, thinking. "Two . . . no, three times. Twice here at the university and once I went out to that wonderful little farm of hers. We talked for hours, and I was convinced that she had a lot to say that people should hear. It was quite an honor to hear the story from someone who was actually on the front lines of the peace movement. I did my homework and I found out that Rocky made a name for herself back in the day. She was part of the Young People's Underground for Peace."

When I looked at her as if I didn't know what she was talking about—because I didn't—the professor shook her head.

"You had lousy history teachers," she said. "Or history teachers who were so caught up in the far-distant past, they didn't understand the implications of the early '70s to everything that's happening today. YPUP . . . Young People's Underground for Peace . . . they were real movers and shakers back then. They worked to end the war in Vietnam. They fought for equality between the races."

"And Rocky was one of them."

"From what I could gather from the little information there is, she ran the movement in the Midwest."

I wasn't surprised; Rocky was one smart cookie.

"So what happened?" I asked.

"That's what I hoped Rocky would explain during her talk. But I imagine the movement broke up because of what usually happens in groups like that. Political differences, ego wars. I was counting on her to fill us in. She said she would. Now . . ." She lifted her hands, then dropped them back in her lap. "I suppose a lot of what she knew is lost. That's how we lose our history. It gets forgotten along with the people who made it, and that's a real shame."

I thought about the hang-up phone calls, the prowler, and that note stabbed into the dressing screen. "So you don't know exactly what she was going to say at the symposium."

"Not in detail, but if those research materials of hers were any indication, it was going to be one blockbuster of a presentation."

I sat up. "Research materials? Like? . . ."

"Scrapbooks, old newspaper articles, flyers that she'd hand out back in the day at peace rallies at universities across the country. She showed me a lot of it. Upstairs in that room of hers, the one that has all those wonderful old botanical prints on the walls."

The botanical prints. And that big old table that was perfectly clean and completely empty.

Interesting, yes? Especially in light of the fact that Declan and I had been from one end of the house to the other.

And we hadn't found one scrap of anything that looked like research for a talk on the '70s peace movement.

Chapter 10

I arrived at Pacifique just as the sun was coming up and yes, I will confess that before I got out of the car, I took a good look around and made sure Minnie Greenway wasn't lurking anywhere nearby. As it turned out, there was no sign of her, no sign of anyone, in fact, and there was a profound silence in the yard that seemed in keeping with the day's event.

Rocky's memorial service.

There was a nip in the early-morning air, but I didn't pay it much mind. For a few minutes, I stood in front of the house, my hands poked into my pockets and my head thrown back, listening to the silence and letting the truth wash over me.

Rocky's memorial service.

It was a day to mourn and a day to celebrate a remarkable life, and feeling more at peace with the thought than

I had since Saturday night when Declan and I arrived at the house and found Rocky dead, I reminded myself that none of that mourning or celebrating was going to happen if I didn't get my act together.

Ready to face the day and whatever it might bring, I got to work.

It would have been crazy for me to drive all the way to Cortland without bringing something along that we needed to host the one hundred or so folks we expected for the service, and I unloaded the boxes from my car: silverware and plates and the white linen tablecloths we'd put on the long serving tables and the round tables where guests would be seated. A couple of boxes hoisted in my arms, I headed back toward the barn, and wisps of fog floated in front of me and to my sides as I passed, as if Nature itself was asking me to dance.

Once around the house, I stopped cold and stared at the white tent that had been erected the evening before. There, too, drifts of sun-warmed fog floated in the morning air, tinted with the same pink light that touched the clouds above me. The fog wrapped around the base of the tent and climbed up its sides like the icing on a wedding cake.

It was so pretty.

And so quirky.

Rocky would surely have approved.

Suddenly smiling on a day when I would have sworn I never could, I stowed the boxes and went back for a second load. Once I was done, I took a minute to sit on the stone step near the back door. Sophie, George, Inez, and Misti had left the Terminal right behind me, but with Sophie driving, I knew they'd be a few minutes, so I took advantage of the quiet and drank in the beauty of the way the light filtered through the last of the leaves on the trees.

I was lucky to have had the luxury of a few minutes' peace. Once my coworkers arrived, the rest of the morning was a whirlwind of activity, what with getting George set up in Rocky's kitchen, giving Inez and Misti last-minute instructions and a friendly reminder that serving at a function like this was nothing like slapping food down on Terminal tables, and helping Sophie arrange and distribute the vases of orange roses, purple mums, white stock, and sprigs of cut-right-from-the-garden lavender we put on each and every table.

With everything done and our guests due to arrive at any minute, Sophie had zipped back into the house to change. Never one to worry about style, what was in, what was out, or how others would judge her based on what she was wearing, she had chosen the sort of classic outfit I knew Rocky would approve of. Black skirt, creamy colored blouse, and a black-and-white herringbone blazer that looked as if it had been made to complement her hair, which was definitely more salt than pepper.

Sophie wound an arm through mine. The weather had warmed up considerably since I'd arrived at Pacifique, and her cheeks were pink. "We did it, Laurel. It's beautiful. Just like it should be. Just like Rocky would have wanted."

It was a good thing we heard the first car pull up the drive; Sophie didn't have the chance to get sentimental and I was grateful. Later, we'd both have the luxury of shedding a few tears and feeling sorry for a world without Rocky in it. For now, we had work to do.

As it turned out, that first car wasn't filled with guests at all. It was Declan (sans motorcycle that morning) who had his two oldest nephews with him. The boys (under the watchful eye of Uncle Declan) would park our guests' cars behind the barn in an open field where in the summer, Rocky grew sunflowers that always made me think of the van Gogh painting.

I had just enough time to change, too, though since I would be working behind the bar that day, I opted for black pants and a white blouse.

The first of our guests started to arrive just as I stepped out of the house and scooted behind the bar, and in what seemed like mere minutes, Pacifique was filled with friends and neighbors, including Tony Russo, who was out of uniform and hung toward the back of the crowd, keeping an eye on things. There was no use asking Tony what he was really doing there because I knew he would never tell me. Still, I liked to think that even here where we honored her memory and celebrated her life, he had an eye out for Rocky's killer.

Declan's parents were there, too, as were Mike and John from the bookstore and Carrie, the woman who ran the boutique across from the Terminal. From the conversations I heard all around me, I knew some of the other guests attended St. Robert's church along with Rocky, that some were farmers she dealt with and others were merchants at the local stores where she shopped and always made their day with a smile and a bit of friendly conversation.

Otis Greenway showed up, his bald head gleaming in the morning light. I never did see Minnie, and I wondered who watched her when Otis was gone and how he knew she'd be where she was supposed to be when he got home. Ben Newcomb and Muriel Ross made something of a grand entrance, arm in arm, and call me cynical, but since I remembered Rocky mentioning that she really didn't travel in their circle, I wondered if their attendance was just for show.

I poured côtes du rhône rouge and for those who didn't like red wine, gentil, from behind the makeshift bar, really just a table set up at the back of the tent, and Misti and Inez passed baked brie, olive tapenade, and the allumettes I'd made from one of Rocky's recipes, wonderful little puff pastry twists served with a sprinkle of goat cheese.

"Nice!" Declan zipped by with a plate of appetizers for a group of seniors seated near the podium we'd set up against the backdrop of the garden nearest to the house. "Everything is perfect."

Though I hadn't had a sip of wine, I must have been feeling particularly mellow; knowing Declan approved of all the work we'd done made me smile.

It was the same smile I turned on Tony Russo when he stepped up to the bar.

"White or red?" I asked him.

He glanced at the wine labels. "I'm not on duty. I'll go with the red."

I poured and he sipped and when a group of guests stepped up and were served, he hung to the side. Once they were gone, he came to stand next to me behind the bar.

"Thanks for pointing out that date book," Tony said.

I knew it wasn't in the nature of cops to share, just like I knew if I didn't ask, I'd regret it. "Was there any useful information in it?" I asked, playing the innocent and pretending I hadn't looked through the date book. "Were you able to get anywhere with it?" Tony pressed his lips together. "She made a note about a prowler on the farm, but I wish Rocky would have called into the station about it. It would help to have a police report. That would make it official, not just a notation on a calendar that might—or might not—be true. It would have also helped if we knew about that note up in her bedroom. 'Leave the past in the past.' What do you suppose it means?"

I was surprised he'd asked for my opinion. Which didn't mean I was reluctant to offer it. "I've been going around and around about it. It might have something to do with Aurore Brisson and Marie Daigneau. Marie has been dead for three years. Her letters to Rocky were in the past."

Tony nodded but didn't comment.

"Or it might have something to do with Andrew Mac-Lain."

"He's not exactly in the past," Tony said.

He was right. "But maybe something to do with the Statue of Liberty . . ." Even I knew it was a stretch and I dismissed the train of thought with a shake of my shoulders. "Then how about the symposium at Youngstown State?" I suggested. "Rocky was going to talk about her past in the peace movement."

"It's possible," he said. "But to me, her death has the feeling of something more personal than that."

"You mean Minnie Greenway."

Tony had just taken another sip of wine and he looked at me over the rim of his glass. He was a nice-looking guy—I mean, not nice-looking like Declan, but then who is?—and the gleam in his eye told me this was not a conversation he'd be having with just anybody. I suppose I had Declan to thank for that. Or maybe Detective Gus Oberlin back in Hubbard, who'd never come right out and said it to me (and never would), but who might have confided in a fellow professional about how I'd helped with that investigation a few months earlier?

"Minnie Greenway." Tony's voice snapped me out of my thoughts. "Did I say anything about Minnie Greenway?"

"You didn't," I admitted. "But there's no denying she's—"

"We're plenty familiar with Mrs. Greenway," Tony said, and I knew the *we* referred to the entire Cortland Police Department. "She's got a reputation."

"For threats." I realized at the last second that I might have betrayed a confidence and figured I might as well fess up. "Declan told me. He said that you said that Minnie Greenway—"

"Has made some threats against her neighbors. It's true. Some guy down the road, she didn't like the way he kept his cows out later than Minnie thought he should. She told him that if someone burned down his barn, that would teach him a lesson. And one of the store owners in town, well, Minnie didn't like the way he packed her grocery bags. She told him it would serve him right if word went around that he was selling spoiled food."

"So she's perfectly capable of being the one who made those harassing phone calls," I said. "And she did say she did something to Rocky. She could have—"

"But here's the thing . . ." When Ben Newcomb stepped forward for wine for both himself and Muriel, Tony clamped his mouth shut.

"Lovely affair," Ben told me with a smile. "And what a beautiful setting! I hear the Terminal handled all the arrangements."

I told him he'd heard right.

Ben gave me a smile. "Muriel's looking for someone to cater a fund-raiser in a couple of months, ahead of next year's election. She'll give you a call."

A couple of months.

I didn't tell him that with any luck, I wouldn't be the one he'd be dealing with.

But I couldn't help to think it and take heart.

That is, until Tony reminded me that we had other, more important things to think about. At least for now.

"Minnie likes to cause trouble," Tony said once he was sure Ben Newcomb was well out of hearing range. "She likes to spout off about how she's going to get even with people she thinks have offended her. But she's never carried through. Not with any of it."

"Not that you know of," I said.

He acknowledged the possibility with a curt nod.

"And she did tell me she'd done something to Rocky," I reminded him.

"I don't doubt for a minute that's what she said. But I've talked to her since then, and she didn't say a thing about it to me, not even when I came right out and asked her. It was like she had no memory of ever saying that to you, and you know what?—I don't doubt that, either. Minnie's got problems."

I was almost afraid to ask. "So where does that leave us?"

If Tony was offended by my use of *us*, he didn't show it. "Now that we know about the note and the prowler and the possible burglar, we're not going to let it go," he said. "Declan said he found some letters."

"From Marie Daigneau. They're in French."

"And we're pathetically understaffed," he admitted. "If you could help us out and find someone who might be able to translate them . . ."

When he held it out to me, I refilled his glass and stepped back and away from the bar when Sophie made the announcement to tell our guests to find a seat.

I had helped her plan what there would be of a formal program, and I knew that Father Frank from St. Robert's would make some comments first. After that, Declan was scheduled to say a few words, then members of the crowd who wanted to could step forward and share their memories of Rocky. I'd put aside a chair for myself just at the spot where the tent ended and Rocky's herb garden began, and I sat down and like the rest of the people in attendance, bowed my head when Father Frank said a prayer. Unlike the rest of the crowd, I had the added advantage of being able to breathe deep and catch the fragrance of rosemary and thyme and the wonderful and very French scent of lavender.

No sooner had Father Frank finished and the last muffled *amen* faded into the autumn air than I raised my head, opened my eyes, and saw something curious back behind the barn.

Or I should say more accurately, *someone* curious.

It wasn't one of Declan's nephews. Now that all the guests were here, the two boys who'd been parking cars had joined us under the tent, and just to be sure, I double-checked and saw them sitting where I'd last seen them, beside their grandparents.

It wasn't George. I knew that for sure. Even though I suppose he could have been taking a break while the quiches baked, the man I saw prowling the edges of the memorial service wasn't as tall as George and not nearly as bulky.

I squinted for a better look.

It was a man, surely. A slim man with a beard.

I sat up like a shot, but by that time, the person I'd seen had slipped completely behind the barn and out of my range of vision.

I inched out of my seat and thanked my lucky stars that the bar was at the back of the crowd. The way I figured it, the only ones who saw me get up and head out were Father Frank, Sophie, and Declan.

As quickly as I could, I headed for the barn, making a wide circle around the tent so that I wouldn't distract from the story Father Frank was telling. Declan, waiting in the proverbial wings, caught sight of me and raised his eyebrows, and I waved a hand as a way of telling him he had nothing to worry about because nothing was wrong.

Now all I had to do was convince myself.

Behind the barn, I glanced around, but since the Fury boys had done their work and done it efficiently, there wasn't much to see except row after row of perfectly parked cars.

I stood on tiptoe and scanned the area, past the cars and over to the plot of land Rocky used for her griselles, and that's when I saw him again.

"Andrew MacLain," I told myself, though from this distance, I really couldn't be sure.

As much to prove my theory to myself as to catch up to the man and find out what he was doing there, I took off running, darting through the lines of cars, but before I ever made it to the griselle garden, the man looked over his shoulder, caught sight of me, and took off.

Lurking at a memorial service and running when seen?

My curiosity ratcheted up a notch and I took off, too, running for all I was worth through the endives and the shallots and the last of the year's leeks and fennel that Rocky would never have a chance to pick.

I'd just negotiated my way through the pumpkin patch near the border of her property when the man ducked into the thick woods that marked the boundary of Rocky's farm and I lost him.

Hands on my knees, I bent to catch my breath, looking right and left as I did, hoping for some clue as to which direction the man went.

Andrew MacLain.

It sure looked like him.

Which left me with only one question to ask as I made my way back to the service, my heart beating double time and my breaths ragged.

Why would Andrew MacLain lurk in the background of Rocky's memorial service?

I BARELY HAD a chance to think about it. I'd run farther than I thought and it took me a while to make my way back to the tent, and by the time I got there, Declan was already done speaking and a woman who introduced herself as Jo was telling us how Rocky had once tried to teach French to a group of women who met each week at the library.

"We didn't learn a whole lot of French," Jo said with a smile. "But we sure always had a good time."

Jo took her seat and as we planned, we allowed a minute for the next speaker to come forward.

This time it was a man named Greg, a restaurant owner all the way from Cleveland, who told us that for the last three years, he'd tried to talk Rocky into moving closer to the big city so that he could get all his produce from her.

"She wouldn't hear of it," Greg said. "She said her home was here at Pacifique. That this was her love. And, you know, I couldn't argue with her. Once a week, I drove all the way out here for whatever Rocky would sell to me. It was worth every mile of the trip."

Greg went back to his seat and again, we waited to see if anyone else would step up and share a memory. Sophie and I had already agreed that neither of us wanted to speak. Me, because let's face it, I was a relative newcomer to the area and I didn't have nearly the relationship with Rocky that many in attendance did, and Sophie, because she said she'd dissolve into a puddle of mush and she didn't want to put a damper on the spirits of the crowd. We all felt the loss of Rocky in our own way, Sophie had said. There was no use making everyone feel even worse.

I'd asked Declan to keep an eye out, and if it looked as if no one else in the crowd was going to come up to the podium, to step forward and let everyone know that lunch would be served in just a minute. He'd just stood up to do that when Minnie Greenway hotfooted into the tent like the Road Runner on speed.

"I've got something to say!" she announced even before she made her way up to the microphone, and I guess more than a few of the people there knew who she was because a buzz started up in the crowd. A little bit of excitement, a little bit of nervousness. People looked around at one another and pointed at Minnie in her ragged jeans and that maroon sweater of hers. Her hair was a fright and she wasn't wearing shoes.

It took Otis a minute to catch on and really, who could blame him? By the time he was on his feet, his forehead sweatier than ever, Minnie had grabbed the mike.

"You're talking about that Frenchy? Well, I've got plenty to say about her!"

Declan stepped up behind Minnie, and Tony materialized out of the crowd, too, and walked up to her side.

"Just the man I wanted to see," Minnie growled, and looked at Tony. "You're going to want to hear this."

"I'm sure we are." How Tony made himself sound so calm and so completely unabashed when the rest of us were watching the scene with our mouths hanging open was a mystery, but then, I guess that sort of thing is second nature to a cop. "Come on, Mrs. Greenway." He gave her a tiny tug. "Let's talk over here where we won't interrupt everyone's lunch."

She yanked her arm away from him. "Oh, we're going to talk, all right," she told him, and raised her chin to glare at the crowd. "But before we do, there's something I need to say. That Rocky? You need to know something about her. You need to know I killed her."

Chapter 11

A couple of things happened all at once—
Our guests sat frozen for a few, stunned seconds, then erupted, leaping out of their seats. Some of them shouted, a few of them cried, more of them stood there with their mouths hanging open, staring at Minnie, pointing fingers, some of them whispered among themselves, and I heard the hissed words.

"Crazy."

"Dangerous."

"Told you so."

And Minnie?

It was hard to see over the crowd that spilled into the aisle way at the center of the tent, and believe me when I say I desperately wanted to know what was going on, so I pushed my way through to the front just in time to see Tony put a firm hold on Minnie's arm. She was wiry, and apparently a lot stronger than she looked. Minnie squirmed, she spat, she kicked, and she wormed her way out of Tony's hold. She took off, straight down the aisle, and she didn't care who she bumped into or who she ran down.

Until she saw me and froze like a deer in headlights.

In that split second, I wondered if she recognized me from the times I found her lurking at Pacifique.

Or if maybe I reminded her of someone else.

I never did find out. I only know that when her eyes locked with mine, Minnie somehow saw her salvation. She raced forward, threw her arms around my neck, and hung on like a limpet, and not even Tony and Declan coming to my rescue could help. When she realized they were trying to pull her away from me, Minnie dug her bony fingers into my skin. She held on hard and refused to let go, even when (believe me!) I tried to push her away.

"You have to help me! You have to help me!" she cried out above the buzz of noise coming from the people who crowded around us to see what was going to happen next. "I won't go with them," she insisted when Tony took hold of her once again, and just to prove it, she slid behind me, her chest to my back, and kicked him in the knee.

"I won't go!" Minnie screamed when Declan moved in to take Tony's place so Tony could take a moment to wince in pain. "I won't come with you and tell you what I did to Frenchy." She gave me a series of rough shakes that made my head bob. "Not . . . unless . . . she . . . comes . . . with . . . me."

At that point, neither Tony nor Declan was going to argue, and I wasn't sure fighting about it would get me anywhere. I nodded my consent, though how Minnie could see me, considering she was dodging left to right, right to left behind me in order to evade first Declan, then Tony, I don't know. I finally managed to plant my feet and spin around so that my back was to them and they had a better chance of grabbing hold of Minnie.

Tony pried her fingers off my neck one by one, and slapped the cuffs on Minnie (he carried handcuffs even when he wasn't on duty?). Declan held back Otis, who fought his way through the crowd, both arms flailing, like a swimmer trapped underwater and desperate for air. He watched the proceedings in horror, his face ashen and his whole body shaking like a plate of aspic. Once Tony had Minnie firmly in hand, Declan rushed over to see how I was. Truth be told, aside from shaken, mashed, and bruised, I wasn't really sure.

I waved him off and fought to catch my breath. In spite of my rubbery knees and my insides that swooped a time or two before they tied themselves into about a million knots and because I said I would, I walked along at Minnie's side when Tony escorted her out to his car. Sophie hobbled over and I assured her I was fine, then reminded myself she'd never believe it if I didn't stop massaging the spots on my neck I knew would be black and blue by morning. On my way out of the tent, I gave Inez and Misti last-minute instructions about serving the quiche. Heck, murder suspect or no murder suspect, I wasn't wasting good food, and now our guests would have plenty to talk about over lunch.

"You uncomfortable sitting in back with her?" Tony asked me when we found his car.

I was about to say that any person with a brain would be uncomfortable being that close to Minnie when she looked my way. Her bottom lip quivered, and she burst into tears.

I rode to the Cortland Police station in the back seat with Minnie. Declan and Otis followed in the car behind us.

Never having been in a police station with a murder suspect, I can't really say what normal procedure might be. I had the feeling that maybe the Cortland cops bent the rules just a little, considering how fragile Minnie was, how upset her husband was, and how the suspect in question absolutely, positively refused to do anything or say anything or move a step from inside the front door unless I was with her.

Go figure.

After I pinkie swore (Minnie's idea) that I wouldn't leave her side, we found ourselves in a utilitarian room that contained nothing but a metal table and four chairs. Minnie and I sat down on one side of the table. Tony took the seat opposite hers. Otis stayed in the outer office to talk to another of the officers, and Declan said since he was an attorney—and definitely not Minnie's representative—he should stay well out of it. No one argued with him and he offered to call legal aid on her behalf.

"So . . ." I knew there was a video camera running because Tony had explained all that to Minnie when we sat down. It would record everything she said and every move she made, and later, would be used as evidence against her. Still, Tony was all set to jot down notes. His pen poised over a yellow legal pad, he gave Minnie a soft smile. "You need to tell us more, Minnie. About what you said back at the memorial service."

The sound she made was half sniff, half snort. "Ain't no memorial service unless you have it in a church," she grumbled. "And they were drinking wine. You saw that, right? Write that down." Tony had removed the handcuffs once we were in the room, and Minnie pointed to his legal pad with one bony and not very clean finger. "Write down that they were drinking wine."

Tony pretended to do just that.

"So while they were drinking the wine . . ." He glanced up at her, his look as placid as the proceedings at Pacifique had been before Minnie showed up and dropped the mother of all bombshells. "You said something to everyone who was there, Minnie. You walked up to the front and you said—"

"Said I killed that Frenchy." She narrowed her eyes and gave him a laser stare. "That's what I said 'cause that's what I did."

"You're telling me you killed Raquel Arnaud."

Minnie glanced my way and spoke to me out of the corner of her mouth. "He's cute, but he must be hard of hearing."

Before I said anything, I looked at Tony to make sure it was all right. He gave his permission with a nod.

"I think they just want to make sure they have all the facts straight," I told Minnie. "Because, you know . . . sometimes the cute ones . . . they're not all that smart."

Tony's sour smile might have been justified if my little joke didn't work. But it did. Pleased with herself for bringing it up and with me for going along with talking about how cute Tony was, Minnie sat up straight and pulled back her scrawny shoulders.

"Well, if that's what they need to know," she said, "then that's what I'll tell them. I'll tell them what I told all those wine drinkers back at the Frenchy farm. I killed her. I killed that Rocky."

"By Rocky, you mean Raquel Arnaud."

It wasn't a question, but when Tony said it, Minnie rolled her eyes. "Yeah, yeah. If that's what you're waiting for me to say, all right, I'll say it. I killed Rack-el Air-nooooo." She exaggerated the accent and grinned, proud of herself.

"All right then." Tony made a note. "Want to tell me why you did that, Minnie?"

Minnie scratched her nose. "Ask Otis," she said.

"Otis. You mean Mr. Greenway."

I knew Tony was just trying to get the facts straight for the sake of the video, but Minnie couldn't have cared less. She squealed with delight. "Mr. Greenway! The way you say it makes him sound important. He's not." She spat out the last two words. "He's a cheatin', low-down two-timer."

"Otis?" I couldn't help myself. Her assessment was not in keeping with the sweating, concerned man I'd seen at Pacifique, the man who needed to lean on Declan when we walked into the station and sat right down when we got inside because it looked as if he might collapse on the spot.

"You know about them, don't you?" Minnie asked, looking my way.

I ran my tongue over my lips. "Them. You mean Otis and Rocky?"

Minnie's top lip curled. "Got what she deserved."

Let's face it, in his time on the force, Tony had probably heard plenty of strange things from plenty of people, but even he needed a moment to process this information.

He cleared his throat. "So you're telling me you killed Ms. Arnaud because she was having an affair with your husband."

"No." Minnie shook her head so violently, her haystack

hair shimmied around her shoulders. "She wasn't having an affair with him. Can't you get anything straight? *He* was having an affair with *her*!"

Maybe Minnie wasn't so crazy after all; in the great scheme of things I think she was technically right, since Otis was married and Rocky wasn't.

Tony took a note, then sat back. "How did you get into the house?" he asked her.

Minnie puckered up like she'd just sucked a lemon. "How do you think you get into a house? Through a window?" This struck her as particularly funny and she laughed like a loon.

Tony was not as amused. "Did you get in through a window?" he asked.

She looked away from him.

He planted his elbows on the table and leaned forward. "Had you gotten in through a window another time? Had you been in Ms. Arnaud's house when she wasn't there? Or when she was sleeping?"

Minnie flinched as if she'd been slapped. "Who told you?"

"We're the police, Mrs. Greenway. We have ways of finding things out."

She slumped in her chair. "About the phone calls?"

"Yes," he said. "We know about the phone calls."

"And the rabbits?"

Tony glanced my way, and I shrugged.

"Tell us about the rabbits," he said.

Minnie's laugh started out small, like the rustle of autumn leaves. She glanced at Tony through her fringe of bangs. "Got 'em from Butch Norris over near Oakfield.

Three little bunny rabbits." She looked at me and whispered. "Let them loose in Frenchy's garden!"

This was not something Rocky had made note of in her date book, which led me to believe either the bunnies weren't as hungry as Minnie counted on them being, or Minnie was simply making up the story.

Tony wrote it all down anyway.

"So the phone calls and the rabbits . . ." Tony pretended to consider this. "Was there anything else you did, Mrs. Greenway? Were you in Ms. Arnaud's house?"

"Went there for tea." Minnie cocked her head. "Like the friggin' queen at Buckingham Palace!"

I didn't believe this, either, but Tony made note of it.

"And this was when?" he asked.

"You ask her." Minnie's lips folded in on themselves. "You ask that Frenchy. She'll tell you. She knows all about it."

Tony cleared his throat. I wondered if he was trying to get Minnie's attention or just giving himself a second to sort through her verbal meanderings. "Minnie, we can't ask Ms. Arnaud. You told us you killed her."

Minnie lifted her chin. "Killed her. Oh yeah. I killed her, all right."

"When did you do this, Mrs. Greenway?"

She wrinkled her nose. "Nighttime."

"Which night was it?"

Minnie looked to me. "She was there. Ask her. Go on. You ask her."

I gave Tony a shrug so he'd know I wasn't making any more sense of all of this than he was. "I saw Minnie at Pacifique on Sunday," I said. "And again when I stopped in on Monday. But of course, I was also there on—"

Tony knew what I was going to say and he cut me off

by clearing his throat. I realized almost too late that I'd nearly said too much. He didn't want me to influence anything Minnie told him; he didn't want her to know I was there on Saturday, the night Rocky died. I clamped my lips shut.

"I need to ask you these questions," he told Minnie. "We have to make sure we know the whole story. So you need to tell me, Minnie, when were you at Ms. Arnaud's farm?"

She sat back in her chair. "Don't know what you're talking about."

I'll say this, Tony Russo must be the most patient man on planet Earth. I was just about to scream. Tony, though, he took it all in stride.

"Let's talk about something else," he said, and as if to signal the change of subject, he flipped the sheet on the legal pad and ran his hand over the blank page in front of him. "Tell me how you did it, Minnie. How exactly did you kill Ms. Arnaud?"

The grin that touched Minnie's lips was as cold as ice cubes. "Shot her in the head. Stabbed her with a knife. That's what she gets. That's what she gets for trying to steal my Otis."

Tony and I exchanged looks and we didn't need to say a thing.

Shot her in the head.

Stabbed her with a knife.

When Rocky had been poisoned?

I think both Tony and I would have groaned if at that moment, there wasn't a sharp knock on the door.

Another of the cops stuck his head into the room. "Hey, Tony, can you step out here for a minute? I need to talk to you."

The thought of being left alone with Minnie was too much for me. Before she could remind me about that pinkie swear and because Tony didn't say I had to stay, I hurried out of the room right behind him.

Otis Greenway stood next to the cop outside the door.

"Go ahead," the cop said. "Tell Officer Russo here what you just told me."

Before Otis could say a word, Tony stopped him.

"Maybe we should start at the beginning," Tony said. "Your wife . . ." He glanced at the window on the wall where we could see Minnie sitting and staring into space. I knew she couldn't see us from the other side. "She claims you and Ms. Arnaud were having an affair."

Otis swallowed hard. "I was afraid that's what she'd say. I was afraid that's what she thought." He shook his head sadly and a tear streaked down his doughy cheek. "Minnie . . ." He sobbed. "My poor Minnie. I never meant to hurt her."

Maybe I was supposed to keep my mouth shut, but I couldn't help myself. "So you and Rocky were having an affair?"

Again, Otis shook his head, more vigorously this time. "I used to walk over and see Rocky . . . er . . . Miss Arnaud once in a while. It started back a couple of years ago. I was reading this magazine article about herbs, about how some herbs, they might be able to help people. People like Minnie."

"You were drugging her?" Tony asked.

What little color there was in Otis's face washed clean away. "No! No! Nothing like that. Minnie sees a doctor regularly. And she takes all the medication she's supposed to take. But nothing works." Again, he looked at his wife through the glass, his eyes empty and his voice drained of hope. "Nothing works. Then I read that article and it talked about making tea from herbs. So I went and talked to Rocky and she gave me some of the herbs that were mentioned in the article."

"Did it help?" I asked, though, honestly, from what I'd seen of Minnie, I couldn't imagine it had.

"It didn't hurt," Otis admitted. "Chamomile in the evening. She likes it with honey. It helps her sleep. And mint tea in the afternoon . . . Well, I can't say for sure, maybe it's just wishful thinking. But I think it calmed her down a little."

"And that's how you and Ms. Arnaud got to know each other?"

Otis glanced at Tony. "We weren't having an affair," he said. "I'd go over to her farm to get herbs and a couple of times, I walked over in the evening after Minnie was in bed. You know, just to have someone to talk to. Just so . . ." He glanced away. "Just so I wasn't so lonely all the time. But that's all it ever was," he added, looking back at Tony, his shoulders a little steadier and the ring of truth in his voice. "There was never anything between me and Rocky, never anything except friendship. I guess Minnie thought otherwise and for that, I'll be forever sorry. But no matter what she thought of Rocky, you've got to know, Officer, my Minnie, she didn't kill Rocky."

"She told us she did," Tony said. "She told us she shot her, then stabbed her."

By now, Otis was crying all out. "Maybe it was wishful thinking," he sobbed. "Maybe that's what she would have liked to do to Rocky because she thought she had reason to be jealous. Or maybe Minnie just dreamed it all and thought it was real. Some of the drugs she takes, they can have that sort of side effect. Maybe my poor Minnie was so angry at Rocky because she thought . . ." He couldn't say another word, and we waited for him to pull himself together.

Otis did but not until after he took a deep breath that made his entire body shudder. "Here's what I told the other officer," he said. "What he wanted you to hear before you went any further questioning Minnie. She couldn't have done it. Not any of it. Oh, I heard what she said about the phone calls and the rabbits, and I ain't denying any of that. That sounds like something Minnie would do, and in the long run it didn't hurt no one or nothing, did it? But she couldn't have killed Rocky. No way. See, all day Saturday— the day Rocky died—me and Minnie were at a church harvest festival over at Mosquito Lake. I got pictures."

Otis pulled his phone out of his pocket and messed with it for a few seconds, then turned it so Tony and I could see. The pictures were date and time stamped—the day Rocky was killed. They showed Otis and Minnie carving a pump- kin, Otis and Minnie eating lunch, Minnie chomping on a donut, her top lip covered with powdered sugar.

"You see, Officer, no matter what she says, Minnie couldn't have done it. She was with me all of that day and into the evening. I never took my eyes off her. Not once."

Chapter 12

Yes, it looked like we were right back where we started from, and when Declan and I drove back to Pacifique, I vacillated between moping and complaining, complaining and moping. About halfway to the farm, though, I stopped obsessing about how a perfect opportunity to solve the case had slipped right through our fingers. A thought hit and I sat up like a shot.

"We've still got the bank statements," I said, more to myself than to Declan. "And they might lead us to the safe deposit box. And who knows what we might find there!"

"And we've got the letters from Marie," he said, because apparently he'd been thinking we were at the end of our rope, too. Or maybe he was just tired of me moping and complaining. "The whole Minnie thing," he admitted. "We should have known from the start that it was too good to be true. Getting a confession like that—it was too easy."

He was right, but oh, how I wanted Minnie to be our killer! Not because I had anything against her, but because if she were, we could put the question of Rocky's murder to rest once and for all.

Instead, when we arrived back at Pacifique and found our guests finished with lunch and just beginning to head out to their cars, Declan went out back to help the boys handle the traffic and I walked up to the microphone and told everyone the news.

"No matter what she said, it isn't true. The police have confirmed that Minnie Greenway did not kill Rocky." They had the right to know the truth, and besides, I hated the thought of them running home and spreading the story that they'd been on hand when the killer was caught and hauled away. It was a disservice to Rocky's memory and it sure wouldn't do much for Minnie's reputation, either. As long as I was at it, I added, "If any of you knows anything about Rocky or the farm or who might have been here last Saturday, no matter how small it seems or how insignificant, please share the information with the Cortland police."

I couldn't tell if our guests were relieved to hear there wasn't a murderer living nearby or disappointed that the dramatic scene that had been played out before them earlier in the afternoon had resulted in nothing more than a phony and fizzled confession.

An appropriately sad smile firmly in place, I watched them leave, saying my good-byes and thanking each person who happened to glance my way.

It wasn't until every last one of them was gone that I caught sight of Sophie hanging around near the bar.

Her herringbone blazer was off.

So were her shoes.

I headed toward the back of the tent. "Sorry," I said, and when she poured a glass of côtes du rhône rouge for herself and one for me, I didn't argue. "That was the last thing we needed."

Sophie took a sip of wine, her gaze trained on the leaves outside the tent that fell like raindrops from the surrounding trees on the heels of a breeze that had the cold nip of the end of October in it. "The quiche was good," she said.

I laughed. "All that angst and you remember the quiche."

"All that angst is why I remember the quiche." She turned a watery smile on me. "Thanks for making today special for Rocky."

I touched my wineglass to hers. "Thanks for having such a great friend."

We didn't plan it, but at the same time, we plopped into the two closest chairs.

Sophie stretched. "We've got to help with cleanup."

"We will." I pointed to her glass of wine. "After you're finished."

She didn't protest. I didn't expect her to. Instead, she gave the house a wistful look. "I guess I'll have to distribute everything in whatever way the will says. It will feel funny never coming here again."

"It's a special place." We were near the herb garden, and I caught the aroma of lavender in the air. "I'll miss it, too."

I pretended not to notice the look she shot my way. At least until I could feel her eyes just about drilling through me.

"What?" I asked.

She pursed her lips and looked up at the canopy of tent above us. "Oh, nothing. For a moment there, I thought you were going to say how much this place feels like home."

I sipped my wine. "Unlikely, since I'm not exactly sure what home feels like."

"Nina's was home for you."

She was right. For four years, her sister had given me a place where I'd felt safe and cared for. "Four years that I'll never forget and that I'll always appreciate. But four years, it's a drop in the bucket," I told her and reminded myself.

With one finger, she traced an invisible pattern over the white tablecloth. "So you'll keep on looking. For a home, I mean. For a place where you can settle in and stay."

I was in no mood for games. "I always told you I would."

"And you haven't changed your mind."

I finished my wine and stood. "Let's get these tables cleared," I said. "And get everything back to the Terminal."

Along with Sophie, Misti, Inez, and George, who pitched in since all the cooking was done, we loaded dishes into crates, gathered napkins, folded tablecloths. Before they left, Sophie had given most of the flower arrangements to people she knew were special friends of Rocky's, but there were a few still around and I made sure to tell Inez and Misti to each take one home and offered one to George, who instead of saying thanks or no thanks just snorted at the very idea.

I left one for Sophie and took the two remaining vases and set them on the front step of the house.

"Nice."

Declan came up behind me and slipped his arms around my waist. If I weren't so drained by the day, I might have protested, but the way it was, the heat of his body felt good in the chilly autumn air and the strength of his arms reminded me that no matter what happened in the investigation and where I ended up looking for that home Sophie talked about, there were people who cared, people who wouldn't let Rocky's memory be forgotten and wouldn't let her murder go unpunished.

I leaned my head back against his shoulder. "Rocky liked flowers. I only wish . . ."

I guess he knew what I was going to say. He gave me a quick squeeze. "You're going to figure it out, Laurel."

I wasn't so sure, and my sigh gave me away. Declan propped his chin on the top of my head. "I've been thinking about those letters," he said. "I know a woman named Amanda Blake who might be able to help. She's a French teacher over at the high school."

If I were planning on sticking around Hubbard, I would have asked: Who is she? How do you know her? Is she someone you used to date? Someone you're currently dating?

But I wasn't planning on sticking around, was I? I swallowed the questions and turned in Declan's arms.

"She could translate the letters for us?"

"I just called her." A few more questions sprang to my mind—*You know her number? She took a call from you during the school day?*—and I kept them to myself. Like the others, they had no business in the vocabulary of a woman who was hoping to work for Senator Katherine Stone. "She says if we drive over to the school now and drop off the letters, she's got some time tonight and she'll look them over and see what she finds."

It was good news and I should have smiled, but somehow when I looked into Declan's face, that was completely impossible. I stood motionless, studying the way the light added kaleidoscope colors to his eyes. Little flecks that were nearly black, a slash of blue reflected from the sky above us, a hint of topaz sparked by the afternoon sun.

I'm not sure which of us moved first.

I'm not sure it matters.

I only know that I found myself leaning forward just as he did.

A second later, he kissed me and I didn't do a thing to stop it.

In fact, I relished the warmth of his body and enjoyed the tiny zip of heat that built in mine.

It was going to be as awkward as hell when the moment was over and I had to say something to explain myself, to tell him it had all been a mistake. I knew that as surely as I knew my own name.

As surely as I knew I didn't care.

Like all good things, this one ended and I found Declan grinning down at me.

"What?" I asked the same question I'd just asked Sophie when she tried to pin me down about finding a home. "What's so funny?"

"Not funny, nice. And long overdue. You didn't think so?"

I'm a lousy liar, so rather than pretend, I didn't say anything at all. I backed out of his arms. "We've got to get the cars loaded," I told him.

He gave up, but he didn't stop smiling. "Then I'll help. That way, we can get over to the high school faster. I've got that hatbox with those letters in it in my car. I thought I might have a chance to stop and see Mandi with them eventually."

Mandi.

I bit my lip.

But I couldn't argue. He was my introduction to the French teacher and I was anxious to hear what she might have to say about the letters.

Thirty minutes later, Inez and Sophie were in my car and Misti and George were in Sophie's and headed back to the Terminal with the supplies we'd brought over. Declan and I were in his car and on our way to Hubbard. A little while after that, we walked into the high school.

Outside the principal's office, where Declan popped in to say we had an appointment to see Amanda Blake, the first person I saw was Andrew MacLain.

It had been a busy and an action-packed day. I hardly remembered that I thought I'd seen MacLain lurking around on the edges of the memorial service.

But now that I did, I wasn't going to let the moment pass.

"Mr. MacLain." I held out a hand and introduced myself and wondered if he recognized me as the woman who'd chased him across Rocky's property earlier in the day. "Nice to see you. Again."

His smile flared up quickly and dissolved just as fast.

"I was at the library Sunday night," I said, as friendly as can be. "And that was me you saw this morning over at Pacifique. You know, at Rocky's memorial service."

Two spots of bright color popped up in MacLain's cheeks. He was a scholar, after all, not an actor. He blinked at me. "Memorial service? I didn't attend a memorial service this morning."

"You didn't," I conceded. "Not with the rest of the guests, anyway. But you were at the farm." Declan chose that moment to walk out of the office, a hall pass in his hands. Since he was coming to the conversation late and since I hadn't had a chance to tell him about the man I'd seen during the service, I filled in the gaps.

"I was just telling Mr. MacLain that I caught sight of him this morning. Over at Pacifique. It was when you and

Father Frank were speaking," I told Declan. "He didn't officially attend the service. He was outside the tent. Out of sight behind the barn." I turned back to MacLain. "You have to understand that I'm curious. I mean, why didn't you want anyone to know you were there?"

When he lifted his chin, MacLain's beard bristled. "You obviously have me mixed up with someone else. Good afternoon."

Declan and I watched him walk away.

"Was it him?" Declan asked.

"I wish I knew for sure." Annoyed at the thought, I shook my shoulders and reminded myself there were only so many things I could control. "Where's this Amanda Blake of yours?" I asked.

"She's not exactly my Amanda Blake." Declan laughed and led the way. "She used to date my brother Brian."

"But it didn't work out because she wasn't Irish."

"Oh, she was. She is. Back before she was Mrs. Blake, she was Amanda O'Donnell. Nice girl, but she and Brian, they went their separate ways. They're still friends, though."

"And you're friends with her, too."

He took my question at face value, which was a good thing because I hated myself for letting the words slip past my lips. I'm not the jealous type and really, I had nothing to be jealous about. No reason to be jealous. No cause to be jealous.

Did I?

Amanda was just finishing up a class, and we waited for a stream of noisy teenagers to scamper out of the door before Declan gave the teacher—who was very pregnant and looked to be dead on her feet—a big hug.

They exchanged the kinds of pleasantries old friends

do, asking about her kids, his family, the Irish shop. A minute into it, Declan grabbed my hand and literally pulled me into the conversation.

"Laurel is Sophie's niece," he said. Technically wrong, but I was tired of defending myself and the family ties Sophie and I didn't share. "She's the reason I'm here."

"The letters." Amanda was in her midthirties and dark haired. She glanced at the hatbox under Declan's arm. "The boys are at Scouts tonight," she said, "and Zoe will be at her swimming lessons. That gives me a few hours to myself to devote to the letters." She glanced my way. "What am I looking for?"

I threw my hands in the air. "I wish I knew! You know about Raquel Arnaud?"

"The woman who died last weekend?" Amanda nodded and put a hand to the small of her back. She shuffled around to the other side of her desk and sat down. "This has something to do with her death?"

This time, I shrugged. "We don't know. But Rocky . . . Raquel . . . she said something about Marie, the woman who wrote those letters. She said something about her and that book, *Yesterday's Passion*, and—"

"And I was there!" Amanda's mouth fell open. "I was at the Book Nook that evening when Rocky caused the scene. I was getting my autographed copy of *Yesterday's Passion*. You mean, you think there might be something to what she said? About how Aurore Brisson stole the book from her friend Marie?" Amanda rubbed her hands together. "Oh, this is delicious! Like a mystery novel!" Declan had put the hatbox down on her desk and she popped the lid open and peeked inside. "Where do you want me to start, with new letters? Or the old ones?"

Where?

I walked closer so I could ruffle a hand through the letters. "Well, Marie died three years ago so there really aren't any new letters. And if there was any truth in what Rocky said about Aurore stealing the book from Marie . . ." I thought through the problem. "It has to take a while for a book to get published, right? I mean, it must take at least a year." The frustration built along with a wave of exhaustion that made me feel as if all the air had been sucked from my lungs. "What do you think, Declan?" I asked him.

"I think . . ." Again, he took my hand, and this time, he didn't let go. When the classroom door popped open and a group of kids walked in, he tugged me toward the door. "I think you've had a long day and Amanda has one more class to teach this afternoon. Start with the newest of the letters," he told her on our way out the door. "But don't worry too much about it. Glance over them. Anything you can tell us, anything might help."

"Are you kidding me?" She plopped the lid back on the hatbox and slid it to the side of her desk. "Now that you've whetted my appetite, I'm going to dig right in. I can't wait to see what I might find."

We thanked her and left the room just as the bell rang for the start of the next class. It wasn't until we were already out at the car that I realized Declan was still holding my hand.

I untangled my fingers from his so I could get in the car. "Are you always so nice?" I asked once he was behind the steering wheel.

This amused him. "Am I? Nice? I was afraid you were never going to notice."

I snapped my seat belt in place. "Everybody likes you, even your brother's old girlfriend."

"I'm a likable guy."

"There have to be some skeletons in your closet."

"You mean *my* old girlfriends."

I was glad I wasn't the one who brought it up. "So why aren't you dating anyone?" I asked him.

"I am." Good thing he was driving and he didn't look my way right at that moment or he might have seen me catch my breath. "You."

"We're not dating."

"You let me kiss you."

I had, and I would again. In a heartbeat.

If I wasn't leaving.

I couldn't tell Declan. Not before I knew for sure that I'd be joining the senator's staff. And even then, I owed the information to Sophie first.

"Look . . ." I turned just a bit in my seat, the better to keep an eye on Declan. "It's not that I don't like you . . ."

"Then it's settled."

I didn't know if I should laugh. Or scream. "It's not settled. You know I have no intention of staying in Hubbard."

There. I'd said it. Without giving too much away.

He considered this for a moment before he announced, "You can't leave."

"Why not?"

"Because people here are depending on you."

"People here got along fine without me before I showed up."

"They did."

I let go a breath of relief. Finally, he was being logical!

"But now that they've met you," he added, "things can never be the same. Not for Sophie." Without taking his eyes off the road, he slid a hand across the seat and captured mine. "Not for me."

"You hardly know me."

"I'd like to. If you'd let me."

"And if I let you . . ."

We'd just pulled into a parking place in front of the Terminal, and I waited until he cut the engine. I chewed on my lower lip. "Once you get to know me," I told him, "you'll change your mind. That's what always happens."

"Happened. Past tense."

"Grammar doesn't change anything."

"Don't you get it?" He tightened his hold on my hand. "You changed everything. By coming here. Things aren't the same as they used to be. They never can be. Not ever again."

Chapter 13

The first person I saw when I got to the Terminal the next morning was Amanda Blake. She was waiting out front in her car, and I unlocked the door of the restaurant and waved her inside.

"What's up?" I asked as soon as I turned on the lights. "And do you want some coffee?"

She had that hatbox of Rocky's in one hand and she touched her other hand to her tummy. "The doc says I should limit my caffeine, but if you've got orange juice . . ."

We had orange juice, and I knew it was the least I could do for her since she must have had news. Why else would she be here just as the sun was coming up?

I left Amanda at a table near the door and got her a glass of juice. Just as I delivered it, George tromped in, and since he was there to cook, I offered Amanda breakfast.

"Can't." She drank her juice. "I've got to be at school

in just a little while. This is my last week before maternity leave and I've got plenty to do."

"But you stopped here first." I tried to keep the buzz of anticipation out of my voice, but honestly, it wasn't easy. No way would she be there, not if she hadn't found something interesting in Marie's letters.

I leaned forward in the seat across from hers. "So . . ."

Amanda finished her juice, set down the glass, and laughed. "I guess it's pretty obvious that I've got something to tell you."

"And it's driving me crazy!" I admitted. "What did you find?"

She set the hatbox on the table and she opened the lid and took out three stacks of letters, each tied with pink ribbon. "I hope you don't mind that I shuffled the letters around a little. It was easier sorting out what was in them this way."

"Of course not," I said, eager for her to get to the meat of her visit.

"These letters . . ." Amanda touched a hand to the pile of letters on her right. "From what I could see, these letters are pretty much what you'd expect from one old friend to another. Marie talks about the latest news in town. You know, gossip and chitchat, who's getting married and who died and all the latest small-town scandals. She talks about the weather, about clothes she's bought, movies she's seen, books she's read."

"And those?" I asked, pointing at the bigger, middle pile.

"Ah, these." Amanda hefted the stack of letters in one hand. "Now, I want you to know, I didn't have time to go over every one of these letters, word for word with a fine-tooth comb. I can do that. I'll have more time beginning next week, at least until the baby comes. Last night I pretty much just scanned them."

"Why do I feel as if this is some sort of disclaimer?"

"Well, it is. Sort of. I mean, I can tell you what Marie wrote. But I'm just saying, maybe we don't have the full story. Maybe that won't come until I've had a chance to take a closer look."

I nodded by way of letting her know that I understood. "Still . . ." I clutched the edge of the table.

"Still . . ." The smile she shot me across the table practically vibrated with excitement. "It started about ten years back," she said. "That was the first time Marie told Rocky that her dream was to write a book."

For a couple of seconds, I didn't dare breathe. "A book about—"

"Medieval France. With a heroine named Cecile." Too charged up to sit still, Amanda wiggled in her chair and tapped her hands against the table. "Laurel, you know I was at the book signing the other night. I bought a copy of *Yesterday's Passion* and I started reading it over the weekend. Everything Marie talks about in her letters all those years ago . . . everything she told Rocky about her plot and her characters and the setting . . . it's all in there. It's *Yesterday's Passion*, all right. Just like Rocky said it was."

I sucked in a breath of astonishment, but warned myself not to get carried away. "Okay, okay." I did my best to calm the sudden clatter inside my chest. "But let's not get ahead of ourselves. Maybe Aurore Brisson was working on the book years ago. Maybe somehow she and Marie knew each other and maybe Marie read what Aurore wrote and maybe Marie was trying to impress Rocky or something so she said she was the one who wrote the story?"

"It's what I thought, too. At least at first." Amanda put a hand on the final stack of letters. "Until I read these. They're the newest of the letters, and by the time Marie wrote them, she was very sick. Lung cancer."

From the tone of Amanda's voice, I knew there was something disturbing in the letters aside from the news of Marie's illness. I eyed the letters carefully. "What does her being sick have to do with *Yesterday's Passion*?" I asked her.

"I think, everything." Amanda patted the stack of letters. "See, Marie never married and she lived alone. Once she got sick and couldn't take care of herself or her house, she had to hire a caregiver, and once the caregiver was there, Marie started telling Rocky that she was worried, that things had gone missing. Oh, nothing big. A pair of earrings, then a string of pearls that had once belonged to Marie's grandmother, then pieces of silver, a knife here, a fork there. At first, Marie said she thought the chemo was messing with her mind, that she was simply forgetting where she'd put things, but after a while, she got suspicious of that caregiver. In the next letter Rocky received, Marie was in a total panic. She couldn't find the pages of her manuscript. The entire book had vanished, and as Marie said, there was no way she would have misplaced that, chemo or no chemo. She'd worked too hard on the book. She loved her story and her characters too much."

If I'd been surprised before, I was floored now. I sat back. "You mean—"

Before I could try to pin her down, Amanda opened one of the envelopes and pulled out a photograph. It showed Marie in a wheelchair and a woman standing next to her.

I pointed at the women with one shaky finger. "That's her caregiver?"

"That's what it says on the photo," Amanda said, and she turned the picture over to read the inscription on the back. "'Giselle Montot, the girl who lives here and takes care of me.'"

"Giselle . . ." I nearly choked on the name.

And who can blame me?

After all, the lips weren't as plump.

The hair wasn't as blond.

But I'd know that face anywhere.

Giselle Montot was the woman who was rich and famous now, thanks to *Yesterday's Passion*.

Aurore Brisson.

"SHE'S IN CLEVELAND."

I told Sophie this at the same time I grabbed what I needed for the trip. "She leaves for the West Coast tomorrow. I've got to catch her today, Sophie."

"So you can come right out and ask if she killed Rocky because Rocky knew *Yesterday's Passion* was stolen?"

"She did know." I stopped zipping around the Terminal office long enough to look Sophie in the eye. "That's the whole point. Rocky wasn't drunk that night at the Book Nook. And she sure wasn't crazy. She remembered what Marie had told her about the book she was writing, and when Rocky started reading *Yesterday's Passion*, she realized it was the same story, the same characters. Of course Rocky didn't keep quiet about it. Why would she? How could she? From everything I've heard about her involvement with the peace movement, she wasn't the kind of woman who kept her mouth shut when she thought she could right a wrong."

My impassioned speech was intended to put Sophie at ease. Or at least to convince her that I wasn't going off half-cocked on a desperate mission.

It didn't work.

Sophie's brow creased. Her lips puckered. "You can't just go up to Cleveland and accuse the woman. If she . . . If she's the one who . . ." She gulped. "She could be dangerous!"

I had everything together: my jacket, copies of the letters from Marie detailing the plot of *Yesterday's Passion*, and a copy of the photograph of Marie with Giselle (I wasn't dumb, I left the originals with Sophie for safekeeping), along with a map I'd printed from the Internet that would get me to the library in a suburb of Cleveland where that afternoon, Aurore Brisson would be the guest of honor at a readers' luncheon.

"I'm just going to talk to her."

"And I'm just coming with you."

This wasn't Sophie, but Declan, who would have breezed into the Terminal office if the office weren't so small that breezing was out of the question. Instead, he stationed himself inside the doorway, his arms crossed over his chest and his feet planted just far enough apart to make it clear that if I was going to leave, I had to get through him first.

"Sophie's right," Declan said. "If this Brisson lady is dangerous—"

"I'm just going to talk to her," I said again, because maybe neither Sophie nor Declan heard me the first time. "No muss, no fuss. We'll see what she says, then we'll let Tony know. It's a perfect plan."

"Perfect because I'm coming with you."

I gave in, but only because I knew that Declan wouldn't move an inch until I did.

NOT TO WORRY, I had no intention of causing a scene anything like Rocky had at the Book Nook. Declan and I went to the library for Aurore Brisson's presentation, all right, but we walked in after lunch was over and sat in the back, quiet and unnoticed by the guest of honor, and we didn't go anywhere near her while she signed dozens and dozens of copies of *Yesterday's Passion* and talked to dozens and dozens of simpering, adoring fans.

We waited while she donned what looked to be a genuine sable coat, and we stepped back and out of the way when a frazzled-looking media escort opened the door and allowed Aurore to walk outside ahead of her. We followed them into the parking lot at a safe enough distance not to be noticed, watched them get into a sleek, black Lincoln. Then we tailed them all the way to Aurore's hotel.

That's when we made our move.

I gave her five minutes to get settled into her suite at the Ritz before I knocked and was rewarded by a grumble from the other side of the door.

"Yes, yes, what is it you want now? More interviews? More autograph seekers?" Aurore yanked open the door, obviously expecting to see the media escort. Before she recovered from her surprise, I darted around her and walked into the room. Declan was right behind me.

"What is this? Who are you? What you are doing?" She made a move toward the phone by the table next to the couch, but Declan stepped in front of her. "Do you know who I am?" she demanded.

It was just the kind of opening I was waiting for. "I know you're Giselle Montot."

She was dressed in an ivory silk suit, and her face turned so pale, I could barely tell where skin ended and fabric began. It took her a moment to collect herself and stick out her chin. "I do not know what you are talking about. I do not know who you are talking about."

Just what I expected.

Which was why I had that photograph of Giselle and Marie right where I could pluck it out of my purse.

I waved it in Aurore's face, but I guess I held it too close because trying to see it, her eyes crossed. I stopped waving and pulled it a little farther away. "That's you with Marie Daigneau," I said. "Back when you were her caregiver and using your real name. Back when things started disappearing from Marie's home."

"You are saying that I did such a thing?" Aurore pretty much knew she was wasting her time batting her eyelashes and puckering her lips at me so she turned her charms in Declan's direction. "This woman, she is surely *fou* . . . crazy! I would never—"

He stopped her, both his hands out, his palms facing her, and gave her the song and dance we came up with on the hour-and-a-half ride from Hubbard. "Hey, don't look at me! Laurel's got this bee in her bonnet and I'll tell you what, once she's got hold of an idea, there's no stopping her. It's one of the reasons I'm crazy about her."

That last bit was not something we'd planned in the car and I would have given him the sour smile he deserved if

I weren't so busy enjoying the thread of warmth that rushed through me.

Heat or no heat, though, I had to stay on track.

"Marie's earrings, her grandmother's string of pearls. I don't suppose there's any way we can ever prove any of that," I admitted, and I gave Aurora a moment to let relief wash through her before I added, "But *Yesterday's Passion*, that's another thing altogether."

Aurore's mouth opened and closed. There was a pack of cigarettes on the table nearby and even though the sign on the door clearly said hers was a nonsmoking room, she tapped a cigarette out of the pack. It took her three flicks to fire up her lighter. But then, her hands were shaking pretty hard.

She sucked in a lungful of poison, then blew a stream of smoke in my direction. "I tell you, I do not know what you are talking about."

Of course this was exactly what Declan and I anticipated she'd say when we came up with our strategy.

He insisted I take the lead.

Which was fine by me since that what I was planning anyway.

Hey, I hadn't worked in Hollywood for six years and not learned anything. I plunked my purse on the table next to her cigarettes, opened it, and with a flourish, pulled out the translations of the letters that Amanda had been kind enough to jot out for me.

"'My dearest Raquel,'" I read. "'I am concerned and do not know who to share my worries with. Have I lost my mind? I do not think so, my friend. You know of my novel. I have told you all about *Yesterday's Passion*. You know that for the last years, I have worked hard, writing each day when I have the strength, planning the story, dreaming of the characters and their lives and their passions. Oh, my friend!'" Unintentionally, I had added a dramatic and very Gallic twist to that last sentence and I swallowed my chagrin and pretended not to notice Declan grinning at me.

"'Today I went to work on the book, to read over the last of the pages I wrote and—*mon Dieu!*—the manuscript is nowhere to be seen. Believe me, Raquel, this is not something I would easily misplace. It is my heart. It is my soul. Is it possible for anyone to be so wicked as to hide it? I do not think so, not just for the sake of being mean. But Giselle, she has asked about my book in the past. She has begged me to tell her the story, and though I told her it was not ready for anyone to read it, she asked so prettily a week ago—the last time I saw the book—that I could not refuse her. Now it is missing. And I am . . .'" Even in the secondhand translation, it was almost too painful to read. I cleared my throat. "'I am devastated, *mon amie*. My heart is broken in two.'"

I let the words settle in the rarefied air of the Ritz before I raised my head and stared at Aurore.

One corner of her mouth pulled tight and her top lip curled. "You cannot suppose—"

"But I do. And I have the proof back in Hubbard. Marie was no dummy, and something tells me you were counting on that. She sent Rocky entire passages of the book in letters dated five, six, seven years ago. I bet that's long before you sent your manuscript in to your publisher. How much do you want to bet that when we compare those passages to ones in your copies of *Yesterday's Passion*, they're exactly the same?"

Her top lip was still as stiff as a board, but her bottom lip trembled. She pulled in a breath that was just as shaky. "You want money? How much?"

Of all the scenarios we'd concocted on our way from Hubbard, this was not one of them.

Declan and I exchanged looks.

He stepped forward. "You should know that I'm Ms. Inwood's attorney," he said, and though I didn't know where he was going with this, I let him run with it. "Any agreement we come up with in regards to this matter is binding."

"Yes, yes." Aurore hung her head. "I understand."

"And you're willing to cooperate?"

At his question, her head came up and she looked at him. "I asked you, did I not? I asked how much money you want."

"For us to keep silent about the fact that you stole Marie's book."

She shot a look at me. "Is that not what we're talking about?"

"Well, actually . . ." One finger trailing over the shining mahogany table, I walked to the other side of it, more to stall for a little time and draw out the drama than because I needed to go anywhere. "What we're really talking about, Ms. Brisson, is murder."

"Murder!" Aurore slapped one hand to her heart and somehow made it to the couch on rubbery knees. She flopped down, her head back, her cheeks pink, her breaths coming in gasps that shivered through her. "You don't think . . . you can't possibly think . . ."

Declan walked over to stand beside her, and don't think I didn't miss the subtle message. He was a big guy, and he loomed over her. There was nothing at all threatening about his stance, but there was no denying that he was *there*, a firm, unmovable presence.

"What we think is that you've made a great deal of money thanks to *Yesterday's Passion*," I told her, coming up to stand on her other side. "You must have, otherwise, you wouldn't have been so quick to offer us a bribe. Your book is a mega-hit. And the cable TV series that's being made from it is sure to send your sales through the roof. I've seen you on the cover of *People* magazine and you've been on all the talk shows, though come to think of it, you've never had very much to say. I guess now that we know the truth, that's to be expected. How can you talk about the process of writing a book when you've never written one?"

There was an easy chair nearby and I sat down. "So what do you think, Declan?" I asked as casually as can be. "I'm thinking that kind of fame and that kind of fortune is pretty hard to come by."

"And I'm thinking," he said, "that when Rocky stepped forward at the bookstore and told everyone that the book was stolen from Marie, it threatened Ms. Brisson here. It threatened her reputation and it threatened her fortune and if the truth finally came out, it could threaten her liberty, too, because, I'll tell you what, the kind of money we're talking"—he whistled low under his breath—"that's got to make stealing a book like this a major felony."

"It's the perfect motive," I added. "The perfect motive for murder."

"No, no, no!" Aurore flapped her hands as if she were trying desperately to take flight. "I was angry, there at the bookstore, yes. I could not believe that woman had the nerve to say such things in front of so many people when

I knew she could not have the proof. But to kill her? No, no. I did not do this."

"It's a great story." Declan took his phone out of his pocket. "I'll bet the cops back in Cortland will be anxious to hear it."

"No!" She jumped to her feet. "You do not need to involve them. No one needs to know. I can . . ." Her gaze darted around the room and finally landed on a briefcase on a table near the floor-to-ceiling windows that looked out over the center of downtown Cleveland. She darted around Declan and over that way. "I can prove it," she said. "I can prove that I did not kill this woman." She shuffled through the briefcase and came out holding a single sheet of paper.

"See. Here." She shoved the paper at me. "I know from what I heard on the television that this woman, she was killed on Saturday evening. But see this. See here. After the parade, I left. I left immediately. I was not even in that horrible little town on Saturday evening."

Needless to say, Declan took all this talk of *horrible* and *little* personally. Before I had a chance to study it, he took the paper out of my hand.

"It's a time sheet from the media escort service," he told me. "It says the escort took Ms. Brisson from the parade to her hotel in Hubbard. That was at two. It says they immediately drove to Cincinnati."

"Oui." Aurore went back to the briefcase and this time, she came back with a hotel bill. "See this? It is from my hotel in Cincinnati. It shows that I checked in—"

"At six forty-five," I said, looking at the bill, then at Declan. "There's no way she could have gotten to Cincinnati that quickly if she made a stop in Cortland."

"You see!" Aurore's eyes shone. "This is what I told you. This Raquel woman, I did not kill her!"

We'd been so close that my heart sank, and I guess the look I gave Declan told him that because he tipped his head toward the door and we started to leave together.

"But wait!"

Aurore's voice brought us both spinning around.

"I have been honest and I have told you the truth. You know I did not kill this woman. Now you . . . you are not going to tell the police, are you?" The green cast of her face didn't go well with her silk suit. "You are not going to . . . you will not . . . you will not say anything to them about *Yesterday's Passion*, will you?"

Honest to goodness, I didn't know what I was going to say until the words came out of my mouth.

"Of course we're not going to tell the police," I said, in spite of the look of amazement Declan shot my way.

I counted to ten, giving Aurore a chance to catch her breath before I added, "What you don't know is that I have a few connections up my sleeve. I don't need to tell the police. I'm going to get on the phone right now and give Meghan Cohan a call. Wait until she finds out that the movie option she paid a million bucks for went to the wrong person!"

Chapter 14

The bad news?

Well, that was pretty obvious.

The good news?

The Ritz has a snazzy bar. Yeah, we had a long way to drive to get back to Hubbard. That's why both Declan and I opted for iced tea.

"So . . ." He added two packs of sugar to his glass and stirred. "What do we do now?"

"You mean about Aurore? Like I told her, I don't need to call the police, I'm going to call Meghan. You can be sure she'll take care of the rest. This is exactly the kind of scandal Meghan loves to sink her teeth into. The publicity alone will be worth a bundle to her, and Aurore will get what she deserves. So will Marie, come to think of it. I mean, if she's really the author of *Yesterday's Passion*, she'll finally get recognition as an author. Meghan might be a nasty and vindictive—" I swallowed down the rest of what I had to say because let's face it, what was past was past, and Meghan was never going to change anyway. I smiled around my gritted teeth. "Meghan will make sure everything gets taken care of."

"Not what I was talking about," Declan said.

I cupped my hand around the slice of lemon that had been delivered along with my tea and gave it a squeeze. "You mean about the case. Well, there's always the safe deposit box angle."

"There is, but that's not what I'm talking about, either. What I'm talking about is us."

Though I told myself it wasn't smart and it would get me nowhere but in trouble, I couldn't help but remember what he'd said back in Aurore Brisson's suite about how he was crazy about me. After that, it wasn't hard to also remember the cadence of excitement that started up in my chest when he said it, because just thinking about it . . . well, that beat started up all over again.

Just like it did every time I thought about the way Declan had kissed me.

I wasn't caving. I wasn't surrendering. What I was doing—at least what I told myself I was doing—was giving in to a delicious sensation that made a crappy day feel a little better.

"I guess we could consider this a date," I told him. "Not the part about confronting Aurore, since that was a complete bust. But this . . ." I glanced around the room with its plush carpeting, its heavy draperies, and the easy chairs arranged around small, round tables. I looked at the crystal chandelier overhead. "We're here. We're together. Heck, we're drinking iced tea. Yes, it's officially a date."

"Then here's to being official." He lifted his glass and clinked it against mine. "And when we get back to Hubbard, will we still be dating?"

"Your family won't approve."

"My mother's already nuts about you."

"Your father isn't."

"He'll come around."

"People will talk."

"Let them!" He barked out a laugh. "Small towns are great for gossip."

"And you don't mind?"

"The gossip?" He took a long drink of tea and when he was done, he wiped the condensation from the side of his glass with one finger. "They already gossip about me."

It was true and we both knew it.

"And they gossip about you," he added.

Maybe this shouldn't have been news. After all, I was from out of town, from Hollywood, no less. Still, it seemed strange that people would actually waste brain cells on a nobody chef who'd breezed into town pretty much out of nowhere and spent her days at an old train station that always had and always would smell like fried baloney and onions, no matter how many quiches she baked.

I gave my shoulders a shake. "I can't possibly imagine what they say. Or why they care."

He leaned his forearms against the table. They were nice forearms, muscular and as well shaped as the rest of him, forearms that just the day before had wrapped me in an embrace that was unexpected, but no less wonderful because of it. Maybe it was the crazy-making aftereffects of that hug and the kiss that went along with it that clouded my judgment and made my head spin. Maybe I was just looking for comfort after our crash-and-burn visit with Aurore Brisson.

Whatever the reason, I leaned forward, too, my posture a mirror of his. "What do they say about me back in Hubbard?" I asked him.

He slid a hand across the table and covered mine with his. "That you're smart. That you're pretty. That if you'd loosen up a little, you might even be fun!"

When I flinched and made to move my hand away, he laughed and refused to let go. Instead, he massaged my palm with his thumb. "Just kidding!"

I realized it was one of the things I liked about him. Kidding and joking and the kind of friendly banter that left me smiling and challenged me intellectually . . . growing up, things like that weren't part of my world and though they still didn't easily fit—like a jacket that was too narrow in the shoulders—I thought I might like to try to see if I could get used to it.

Just as the thought settled inside me and left a wonderful, warm feeling in its wake, my phone rang. I recognized Fletcher Croft's number and excused myself to go stand near the windows with the view from the hotel's sixth floor.

"Croft," he said, ever the small talker. "The senator has some time on Monday. In New York. Can you be there?"

I'd been so lost in the sweet daydreams that enveloped me back at the table, it took a moment for me to come back to reality. It was long enough for Croft to think he had to repeat himself.

"I said Monday. This coming Monday. Are you there, Ms. Inwood?"

I glanced over my shoulder toward where Declan sat, relaxed and at peace with the world. His dark hair gleamed in the light of the chandelier and I didn't have to get any closer to know his eyes sparkled, too. It was the first I really thought about it, but I realized that they always did when we were together.

"Ms. Inwood?"

I was jolted out of my thoughts. "I'm here. Of course I'm here. It's good to hear from you, Mr. Croft."

Chitchat was not his forte. "Monday," he said, and my cheeks got hot when I realized it wasn't for the first time. "Can you be in New York on Monday?"

I took one more look over my shoulder at Declan and told myself that the ice in the pit of my stomach was the result of drinking my tea too quickly. I mean, it had to be, right? What else could it have been?

"Of course I can be there," I told Fletcher Croft. "I can get there anytime you like. I'm looking forward to finally meeting the senator in person."

"She won't be in the city until two," he told me. "But we'll want you here earlier so you can get lunch started."

This wasn't a surprise. No one in their right mind would hire a personal chef without vetting the chef first, and there was nothing like a meal to take care of that.

"Allergies?" I asked him, and he assured me there were none.

"Food preferences?" was my next question.

I wasn't surprised that he sounded as if he was reading from a list. "The senator has a penchant for blue crab. Fresh only, of course. She hates spinach. And—don't breathe a word of this to anyone because our polling tells us many of her constituents are young and vegetarian—there's nothing she likes better than a thick steak cooked rare."

I'd made a mental note of it all even before Croft said,

"I'll need to approve the menu ahead of time. You can email it to me by Saturday."

I was already two steps ahead of him.

Blue crab cocktail was exactly what the senator would expect, exactly what any other chef might chose as an appetizer.

I'd go with Maryland crab soup instead. A nice, steaming bowl would be perfect on an autumn afternoon. I'd follow it with pepper-crusted filet mignon and add a nice green salad—minus any spinach, of course. And to top it all off? I remembered how one Thanksgiving, I'd served Meghan and her guests sweet potato meringue pie and how they'd raved about my recipe.

"You'll have the menu by then," I assured Croft.

"And we'll have a driver meet you at LaGuardia. Just let me know your flight information."

He didn't say good-bye, but I guess he didn't need to. Our business was concluded.

There was a spring in my step when I neared the table.

At least until Declan looked over, a shadow of concern on his face. He glanced at the phone in my hand. "Nothing's wrong, is it?"

Why did I feel as if I had to cover for what had been a perfectly innocent conversation? An innocent conversation that was none of Declan's business to begin with.

"No, nothing's wrong." I tucked the phone in my pocket. "Not a thing."

"Great." When our waiter came into view, Declan waved him over and paid the bill. "Then let's get back to Hubbard. It's Thursday. What's the special over at the Terminal tonight?"

"Potée champenoise. It's a fancy name for stew."

"Like Irish stew?"

"Not exactly," I told him. "It's got sausage, bacon, cabbage, and potatoes in it along with bouquet garni and carrots. A nice, hot meal for a cool autumn evening."

My own words echoed back at me exactly what I'd thought when I decided to make crab soup for the senator. *A steaming bowl of soup on an autumn afternoon.*

I twitched the thought away.

"Cold?" Declan slipped an arm around my shoulders and I had the perfect excuse for sloughing him off; I needed to put on my jacket.

"So this French stew, it sounds good, but I'm thinking . . ." We were out in the hallway, and he pressed the button to call the elevator and stepped back when it arrived, so I could step inside first. "I'm thinking it's burger night over at the Dew Drop Inn. What do you say?"

What I wanted to say was that it sounded like a date.

And that a woman who was interviewing with Senator Katherine Stone on Monday couldn't afford a date with a man who could easily make her forget that she had plans for her life—plans away from Hubbard.

"Actually, that was Sophie who just called me," I said, refusing to meet his eyes in case he'd see through the lie. "Misti isn't feeling well and we're down a waitress tonight. I'll have to pass on the burgers and get over to the Terminal so I can help out."

"Sure. Okay."

I should have known he'd be sensible about it.

It was one of the reasons I felt so lousy all the way back to Hubbard.

* * *

THE TERMINAL IS not usually open late on Thursday but since we'd been closed on Wednesday for Rocky's memorial service, we made an exception that night. By the time I got back to the Terminal, the evening was in full swing and—hurrah!—the dinner crowd couldn't get enough potée champenoise. The only thing that would have made our French stew even more of a culinary success would be if Inez and Misti could get their pronunciation right.

"Potty champ-enaise." On a short break and gulping down a cup of coffee, Misti tried again and honestly, after correcting her a dozen times already that evening, I didn't much care any longer. We'd sell just as much stew either way, and it wasn't like any of our customers knew the right pronunciation anyway.

Not like Senator Katherine Stone no doubt would.

The thought snuck up and blindsided me, partly because I wasn't even thinking about the senator.

Mostly because I'd never considered myself a snob.

I was just taking a tray of freshly baked baguettes out of the oven and I bobbled and recovered, juggling the tray and plopping it on the countertop.

Me, a snob?

I glanced over at Misti, still enjoying her coffee.

I took a covert look at Sophie, who was plating an order for table eleven, and another at George, who I noticed, just happened to be studying me as if he could read the thoughts that tromped through my head.

Not possible, I reminded myself.

Just like I reminded myself that I had nothing to feel guilty about.

"Oooh, those look delicious!" Sophie rushed by, and I couldn't help but notice that when she did, she was limping.

"I'll take those." She had a dish of stew in each hand and I grabbed them and bumped out the door before she could protest. I set the stew down in front of our patrons on either side of the Eiffel Tower frosted votive holder where the light of a battery-operated tea candle winked against the gold and silver Eiffel Tower confetti we'd dusted over the table. *"Bon appétit!"* I told them, and took a moment to head into the office to catch my breath.

And wonder why just thinking about my interview with the senator on Monday left me feeling as if I were doing something underhanded.

Which I wasn't.

I plopped down in the chair in front of Sophie's desk and grumbled about it for a while. I was going to New York on Monday; I'd already purchased my plane ticket and made up some song-and-dance story for Sophie about how I had a doctor's appointment and was it all right if I took Monday off.

Of course she'd said yes.

Of course she hadn't questioned me.

Of course she took my story at face value because that's what good people do.

People who don't lie to the people who trust them.

I told my conscience to shut up and just to make sure it did, I grabbed a pad and pen and made a list of the things I'd need to take to New York with me. No doubt, the senator would have a fully stocked kitchen, so I didn't worry about the basics like knives and bowls and such. I did check online to make sure I could get really fresh blue crabs delivered to the senator's penthouse apartment along with those filets I planned to grill for her and the greens I'd need for my salad. I would be landing before eight in the morning so I knew I'd have time to grab really good olive oil for the dressing and everything I'd need for the sweet potato meringue pie.

I was going to New York, after all, and as I knew from the times I'd visited the city with Meghan, New York was at the center of the culinary world. I could find everything I needed just minutes from the senator's home, and if I was willing to pay enough—and I was if it meant impressing the senator—I could find it fresh.

What I couldn't find . . .

I thought through the ingredients I'd need and decided there was only one place I could find herbs that were good enough and fresh enough for my bouquet garni—Pacifique.

That taken care of, I spent a few minutes looking over the bank statements we'd found in our search of Rocky's home, searching for any clue as to where I might find the safe deposit box. As it turned out, Rocky did business with three different banks, one for her savings account, one for her checking account, and—

"Voilà!"

I read through the last bank statement and congratulated myself.

There was a charge on it for "other services."

Pretty darned pleased with myself, I made up my mind. Since Sophie was Rocky's executrix, I'd take her to the bank in Cortland to check out the safe deposit box and make some excuse about how because I knew we'd be busy at the Terminal both Saturday and Sunday, I needed to stop at the farm and get herbs as long as we were close by.

Herbs for the senator.

A peek into the safe deposit box for the sake of my investigation.

In the great scheme of things, it was all falling into place perfectly.

At least until I walked back out into the restaurant.

That's when I saw Declan near the front door and realized he must have just walked in—and caught sight of Misti, who I'd told him earlier had to leave because she wasn't feeling well.

In too deep to get out too easily, I closed in on him, a smile on my face.

"What's up?" I asked him.

Over my left shoulder, he watched Misti exchange small talk with a group of regulars, and whatever her patrons said, she threw back her head and laughed.

"I thought we had to skip the Dew Drop tonight because Misti wasn't feeling well."

I guess I could have at least tried to make up some sort of lie that would explain away why I'd backed out of our date, but before I could, Misti zipped by and Declan stopped her.

"Sorry it took us so long to get back here from Cleveland," he said, and was met with a blank expression from her. "Laurel said you weren't feeling well, that you had to get home."

Like Sophie, Misti is pretty aboveboard. "Well, if I'm not feeling well, no one's told me!" she said, and she zoomed over the kitchen to pick up an order.

Before Declan could say a thing, I slipped behind the front counter and took care of the customer who was waiting to pay his bill. I gave him his change, thanked him for coming, and once he was out the front door, I shrugged. I didn't need to look at Declan to know he was watching me carefully. I could feel his eyes watching my every move.

"I guess I got the message wrong," I said.

"Yeah," he said, "I guess I did, too." And he headed out the door.

Chapter 15

Sophie was up for the adventure.

The next morning, we got George set up for the breakfast crowd, reminded Inez that the cash register keys sometimes stick and that she had to be patient with them, and started out for Cortland.

"So . . ." Sophie settled herself in the passenger seat and sat back. I thought she was all set to enjoy the ride. I should have known she had other things on her mind. Sophie usually does. "Declan didn't hang around very long last night."

"Really?" I shot her as much of a look as I was able to considering I was driving. "We're on our way to Cortland to try to get to the bottom of the mystery of Rocky's safe deposit box and all you can think about is Declan?"

"If you were smart, maybe you'd think about him a little more, too." When it comes to having boundaries, Sophie doesn't often know she has a limit, but even she realized she may have gone too far. "That's not what I meant," she insisted, patting the seat between us for emphasis. "I know you're a smart, independent woman and believe me, I don't buy into the old myth that every woman has to have a man in her life in order to be happy. I just meant . . ." Her sigh rippled the air inside my car. "He looked upset when he walked out of the Terminal last night."

He did.

He was.

And it was my fault.

I set my shoulders and refused to think about it, just like I'd refused to think about it all during the night when sleep refused to come and the uncomfortable prick of guilt tapped at my brain and soured my stomach.

"I'm not in charge of Declan's feelings," I reminded Sophie and myself.

I was driving, so I didn't look her way, but somehow, I knew she was smiling. "He'd like you to be."

I sighed. "So he keeps telling me."

"There are plenty of women who would jump at the chance."

"Maybe I'm not one of them."

"Maybe I don't get it."

It was on the tip of my tongue to tell her that she should. After all, I'd made it clear from the start that Hubbard was not and never would be home. No place would be. Not for me. Instead, I shook off the thought. "I hope whatever's in the safe deposit box helps us figure out what happened to Rocky," I said.

Sophie gave up with a grunt. "I bet it's things Rocky treasured and didn't want to take the chance of misplacing.

You know, her birth certificate, her passport. Old pictures, maybe."

Honestly, I was hoping for something a whole lot more interesting if not incendiary. Something that would lead to a killer.

We found out soon enough when we arrived at the bank in Cortland that had charged Rocky a fee for "other services." Sophie produced Rocky's death certificate (not without a sniffle) and the proper paperwork that proved she was the executrix of Rocky's estate, and a young man who barely looked old enough to be out of school led us into a small room off the main bank lobby. Three of the room's walls were lined with niches and in each of those, there was a safe deposit box.

There was a single table in the middle of the room, and the young man carried Rocky's metal safe deposit box over, inserted what he called his guard key, and waited for Sophie to use hers. Once the lock clicked open, he told us he'd be outside if we needed anything, backed out of the room, and closed the door behind him.

Sophie scrubbed her palms over the legs of her black pants and tried her best to chase away the nervous strain that crackled in the air. "So . . . Rocky was a flower child back in the day, you know. What if it's a box full of pot?"

I doubted it.

Sophie ran her tongue over her lips and gave the box a careful look before she glanced up at me. "Are we ready?"

More antsy than ready, but I bit my tongue and didn't mention it. For me, this was just another piece of the puzzle, and I hoped it would provide us something that would help bring Rocky's murderer to justice. For Sophie, it was a glimpse into her friend's private life. I could tell from the way she stared at the safe deposit box and blinked nervously that she was not at all comfortable with it.

I looked to her before I dared put a hand on the box, and when I got a brief nod as a go-ahead, I flipped open the lid.

Sophie caught her breath, but whether it was with relief or surprise, I couldn't tell. "Newspaper articles!"

They were, and they looked old.

Carefully, I retrieved the stack of a couple dozen articles and set them in a pile next to the safe deposit box. There was a scrapbook at the bottom of the box and one of those notebooks like kids use in school, and I took those out and handed them to Sophie.

She dropped into one of the chairs near the table and quickly paged through the scrapbook. "Flyers that Rocky used to hand out at protests and rallies." She tipped the book toward me so I could see the colorful handouts. "And here's a pressed flower. A daisy." Along with the brittle flower, there was a picture of a very young Raquel Arnaud, her hair long and straight and loose around her shoulders, a daisy tucked up behind her ear.

Her eyes bright with unshed tears, Sophie closed the scrapbook, cleared her throat, and grabbed the notebook. "Rocky's handwriting," she said, tracing the letters of the writing with one finger. "It looks like a sort of outline, what she was planning to talk about at the peace symposium."

"And these articles . . ." There were too many to study too closely, not right there, anyway, so I gave them a cursory look. "She's got them dated. September 1, 1970. October 3, 1970. October 6, 1970." I read over the headlines. "They're all about the peace movement and the Young People's Underground for Peace. According to Professor Weinhart over at Youngstown State, that's the group Rocky was part of."

"Yes, of course. Peaceniks, we called them." Sophie smiled across the table at me. "It makes sense that Rocky would have articles about them if she was planning to talk about the movement at the peace symposium. She was probably using all this for research."

"But why hide the articles in a safe deposit box?" I riffled my fingers through the articles.

"Well, if there was a fire . . ." Sophie suggested.

"She could have scanned them," I said. "That would have kept the originals safe. Or she could have copied the articles and kept the copies at home. When we looked through the house . . .We didn't find newspaper articles of any kind."

But Professor Weinhart had mentioned them, hadn't she? She'd told me that Rocky showed her the research materials she'd gathered to support her presentation at the symposium.

I wasn't sure what this meant other than the fact that at one time, Rocky had kept the materials in front of us at Pacifique; that's where Professor Weinhart said she'd seen them.

I pulled out one article at random. It was dated January 26, 1971, and included a picture of a skinny, bearded guy with long hair and wild eyes. The photo was old, grainy, black and white, yet something about it conveyed the intensity of the time and the young man who was identified in the caption as Steve Pastori.

"Steve!" Sophie caught sight of the photo and plucked the article out of my hand. "My goodness, I'd nearly forgotten all about him. He was a mover and shaker on the Ohio State campus, that's for sure."

Yes, I know the young have a hard time picturing older people as ever having lives that included not being old, but it was the first time I'd ever thought of Sophie as young. It was the first I'd ever wondered about what her life was like before she bought the Terminal and devoted her life to providing home-style food to her customers, along with a spot that many of them considered their home away from home.

"You went to college?" I asked her.

She barked out a laugh. "Hard to believe this old hen was ever a young chick, isn't it?" She didn't hold the question against me—I could tell by her smile. She wrinkled her nose. "Back in the day, I thought I wanted to be a nurse, and I attended Ohio State for two years. But the course work . . . well, math and chemistry weren't really my strong suits."

"Cooking is all about chemistry," I reminded her.

"It is, and that kind of chemistry, I understand. The other kind—the real kind—well, I tried. Really hard. But I never quite got it."

"But you were there. At Ohio State with Rocky."

"Sure, that's how we met. She lived down the hall from me in our dorm, and Rocky . . ." Thinking back, Sophie cocked her head. "Rocky was different, maybe a little too different for most of the girls in the dorm. They were put off by her. But remember, I'd grown up with Nina!" This time when Sophie grinned, the warmth of it traveled right through to my bones. "Nina was always the girl everyone noticed, the one who spoke up, the one who pushed the envelope when it came to what she did and what she wore and how she felt about the world in general."

"Just like Rocky."

Sophie nodded. "We hit it off the first time we bumped into each other in the cafeteria line, and after that . . . well, I think both our roommates were relieved that we'd found each other and spent so much time together that they didn't have to put up with us! My own roommate was a party girl who didn't want to bother with a wallflower like me, and Rocky's roomie, well, like I said, she wasn't sure what to make of a girl like Rocky who protested for causes she believed in and wouldn't keep her mouth shut when she thought she could right a wrong."

"And Steve?" I asked.

The smile faded from Sophie's face and her eyes clouded with memory. "Young, impulsive, committed. It's hard for people these days to understand what things were like back then. That's why this peace symposium is so important. It's why I encouraged Rocky to speak at it in the first place. There was a war happening on the other side of the world and so many people here thought it was wrong, that it was immoral. So many people didn't want to send our boys to the jungles of Vietnam to die. There was anger." She passed a hand over her eyes. "There was so much anger."

I glanced over the article in front of us and what looked to be an interview with Steve Pastori. "And Steve was one of the angry people?"

"The angriest." Sophie picked up the paper and looked at the picture again. "Like I said, he was committed and convinced that he was right. Sometimes people like that are impulsive. He was a national organizer, and Rocky, she started out as an organizer on the OSU campus, then worked the entire Midwest region. She and Steve, they bumped heads a lot."

"Ego wars and political wars." When I realized Sophie was looking at me in wonder, I shook my shoulders. "That's what Professor Weinhart said, that a lot of the tension within the peace movement was caused by ego wars and political wars, people who wanted to make a name for themselves, people with their own agendas. Is that what happened between Rocky and Steve?"

"Something like that." Rocky closed the notebook and put it on top of the scrapbook, then grabbed the newspaper articles and piled them on top and gave them a pat. "We'll read these at home," she said. "When we have more time. What do you suppose they'll tell us?"

This I couldn't say. Not for sure.

I knew only that there was something contained here in this small pile of aging paper that made Rocky think she had to keep it from prying eyes.

It was those kinds of secrets that got people killed.

ON THE WAY out of Cortland, I mentioned to Sophie that I wanted to stop at Pacifique and gather some herbs, and she didn't object. Or question me.

Good thing, because I wasn't ready yet to tell her about Senator Stone.

I would, I promised myself. Monday after the interview, I'd assess my chances for the job and if I thought there was even the remotest possibility (even while I was driving I crossed my fingers), I'd come clean and tell Sophie there was a very real chance that I would be leaving, and soon. Until then, she didn't need to know that I was looking for the curly parsley, thyme, marjoram, oregano, sage, and rosemary that I would use in the bouquet garni in the senator's soup.

"I'm going to go inside." As soon as we were out of the car, Sophie headed for the front door. "I'll just make sure everything's all right and I'm going to make a cup of tea while I'm at it. You want one?"

I didn't really, but I told her I'd take one anyway. Making the tea would give Sophie something to do and besides, it was chilly that Friday morning. By the time I was done in the garden, I was sure a cup of tea would be exactly what I needed. As soon as she was inside, I got to work. I went into the barn and rooted around for everything I needed.

A towel.

Gloves.

Some of the small plastic containers Rocky used when she sold live plants.

I scooped them all up in my arms and while I was at it, I grabbed one of the sturdy canvas aprons Rocky wore when she was out in the garden. Once that was on, I was ready to go, and I tromped out into the herb garden.

And stopped cold when I realized there was already someone out there.

Someone who looked remarkably like . . .

I swallowed hard and bent forward for a better look at the woman who tracked through the garden with her back to me, a straw sunhat on her head and an apron similar to mine looped around her neck and billowing around her on the end of the stiff October wind. She walked with an easy gait, one hand out to brush through the knee-high lavender that grew all around her. Even from here, I could tell she was relaxed and at peace in the garden, and at the same time I envied anyone who could be so at one with her environment. My heart bumped and my stomach swooped.

"Rocky?"

The name came out of me more like a squeak than an actual question, but the woman heard it and whirled around.

I braced a hand to my heart and nearly collapsed from the relief.

Until I realized I shouldn't be so quick to dismiss my fears.

"What are you doing here?" In clean jeans, a white sweater, and that apron, Minnie Greenway looked like a different woman, but she sounded like the same old Minnie when she confronted me. "What do you want?"

I held up my trowel as if for proof. "Just digging up some herbs. How about you, Minnie? What are you doing here?"

I had closed in on her. Minnie's hair was combed and pulled back into a ponytail. There was color in her cheeks. "I . . . I was just walking, enjoying the sunshine." As if it were the first time she realized exactly where she was, she glanced over at the house and bit her lower lip. "I'm sorry. Maybe I shouldn't be here. I just started walking and I guess I just lost track of the time and where I was and . . ." She stepped over a row of neatly planted parsley. "I'll go home now."

"You don't have to." I thought about the last time I'd seen Minnie in the Cortland police station when she made her phony confession. "How are you, Minnie?"

It took her a little while to think about it. "They put me . . ." She drew in a breath. "I was in the hospital. For two nights. And they changed my medication and I promised them I'd take it every single day like I'm supposed to, and I have. I haven't missed even one dose. Otis makes sure."

"That's good. It shows."

She touched a hand to her hat. "Does it? That's what Otis told me this morning. He said I looked like a new woman, and I told him . . ." Again, her gaze darted to the house and this time, her eyes filled with tears. "I told him that I understand now that when he came to see that

Frenchwoman, he wasn't looking for a new woman, just a friend he could talk to. He says . . ." She looked down at the earth at our feet. "He says this old woman he has is just fine with him."

"I'm glad, Minnie." I thought about giving her a hug and decided that might be too much for Minnie, so I kept my distance. "I'm glad you're feeling better."

"And you know I didn't kill that Rocky woman, right? The police, they told you that?"

"They told me that you thought maybe you did."

She nodded. "But I wouldn't. Not really. That's what my psychiatrist told me. She said I might have fantasies, but I'm not a violent person. I would never really kill someone."

So what's a person supposed to say in response to a comment like that?

That's good?

Hoorah for you?

Because I didn't know what to say, I didn't say anything at all.

"I sometimes pick the lavender. That Frenchy, she never minded." There were a few sprigs of it in Minnie's hand and she showed them to me. "Otis puts it next to my pillow. He says it helps me sleep. I like the way it smells. Do you think I'll get in trouble for being here? For picking the lavender?"

It was another one of those questions that's impossible to respond to.

I shrugged. "Eventually, the house will belong to whoever Rocky left it to in her will. Or it will be sold and belong to some stranger. Then . . . well, maybe those people won't want you here picking the lavender. But right now, Sophie's in charge of the house and I know she won't mind."

Minnie smiled. "I'm just going to pick a little more and then I'm going to leave. Can I pick a little more?"

I assured her she could and while she was at it, I got busy and got to work.

I'd already dug up three curly parsley plants and plopped them in plastic containers when I realized Minnie was standing over me.

I sat back on my heels and looked up at her just in time to see her hold a wand of lavender to her nose and sniff.

"I was here. I was picking lavender," she said. "The night I saw the man."

Coming from anyone else, this might have been something to sit up and take notice about. But remember, this was Minnie, and medication or no medication, I knew the things Minnie said couldn't always be trusted, that they weren't always sensible. Or true.

Tell that to the sudden thumping inside my rib cage.

Slowly, so as not to startle her, I got to my feet. "The night you saw the man?"

She nodded, then held out the lavender to me. "It smells good."

I took a sniff and nodded. The lavender smelled heavenly and as long as I was here, I'd take some home for myself and some for Sophie, too. But that was a thought for later. For now . . .

"What man are you talking about?" I asked Minnie.

"He came in a car, and he didn't see me." Minnie shook her head so hard, her straw hat went cockeyed and she didn't straighten it. "I was in the garden. She was in the garden, too. Earlier."

"She?"

"Frenchy. Always in the garden. Morning, afternoon, and evening."

"And was it morning, afternoon, or evening when you saw the man?" I asked Minnie.

"It was evening. Late. But she wasn't in the garden when I got here. He was. He parked his car over there." She pointed behind us toward the barn and the little outbuilding beyond where I knew Rocky stacked firewood for the winter. "He didn't see me because I went into the barn and I hid in one of the old horse stalls." Minnie bent nearer and whispered, "I'm smart."

"You are smart," I told her. "But you forgot to tell me when this was, Minnie. You say there was a man here. He must have been visiting Rocky."

"She wasn't dead yet." Apparently, I was as dumb as dumb can be because Minnie rolled her eyes. "She wouldn't have a visitor if she was dead."

Not dead.

Then at least a week before.

Which, of course, meant nothing.

I did my best to control my excitement, but let's face it, I had to know more. I remembered those pictures Otis showed us at the police station, the ones that proved that he and Minnie were at a harvest festival the evening Rocky died. "It wasn't the day you and Otis were at the church festival, was it?"

I got another eye roll for my efforts. "The police know I didn't kill her," Minnie said. "Because we were at the festival and we got home late. Too late for me to kill her. But not too late for me to see the man."

I could only imagine the jumble that was Minnie's brain,

and it was frightening. The best I could do was try to step my way through and make some sense of it all.

"Then it was the night of the festival?" I asked her.

Minnie giggled. "Before you came here with that good-looking guy."

My heart thumped. Me and the good-looking guy—Declan—we were here Saturday night. We found Rocky's body.

And unless Minnie was here and watching, she had no way of knowing that.

As much as I tried, I could barely control the shiver of excitement in my voice. "You were still here when Declan and I showed up?"

She nodded. "I was in the barn, and nobody knew it. Saw you go inside. Saw the police come, too. That's when I skedaddled home."

"But before you did that, before I got here with Declan—"

"The good-looking guy."

It was my turn to nod. "The good-looking guy. Before we showed up, you saw someone else here."

"He went inside. But not for long." One corner of Minnie's mouth crinkled. "Went inside, came outside. He got in his car and left and then a little while later, that's when you and that good-looking guy—"

"You should have told the police about this, Minnie."

"I didn't remember. Not until now. Because now I'm taking my medication. And I'm picking lavender." Again, she held out the stems for me to see. "Can I pick more lavender?"

"Sure, Minnie, only . . ."

She was already walking away and she turned back around.

"Can you tell me what the man looked like?" I asked her.

"Don't need to think about it." She grinned. "I'm smart."

"And the man?"

"The man," she said, "he had a beard."

A man with a beard. Here at Pacifique the night of the murder.

This was exactly the kind of break in the case we'd been waiting for, and anxious to give Tony Russo a call, I took my parsley plants out to the car. By then, Minnie was nowhere to be seen, so I turned toward the house. I was almost there when I heard a curious noise from inside, like something heavy falling over.

Or something being thrown.

Before I could decide which it was, I heard Sophie's high-pitched scream and broke into a run.

She was somewhere upstairs, and she screamed again just as I burst through the kitchen door.

"I'm here, Sophie," I called, and took the steps two at a time. "I'm coming!"

I dashed into Rocky's neat little library and found no one. I looked into the room filled with botanical prints and it was empty.

Sophie was in the guest bedroom, lying facedown on the floor, and I raced over to her and knelt down at her side.

In the great scheme of things, I guess I should have looked around the room first.

The blow hit me from behind even before I knew it was happening, and in an instant, stars burst behind my eyes. Novas exploded inside my head.

And then everything went black.

Chapter 16

The first thing I saw when I woke up was a straw hat. It was a little crooked.

Or maybe it just looked a little crooked because the room was spinning in front of my eyes.

Then again, the expression on the face of the woman wearing it was a little off-kilter, too. Like she wasn't quite sure what to do.

"Minnie?" A wave of nausea nearly took my breath away. I was on my back, and I tried to prop myself up on my elbows and promptly fell back on the floor. "Minnie, what are you doing here? What happened? And where's—"

A memory like the cold slap of a tsunami washed over me, and inside my muddled head, I pictured Sophie as I'd seen her when I walked into the room.

Facedown and on the floor.

"Sophie!" Nausea be damned! I sat up as quickly as I

could, ignored the scene in front of me when it tipped right then left then right again, and scanned the room. Sophie wasn't where I'd seen her last, and at the same time as my heart skipped a beat, I looked over my shoulder.

She was sitting up on the edge of the bed, one leg propped on the mattress. Her face was ashen.

"What . . ." I tried to stay upright, but it was a losing cause from the start. Before I could flump down like a dead fish, I lowered myself back on the floor. "What happened?" I asked her.

There were two spots of high color in Sophie's cheeks, but—thank goodness—I saw no sign of injury, no sign of blood. She pressed a hand to her heart. "I walked into the room and someone . . ." When she shivered, I felt the tremor of fear all the way over where I lay. "Someone was in here. Behind the door." She looked that way and swallowed hard. "That person . . . he . . . she . . . he pushed me down and I landed . . ." She put a hand to her knee and winced.

Well, that explained the screaming.

"I fell over on my face and just kept screaming, and I don't know what would have happened if you didn't get here. But you did." Her shoulders lost some of their stiffness. "I heard you say you were on your way and I heard you come into the room, Laurel, and then I heard a sort of sickening thud and . . ." She pressed her fingers over her lips.

"Did you see who did it?" I asked her.

Her lips puckered and her gaze traveled over to where Minnie knelt at my side, and automatically, I found myself scooting over on my butt, putting a pathetically few safe inches between me and Minnie.

Sophie made a face. "I can't say for sure, of course. I don't know for sure. I was too afraid to look," she admitted.

"And I was in too much pain to move. I waited until I heard the person run out of the room and down the steps and out the front door. Then I dragged myself over to where you lay and the next thing I knew, Minnie was here."

Minnie nodded like a bobblehead, and I had to put a hand on her arm to stop her before all that movement got the better of my stomach.

"Minnie, how did you—"

"Told you I was smart," she said. "I heard the screaming. In the garden. I was picking lavender." Like a fairy godmother brandishing her magic wand, she waved those lavender stems in front of me, and the scent that had been so clean and pleasant outside stuck inside my nostrils, cloying and sickening.

My own hand shaking, I pushed the lavender away.

"What did you see?" I asked Minnie. "Who did you see? When you came back into the house, who was here, Minnie?"

Her lips folded in on themselves. "Nobody," Minnie said. "But someone out there."

She pointed to the window in the guest room. "Someone running toward the road."

Not someone who'd parked anywhere where we might have seen the car.

I grumbled a curse at the same time I tried again to drag myself up off the floor. Before I could, we heard cars pull up the drive and a second later, running footsteps inside the house.

"What happened?" Tony Russo asked almost before he burst into the room. "Who's hurt? What happened? Who did it?"

I passed a hand over my eyes and while I was at it, I

managed to scoot back so that I could sit up and lean against the bed. A simple enough movement, but it took a lot out of me and I closed my eyes. When I opened them again, Tony was peering into my face.

"The paramedics are coming," he said.

By way of telling him what I thought of this idea, I made a move to push him back. It was a noble effort. Really. Too bad I passed out before I knew if anyone was going to pay any attention to it.

I WASN'T IN Rocky's guest room.

I knew that the moment I next woke up and saw the color of the wall over on my left. No more creamy white, soothing ivory, gentle shades of ecru. No more pooling draperies or light filtering through windows that looked out over the gardens.

The wall was green and there were metal blinds on two windows with a view of a blacktopped parking lot. When I turned my head (oh so carefully), I saw that the tile on the floor was green, too.

Hospital room.

I groaned and when that didn't change anything, I added an especially colorful curse.

"Nice way to talk!"

I hadn't realized Tony Russo was in the chair next to my bed until he spoke, but believe me, I didn't waste any time on being embarrassed. Or on taking back the words I'd muttered.

"What am I doing here?" I asked him, struggling to sit up. "I don't belong here. I'm fine."

"The paramedics said otherwise." He didn't look

especially upset by my outburst, just a little amused when he handed me the gizmo that made the head of the bed rise. The curtain was pulled around my bed, enclosing the two of us in a world bordered by that green wall, the windows, and a whole lot of white fabric. "They're keeping you for observation."

I did as quick a mental computation of the days as my scrambled brain could manage. It was still light outside, still Friday. I didn't have to leave town until early Monday morning for my interview with the senator.

I couldn't be gracious about the hospital stay, but I could be cooperative. At least to a point.

I raised the head of the bed and settled back against the squishy pillow. "Have you figured out what happened?"

"I was about to ask you that." When Tony shifted in the guest chair, the green vinyl cushions creaked. "What did you see?"

I thought about shaking my head and decided that was probably a bad idea. "Not a thing. I walked into the room and the next thing I knew, wham!"

"Could you have been struck by Minnie Greenway?"

I had to admit, the thought had crossed my mind back at Pacifique when I found Minnie bent over me. "But why?" I asked Tony and myself. "There doesn't seem to be much point in her leaving me out in the garden and going into the house so she could attack Sophie and then me. And she seemed better, didn't she?" I thought back to my brief visit with Minnie. "She said she's been taking her medication and she seemed more . . . I don't know . . . more together."

His head didn't feel as if there were elephants in it doing the conga, so Tony was able to nod without wincing. "Pretty much what I was thinking. And she is the one who called us. Why attack you and Sophie, then call us to come help you? That's just . . ."

We both knew he was going to say *crazy* and there didn't seem much point in belaboring the subject.

"So if not Minnie," Tony asked, "who?"

"Somebody who was already in the house when Sophie went inside." This was a new thought and it just sort of fell out of my mouth at the same time it popped into my head, but I guess I had an excuse, what with my brain feeling like Jell-O. "Whoever it was, that person didn't want Sophie to see him . . . or her. My guess is the person thought she . . . or he . . . or whatever . . . that the person thought he could lay low until Sophie and I left, but then Sophie went upstairs. So when she walked into the guest room, where the intruder was hiding, that person shoved her down and probably would have left the house right then and there if I didn't come running. Once I was there—"

"You were a threat. Younger than Sophie, more likely to fight back and get a look at your assailant. Conking you on the head was the logical thing to do. Hey," he protested as soon as I shot him a look. "I didn't say it was right, or good. I just said it was logical from your attacker's point of view. It was better than some of the alternatives, that's for sure."

Some of the alternatives were things I didn't want to think about.

I shivered and pulled the lightweight hospital blanket up around my shoulders. It was the first I registered that I was wearing one of those flimsy blue and white hospital gowns that tie in the back and pretty much don't cover anything that should be covered. I tugged the blanket up a little farther.

"So the real question . . ." I thought it through. "Who was it in the house? And what was the person doing there?"

"My guess is he was looking for something," Tony said.

"Like he was the night he broke into the house, the night Rocky made note of on her calendar."

"Could be." He rose to leave. "In the meantime, if you think of anything, if you remember that you saw someone or noticed something odd, you'll call me, won't you?"

I promised I would, only before Tony could lift one edge of the bed curtain so he could scoot around it, I stopped him.

"But what about Sophie?" I asked.

Tony smiled and whipped back the curtain to reveal that I was in a two-person room. My roomie was Sophie.

Relief washed through me. That is, until I saw that her leg was encased in some kind of contraption designed to keep it immobile.

"How are you feeling?" I asked her.

She smiled and waved good-bye when Tony walked out of the room, but the moment he was gone, she harrumphed. "Stupid," she said.

"You can't think—"

"That I could have done something?" Sophie clutched her hands together on top of the cotton blanket that matched mine. "I should have. I could have at least taken a look and seen who did it."

I wasn't about to argue that point with her. Whether she realized it yet or not, I was convinced that the fact that she kept her head down and her face averted was what kept her from further harm. There was no telling what our attacker might have done if Sophie could identify him.

"It doesn't matter now," I told Sophie, both to soothe

her and because it was true. "All that matters is that you're okay. How's the knee?"

She winced, so that told me something.

"You called George?"

She nodded. "Talked to Inez, too. They've got everything under control tonight, and Declan and his family, they're coming in to help."

My protest hadn't even made it to my lips when Sophie stopped me. "This has nothing to do with you. Declan heard what happened, that's all. My guess is by now, everyone in Hubbard knows the story. He heard what happened and he knew since it's Friday we're going to be slammed tonight. So he said he'd come over and help out, you know, with cashing out customers and such. And he said his mom and dad don't mind helping, either, and there are a few nieces and nephews who can bus tables and a couple of cousins who might be able to pitch in."

I suppose I should have been grateful, and deep down inside, I guess I was.

Except I couldn't help but picture the Fury family turning the Terminal upside down. Maurice Chevalier would be replaced by the Chieftains and every tartine would come with a side of colcannon.

And I couldn't worry about any of it.

Not from a hospital bed.

"Misti says she can be there early tomorrow to help with the breakfast crowd," Sophie said.

"I hope we're out of here by tomorrow," I grumbled.

Sophie sniffled. "You could have been really hurt."

"It's just a headache."

"But if something happened, Laurel, because you were coming to help me . . ."

If I could have reached across the space that separated our beds, I would have patted her hand. Instead, all I could do was try to talk her down. "Something didn't happen. At least not something too horrible. But what was the person doing there in the house?"

"I heard what you said to Officer Russo. It was the killer. It had to be. And he had to be searching for something."

Hey, three cheers for my brain. At a time when it was hard to think of pretty much anything at all, it managed to nudge a memory out of me.

"The stuff we found in Rocky's safe deposit box," I said.

"But he couldn't have known we had it," Sophie insisted.

"No, he couldn't have. For all the killer knew, all that stuff was still in the house. He didn't know about the safe deposit box." It's funny how the mind works, or maybe the fact that mine had been recently jumbled actually helped. A distant memory bubbled up to the surface.

Rocky's date book and the notation of the break-in.

"You don't still have those papers from the bank with you, do you?" I asked Sophie.

She nodded and reached into the top drawer of the bed-side table for her purse. "Here's what that young man at the bank gave us this morning," she said, stretching to hand the papers to me. "Why? What are you looking for?"

"I don't know yet," I admitted, scanning the papers through bleary eyes. I blinked, rubbed my eyes, tried again.

And the truth came into focus.

"Rocky opened the safe deposit box the day after the break-in."

I didn't need to explain; Sophie understood the significance. "So those newspaper articles, the scrapbook, that's what the burglar was after."

I wasn't ready to say that for certain. "It's what Rocky thought the burglar was looking for," I pointed out. "And that's because of the note."

"Leave the past in the past." Sophie exhaled the words on the end of a breath of amazement. "So Rocky did see that note stabbed into her dressing screen."

"And didn't say a word to anyone about it because she wasn't sure what to make of it. She knew there was something she had that someone wanted her to keep quiet about, but what? Maybe even she didn't know exactly what she had that someone might be after."

We sat for a few minutes, but there is no such thing as quiet in a hospital, and there was little chance for us to try to make sense of the puzzle.

"We need to look through those articles again," I told Sophie, who pointed out the obvious.

"They're still in your car. Back at Pacifique."

Declan wanted to help?

I reached for the bedside table and my phone, but stopped before I dialed his number. The last time I'd seen him was when he discovered I'd lied about Misti being sick and the date needing to be called off because I was needed at the Terminal. Something told me he wouldn't appreciate me calling him now because I needed his help.

The same something that told me he had every right to be pissed.

"That doesn't mean I can't call him." When I looked at Sophie in wonder, her face lit with a grin. "Oh, come on, Laurel. It doesn't take a mind reader to figure you out. You need help, you reach for your phone, and the first person you'd naturally think to call is Declan. That's what happens when two people fall in love."

I opened my mouth to protest and when the words refused to form, I snapped it shut again without a word.

It was just as well. Sophie was already on the phone with Declan.

HE ARRIVED AT the hospital with a big box of chocolates for Sophie along with a bouquet of orange, purple, and yellow mums that were in a cute jack-o'-lantern vase and pleased her no end.

No flowers for me, and to tell the truth, I was actually relieved.

At least until the nurse who he'd somehow schmoozed into helping him trailed in behind him with a dozen yellow roses.

"Red is too showy," he said, setting the vase of flowers on the windowsill next to my bed. "Yellow is cheerier."

"I don't need cheering." I could have kicked myself the second the words were out of my mouth. They were bratty and he didn't deserve that. I swallowed hard. "The flowers are very pretty and . . . and thank you for bringing them."

"You're welcome." He perched himself on the side of my bed and maybe I was imagining it, maybe I was thinking that rifts between people could be healed so easily and with so few words. Maybe I knew better. Or maybe at least I should have.

Still, some of the tension seemed to go out of Declan's shoulders. "I hear you're looking for these." He had the pile of newspaper articles, the scrapbook, and the notebook banded together and tucked up under his arm. "Then again, Sophie was the one who called and asked me to go get this stuff out of your car. Maybe she's the one . . ." Even before he'd turned toward Sophie's bed, I had my hand out for the papers.

He pretended to think about it for a moment before he handed them to me and grinned. "So what are you looking for?" he asked.

It wasn't what he was asking about, but tell that to my conscience! "Maybe the chance to explain," I said.

"Then maybe once your head doesn't feel like it's going to crack open, you'll have coffee with me."

"Will it be a date?"

"Do you want it to be?"

Blame my whirling head. For once, the truth seemed like a better option than beating around the bush.

"Yes," I said. "I would like that very much."

He might have replied if a long, dreamy sigh from Sophie didn't interrupt us.

"So . . ." With a quick grin in my direction, Declan got down to business. He pointed at the stack of papers I'd already unbanded and separated into three piles: the scrapbook, the notebook, the newspaper articles.

"I don't know exactly what we're looking for," I admitted. "But remember that note . . . 'Leave the past in the past' . . . We think"—I glanced Sophie's way to indicate that we'd worked through the problem together—"We think these papers might hold the key to that past."

"Makes sense." He nodded. "That's why Rocky wanted to keep all this stuff safe."

"Because someone wanted the past left in the past."

"And these articles, they're definitely all about the past."

"So who'd want to make sure this stuff stays quiet?" I was talking more to myself than to Declan or Sophie and it was a good thing since I knew neither of them had the answer for me.

I shuffled through the articles and once again found myself looking at that picture of wild-eyed Steve Pastori.

"How about him?" I asked, flashing the article at Sophie. "Could Rocky have been planning to say something about Steve at the symposium, something that maybe even after all these years, he didn't want anyone to hear?"

She was chewing on a chocolate-covered caramel, so she simply nodded. Once she swallowed, she said, "Oh, there was plenty she could have said about Steve. You see, he kind of . . . oh, I don't know how you'd say it. I guess you could say he went off the reservation."

Declan and I exchanged looks before we both looked Sophie's way.

"Like I told you this morning, Laurel, Steve was committed to the movement. To the point of obsession. The kids in the Young People's Underground for Peace, they were all about nonviolent protests. You know, real flower power types. It was what made the group so effective. They didn't go out and cause trouble, they wanted to change the world and they thought they could do that through love and brotherhood."

"But not Steve." Somehow, just looking into his eyes in that picture told me it was true. "You said he went off the reservation."

"Well, not at first, of course," she said, plucking another caramel out of the box and popping it in her mouth. She offered the candy our way, and both Declan and I declined. Sophie chewed quietly for a few moments. "I remember one night when I found Rocky in the school library. It was very late, and she was very upset."

"About Steve?"

"About what Steve had become. You see, he was an impatient guy, and he didn't see things changing fast enough, not to suit him. That night we talked at the library, Rocky had just left a meeting of the Young People's Underground, and at the meeting, Steve said he thought it was time to step things up, to take their protests to the next level."

"With violence?" Declan asked.

Sophie nodded. "Rocky was desperate to talk him out of it. She begged him, but he wouldn't listen. A week or so later . . ." Sophie's eyes clouded with the memory. "The campus ROTC building . . . ROTC, I think it's still around but I bet you kids don't know about it. ROTC, it stands for . . ." She had to think about it for a minute. "Reserve Officers' Training Corps, that's what it is. It's college-based officers' training for the armed forces. Well, you can imagine, back in the late '60s and early '70s when there was so much student unrest and so many people protesting about our country's military involvement in Vietnam, ROTC headquarters on campuses around the country were at the center of a lot of the controversy. And about a week after Rocky and Steve had that fight, an ROTC building at a nearby college was firebombed."

This wasn't what I was expecting from a group called the Young People's Underground for Peace, and I gasped.

"Oh yes. Sad but true." Sophie shook her head in dismay. "I bet when we look closely, we'll find articles about it there in Rocky's things. A couple of people inside the building were badly hurt. But that . . ." Her gaze drifted off. "That wasn't the end of it, I'm afraid. A few days later, there was a firebomb attack at a different college and this time, two people were killed."

I looked down at the picture of the long-haired, bearded kid from the old newspaper. "Steve Pastori did that? He killed people?"

Sophie nodded. "The cops were sure it was him, and Rocky, well, she was heartbroken. Just heartbroken. She couldn't understand how someone she believed in, someone who'd preached peace and love, could turn to violence."

"Then Steve Pastori . . ." I flicked the photo with one finger. "Maybe what Rocky was going to say at the symposium had something to do with him. Maybe he's the one who wanted her to leave the past in the past. Maybe he . . ." Again, I couldn't help but look at the photograph. "Could he have killed Rocky?"

"Oh no. That isn't possible." Thinking, Sophie cocked her head, both her hands against the lid of the now-closed box of candy. "You see, a couple of months after the first bombing . . . well, the cops were all over the Young People's Underground, looking for information, searching for Steve. They talked to Rocky over and over and she told them she had no idea where he'd disappeared to after those buildings were firebombed. He was in hiding, and it was true, she didn't have a clue where he was. Then one day I was with Rocky when we got word. There was another firebomb, at an ROTC building at a college campus in Illinois, and Steve, well, he didn't get out of the building fast enough. They found his body in the wreckage."

I didn't realize how much I'd glommed on to the idea of Steve as bad guy until a wave of disappointment enveloped me. "Then Steve couldn't have written that note in Rocky's bedroom. He couldn't have been the one Rocky was looking for."

It was Sophie's turn to look at me in wonder, and I

realized this was one part of the story she didn't know. It wasn't my secret. I turned to Declan.

"A few years ago," he explained, "Rocky came to me looking for advice on how to locate someone."

For a few, long moments, Sophie went very still. She swallowed hard. "Did she say who?"

Declan shook his head. "I asked, but she wouldn't tell me."

Sophie coughed behind her hand. "Did she say if she ever found the person?"

"She never said another word to me about it," Declan told her.

"Well, then, it might have been . . ." For a minute, Sophie wrestled with her words. For a woman who usually let it all hang out (as the Young People's Underground might have said), it was an odd response, and something about it made me feel as if there were a rubber band inside me, stretched tight and ready to snap.

"I mean I can't say for sure because she didn't say anything to me about it," Sophie said. "But it's possible, I suppose and really, I guess it's only natural if after all these years . . ." She set her shoulders and lifted her chin. "I guess Rocky might have been searching for her baby."

Chapter 17

It must have been the smack on the head. I could have sworn Sophie said . . .

"Baby?" I stared across the small space that separated our hospital beds, my jaw slack. "You never told me that Rocky had a—"

"Well, it wasn't my secret to tell." Sophie stuck out her lower lip. "And it wasn't anything she ever talked about. I mean, not for the last forty years or so. You just don't go spreading those kinds of personal stories about your friends. Not for no reason."

"But there might be a reason!" Something told me that the hit-with-a-cream-pie look on Declan's face matched my own. "Did she give up the child for adoption?" he asked.

"Yes. Back in . . ." Sophie did some mental calculations. "It was '71. Or maybe '72. I'm pretty sure it was early '72.

Maybe. I know I'd already left Ohio State and was back in Hubbard. Yes, '72. Winter. I'm sure of it."

Declan whistled low under his breath. "Then that explains who she was searching for!"

"Well, we don't know that for sure," Sophie warned both of us. "But I suppose it's possible."

"Leave the past in the past." Possibility after possibility cascaded through my head and I whispered the words in wonder. "Maybe the baby she was looking for didn't want to be found."

For a few minutes, we let the revelation sink in and when it did, I finally was able to shake my head (carefully, of course!) and order my thoughts.

"You've got a lot to tell us," I said to Sophie. "I think you should start at the beginning."

"The beginning." Sophie considered this for a moment. "Well, I suppose the beginning is when Rocky joined the Young People's Underground for Peace. That's when she met Steve."

"Wait a minute! Wait a minute!" Before she could say another word and make my head spin even more, I waved Sophie into silence. "Are you saying that Rocky and Steve Pastori were—"

"A couple? Well, certainly." She folded her hands on top of that box of candy. "Why else would Rocky be so upset when Steve went rogue? She loved him. Or at least she thought she did. Until she realized the man she was in love with never really existed."

I gave her a squint-eyed look. "You mean Steve—"

"Oh, I don't mean he never existed." Sophie laughed. "Of course he existed. Of course he was a real person. He just wasn't the person Rocky thought he was. Once he resorted to violence to further his cause, he proved that to her and to the world."

"But before that?" Declan asked.

"Well, they were completely and totally into each other," Sophie told us. "Head over heels in love. And they were the perfect couple!" Thinking, she tipped back her head. "He was tall and long haired and his eyes, they were dreamy, like a poet's. And Rocky . . . well, there she was, straight out of some little village somewhere outside of Paris, and she was so interesting and so exotic and so pretty. They got to know each other when they joined the Underground and I think it took exactly . . ." Her cheeks flushed a deep pink and Sophie looked away. "I don't think I'm telling tales," she said, "because Rocky told me about it when it happened. It took exactly one meeting of the Underground and one cup of coffee after and wham! Just like that, they fell into bed together. They knew they were meant for each other, you see."

I didn't like the way she paused after she said that, or the way she stared at me and Declan as if she expected that something inside our heads would instantly click and we'd call for the hospital chaplain to perform the wedding ceremony.

When we didn't (big surprise), Sophie's lips pinched, but she went right on. "From that day on, Rocky and Steve were inseparable. They were both devoted to ending the war in Vietnam. They were both committed to changing the world. There's nothing sexier, is there, than two people who are working together for a common cause?"

Again, her gaze slid from me to Declan.

Rather than be derailed—by her suggestion or by the thoughts that popped into my head because of it—I stuck to the matter at hand.

"And Rocky had a baby," I said to try to get Sophie back on track. "What did Steve think of that?"

"Well, that was one of the terrible things," she said. "With the old Steve . . . well, when Steve was like the Steve she first met, I think Rocky pictured a perfect life. Her, Steve, the baby. She had this dream that they'd live on a little farm somewhere together, grow organic crops, and be at peace with the world."

"Which is what she ended up doing all by herself," I said. Not that anyone needed it pointed out. "And now after all these years, Rocky might have been searching for that baby." I drummed my fingers against the cotton blanket and thought this through.

A tear slipped down Sophie's cheek. "I remember it like it was yesterday. At first, I mean at first when Rocky found out she was pregnant, well, she was so thrilled, she could hardly contain herself. By that time, Steve was already talking about violent protests, about going to war with the police, and about organizing a militant wing of the Young People's Underground. And Rocky was convinced that once he knew he had a baby coming, it would make a difference." When she sighed, Sophie's shoulders rose and fell. "She thought he'd come to his senses and realize he couldn't risk his life and his safety and his reputation by committing criminal acts. She thought that once he knew about the baby, he'd realize that a world of violence wasn't the kind of place they wanted to raise their child. She thought he'd come back around to her way of thinking."

"But he didn't." It was obvious, so I guess I really didn't need to say it.

"Knowing about the baby only made Steve more determined than ever to change the world right there, right then.

He said he owed it to his child. He said he was doing all of it for his child—the rallies and the protests, the rock throwing and yes, the bombs. He told Rocky that if she didn't understand that, then they really had nothing more to say to each other. And after that . . ." Her shrug was casual enough but the tone of Sophie's voice gave her away. Even all these years later, she remembered Rocky's pain. She felt it deep in her bones.

"Steve left and after that, that's when we heard about the first bombing. Rocky was beside herself, desperate. Then once Steve was dead . . ."

She cleared her throat and held out a hand. "Let me see that picture of Steve."

I handed it to Declan, who got up and gave it to Sophie.

"Yes. See." Sophie tapped the newspaper photo with one finger. "It's hard to tell, of course. The picture is black and white and it's old, but you see what Steve is wearing? He had this beat-up old green army jacket with a red peace patch on the sleeve. You know the one." With one finger, she drew a peace sign in the air, a circle with a line cutting it in half and two smaller slanted lines toward the bottom.

"We used to tease Steve about that jacket. We used to tell him that it didn't make any sense that he opposed the military but he wore a military jacket. And he said it made perfect sense because it was the warmest coat he'd ever had and because he wore it to show his defiance. He wore it to show that when you don a uniform, you don't have to go to war. And he added that big, red peace sign patch . . . at least that's what he always said . . . to show that soldiers don't have to conform, that they can still go their own way and make their own choices and listen to their own consciences, that they don't have to obey orders that aren't honorable."

One more look at the picture and Sophie waved the article back at Declan, who got up and took it from her. "That last bombing, when they found him in the rubble, that army jacket with the red patch was practically burned to a crisp." Sophie's voice dropped. "So was Steve."

It wasn't a pretty thought so I decided to set it aside. "And the baby?"

Sophie shook her head. "The baby hadn't been born yet, and Rocky agonized over what to do. Steve was dead and all she had of him, all she had to remember him by, was that baby. But she was young, and she knew she couldn't care for the child the way she should. Once he was born, she put him up for adoption."

"He."

This was a crucial part of the story that Sophie had failed to mention, and Declan noticed it, too. His eyebrows rose, but before he could say another word, Sophie went right on.

"Rocky was devastated. By what Steve had turned into. By his death. By the grief she felt at having to give up her son. She couldn't eat. She couldn't sleep. She'd gone back to school after the baby was born, but she couldn't concentrate and her grades went right down the tubes. By that time, I'd already left Ohio State and I was back in Hubbard so I convinced her to come stay with me for a while. That's when she found the farm, and the farm . . . well, Pacifique saved her. I saw it happen, acre by acre and year by year. She moved on from all the sadness and she made a life for herself. And you think . . ." She raised tear-filled eyes to Declan. "You think that now, she was looking for this boy?"

"It's possible," he admitted.

Sophie's salt-and-pepper eyebrows dropped low over her eyes and I could tell that though she'd never admit it, she was upset. "She never said anything about it to me."

"Maybe she just wanted to get more information before she spilled the beans," I told her. I had no way of knowing that was true, but I knew it would soothe Sophie's hurt feelings.

"It's also possible . . ." I'm not a mind reader, but somehow, I knew what Declan was going to say. Sophie hadn't thought of it yet. I could tell as much from the look on her face. It was all about old memories, good and bad. It hadn't yet registered with her that those old memories might be what Rocky's murder was all about.

Declan put a hand on my knee. A day earlier, I might have sloughed him off. That late afternoon with the last of the day's sun slanting through the windows and the terrible, sad truth of Rocky's story left me feeling chilled. I appreciated the warmth.

"Now that we know Rocky had a son . . . it might explain her obsession with Andrew MacLain," he said.

"And it might explain why MacLain was lurking around at the memorial service," I added.

And still, Sophie wasn't sure what we were talking about. Her gaze swiveled from me to Declan and back to me, and since she was never one to beat around the bush she just came out and said what she was thinking. "What on earth are you getting at?"

"MacLain," I said. "Andrew MacLain. Could he be Rocky's son?"

Sophie gasped and pressed a hand to her heart. "You think . . ." She fanned her face with one hand. "You mean . . ." She twisted in bed, but with that contraption on her knee, she couldn't move very far.

Declan got out his phone and did a quick search. "The dates are right," he announced. "MacLain's the right age. His biography says he was born in February of '72."

"February." Sophie nodded. "Near Valentine's Day."

"The thirteenth." Declan confirmed this with a look at his phone.

"So why would Rocky look for him now?" I asked no one in particular.

Sophie lifted her arms and dropped them back on the blanket. "When you get older, you think more and more of the past. Maybe she just wanted some connection, some closure. Maybe she had something to tell him or something to give him. Maybe . . ." I knew when the pieces clicked because she turned as white as the blanket on her bed.

"Do you think he could have had something to do with Rocky's murder?"

I couldn't say.

I didn't know.

But I sure intended to find out.

WE HAD EXACTLY one opportunity left. Andrew MacLain was speaking at the Hubbard library one last time that Saturday. After that, he was set to leave town, and I didn't need a crystal ball to tell me he wouldn't be hurrying back anytime soon.

I'm convinced it was the only reason Declan let me come along with him to the library instead of going home "where I belonged" (his words, not mine) when I was released from the hospital that morning.

On our way into the Hubbard library, he shot me a side-long look. "You need to rest."

"You weren't paying attention at the hospital. The doctor said I'm fine."

"The doctor said you should take it easy."

I slid him a smile. "I am taking it easy."

We slipped into the meeting room and took seats in the last row. MacLain was already halfway through his program. As with his talk on Sunday, his information was fascinating and MacLain himself was entertaining and engaging. He had charm, that was for sure. If what we thought of his parentage was true, I was pretty sure he'd gotten it from his mother, not his father.

"He's not just going to come out and admit it." The program ended and all around us, people got up to head to the front of the room, meet the speaker, and get their books signed. Still, Declan whispered in my ear when we stood.

"He might," I allowed. "If we play our cards right."

We waited until the last of the crowd was gone, then Declan and I closed in.

"No book?" He looked at our empty hands. "Just want to talk about Lady Liberty?"

"Just want the truth," I said. "And I think we can start in the most logical place. Last Sunday when you signed the book I brought in, I had you make it out to Raquel Arnaud, and you never had to ask me how to spell her name."

MacLain took a good, long time collecting his pen and tucking it in his shirt pocket. He stood and looked toward the door of the meeting room, but if he was waiting for a librarian to come to his rescue, he'd have to wait awhile. We'd left Sophie out front, and since she knew everyone in town and could get away with asking anyone for anything, she promised us we'd be left alone for as long as we wanted. As long as it took.

MacLain's smile was tight. "I'm sorry, I don't understand why we're discussing my spelling skills."

"Because it's an odd name, don't you think? I mean, even if I asked you to sign a book to Mary Jones, I bet you'd ask how to spell it. Any author would. Names are tricky and people like unusual spellings because it sets their names apart. I just think it's odd, that's all, that you know how to spell the unusual name of a woman one day and then a few days later, you were seen hanging around that woman's memorial service."

He huffed out a breath of annoyance. "I told you once before—"

"You did tell me. But I'm not much of a listener. Then again, I wasn't the only child of an übersuccessful engineer who devoted his life to making sure I succeeded."

MacLain was confused, and I couldn't blame him. He sidled around the table and would have taken off for the door if Declan didn't step in his way.

MacLain looked back and forth between us. "I'm afraid I'm a little slow. Or maybe you're just being obtuse. You want to tell me what this is about?"

I was only too happy to oblige, and when I did, I made sure I got up nice and close to him so that I didn't miss even one little nuance of emotion that crossed his expression.

"It's about your mother," I said.

His shoulders went rigid. "My mother is Rose Magdalen MacLain. She lives in Cassadaga, New York, and I can't imagine what you know about her or what you'd have to say about her."

I took one more step closer. "Not your adopted mother," I said. "Your biological mother, Raquel Arnaud."

Sure, I was taking a chance. If I was wrong, the worst that could happen is that I'd be embarrassed (or at least pretend to be) and MacLain would leave town thinking he'd just run into one nutty woman.

If I was right, I'd know the truth, once and for all, and in that one instant between when I spoke the words and when MacLain reacted to them, I knew I was right.

He didn't so much step back as he nearly fell, feeling his way, his hand along the edge of the table, back to his chair. He sat down with a plop.

"I don't know . . . I don't know what you're talking about," he stammered.

But it was too late for that.

"She started searching for you a couple of years ago," Declan told him, and played one of the cards we hoped would get MacLain talking. "I know because I'm her attorney. Obviously, she found you."

MacLain's shoulders went rigid. "This is crazy. And it's harassment. There's no reason for you to be bothering me with this. No reason for you to be asking these questions or making up any kind of crazy stories about me and my family."

"Actually, you're wrong." I perched on the edge of the table. "There's one very good reason. You were seen. At Pacifique. The night Raquel Arnaud was murdered."

He froze.

That is, right before his spine accordioned, his shoulders shook, and his hands trembled.

I would have a few moments before he composed himself, and I intended to take advantage of them. "How did Rocky find you?" I asked him.

"I . . . I don't know." MacLain's voice was tight, his eyes were wild with fear and despair, and in that one moment, he reminded me of his late father in that old newspaper picture. "She never said except that she mentioned she'd hired a private detective. All I know is . . ." He passed a hand over his eyes. "One day I got a letter from a woman claiming to be my biological mother."

"Did you know you were adopted?" I asked him.

He glanced up at me, still working through the shock and talking because of it. "I wasn't supposed to. But years ago . . . I was maybe nine or ten, I found some paperwork with my mother's things. My adoption papers. I shouldn't have been looking through her desk, but she wasn't angry when she discovered me. She was upset. So terribly upset! She swore me to secrecy. Father was in Europe on a business trip and even though it was summer, she made me help her start a fire in the fireplace and together, we burned the papers. She made me promise never to tell anyone. No one." His look was pleading. "You have to promise you'll never tell a soul."

MacLain was a smart guy, but whether he realized it or not, he was digging himself a bigger hole.

"So you don't want anyone to know you're adopted. All the more reason to silence the woman who said she was your mother," I told him.

I didn't think it was possible for anyone to be any paler, but MacLain actually lightened a shade or two. Against the pallor of his skin, his eyes looked huge and sunken. "You can't think . . . you don't think . . ."

"You were there at the farm the night she died. You showed up again the day of the memorial service." I rubbed the spot on my head that was still sore. "I'll bet you were there yesterday, too, probably looking for anything Rocky had that would prove she was your mother."

He shook his head. "The memorial service . . . I just felt . . ." He threw his hands in the air. "After everything that happened, I was just looking for some closure."

Everything that had happened.

Exactly what we were there to talk about.

Declan leaned forward, his hands flat against the table. "So what did happen?" he asked Andrew MacLain. "And why?"

"Not what you think." He twitched his shoulders and raised his chin. "Like I told you, a few years ago, I got this letter out of nowhere from this woman named Raquel Arnaud. She said she was my mother."

"And you weren't anxious for a reunion."

He traced an invisible pattern against the table with one finger. "I never said that."

"You said your adopted mother insisted on keeping the adoption a secret," I said. "Why?"

MacLain made to stand up, but one pointed look from Declan and he changed his mind. "It's awfully personal," he said.

"So is murder," Declan reminded him. "And telling us the story might save you the trouble of explaining it to the police."

This was not technically true, of course, but MacLain was still upset enough not to be able to think things through.

He ran a tongue over his lips. "Father . . . my adopted father. He doesn't know."

As reluctant as MacLain was about reuniting with his biological mother, this didn't surprise me. "He doesn't know Rocky found you."

MacLain looked up at me. "He doesn't know Rocky ever existed. He doesn't know I'm adopted."

Even me, who'd spent her life being reminded day in and day out that I was a nobody without a family, found this a little odd. "Why would your mother—"

With a look, MacLain stopped my question before I could put it into words. "My father is a successful and brilliant and driven man," he said, and I knew he wasn't talking about his biological father, Steve Pastori, the bomber. "But he is also . . ." He drew in a long breath and let it out slowly. "Father has a very strong sense of family. You might call it something of an obsession. I didn't know about that when I was a child, of course. I didn't know about any of it that day I watched my mother burn those adoption papers. But years later, I asked her about the incident, I asked why she was so eager to keep the secret, and she explained. She told me she had never been able to get pregnant. She told me she was desperate for a family and she wanted to adopt. But my father, he said he'd never share his life and his fortune with someone else's child."

I hadn't expected the comment to sting like it did, and I hugged my arms around myself.

"My father was in China working on a dam project when she told him she was pregnant," MacLain continued. "He was scheduled to be gone for a year, so she knew she could get away with the story. By the time he came back home . . ." He pointed toward himself. "There I was."

"And he still doesn't know the truth."

His eyes snapped to mine. "He never will. It would kill him."

"And leave you out of an inheritance?" Declan suggested.

From the way MacLain hemmed and hawed by way of answering the question, I figured Declan was right on the money.

"All the more reason for you to keep Rocky quiet," I reminded him.

"No!" He slapped the table with one hand. "The first time she contacted me, I ignored her. Who wouldn't? It was just so crazy, so out of the blue. I thought by not responding, she'd go away. The second time she wrote to me, I decided to be proactive. I wrote back. I told her she was wrong, but I got another letter after that one. And another and another and another. She told me she was sure her information was right. She told me she knew I was the child she'd given up for adoption."

"Did she say why she wanted to find you?" I asked him.

"I never asked. I never cared. I only wanted her to go away." He clutched his hands into fists so tight, his knuckles were white. "But she told me that she was getting older, and she was thinking about the past, and she wanted to make the connection. She said she didn't want anything, just to see me, to know what kind of man I'd become. She even . . ." As if just thinking about it scared the bejabbers out of him, MacLain swallowed hard. "She suggested a DNA test. Not to prove it to herself, she told me, but just so I could be sure."

"But you didn't want to be sure." It wasn't a question, but MacLain turned to Declan when he spoke, anyway.

"Like I said, I couldn't risk what I had. I couldn't betray my own mother's secret. Not for some woman who popped up out of nowhere and claimed I was the baby she'd given away years before. Then . . ." His shoulders heaved. "Well, when my publicist told me I was going to Hubbard, Ohio, let's face it, I had no idea where it was. I certainly didn't know it was anywhere near Cortland where Raquel's letters had come from. If I did, I would have refused the gig."

"She was so anxious to see you," I told him, remembering Rocky at the Statue of Liberty parade, the color high in her cheeks and her eyes gleaming with excitement. "No wonder she said the past had overwhelmed her that day," I said, more to Declan than to MacLain, since he didn't know that part of the story. "She must have been overcome at seeing you."

"She contacted me right after the parade," MacLain said. "She begged me to come see her. It was the first time I realized she lived in the area, and let me tell you, I was ready to pack up and leave town that night. Then I thought . . . well, I don't know what I thought. I thought maybe I could reason with her. I even thought maybe I could bribe her! I thought if I just went and had a talk with her, maybe she'd be satisfied. Maybe then she'd leave me alone."

"So you were at the farm that night," I said.

MacLain's head shot up. "That doesn't mean I killed her!"

"It sure looks like it does." Since he was smart, I didn't have to point this out, but as I'd come to learn, you can never be too obvious when it comes to murder. "You didn't want anyone to know you were adopted, Rocky wanted to establish a relationship with you. You were there. The night of the murder. You were there."

"But not to kill her! Just to talk to her!"

"And did you?" Declan asked. "Did you talk to her?"

MacLain hung his head. "No. I got to the farm just as it was getting dark. There was no one around, and the music, it was playing really loud. She didn't answer when I knocked so I went inside the house." He looked up at me, his eyes brimming with tears. "And that's when I found her. That's when I finally met my mother. After she was already dead."

Chapter 18

Did we believe Andrew MacLain's claim that he arrived at Pacifique after Rocky was already dead?

It was hard to say.

He certainly seemed sincere enough, but delving into people's souls, ferreting out their secrets and their motives . . . well, though I'd been called upon to do it a time or two, it wasn't exactly my job.

We called Tony Russo and told him what we'd found out, and he ordered Andrew MacLain not to leave town and came to Hubbard to interview him.

In my book, that was pretty much all we could do.

But not pretty much all I had to do.

It was Saturday, and I owed Fletcher Croft a menu. I made dozens of tartines for our hungry lunch crowd at the Terminal, then took care of the e-mail to Croft, and all the while, my thoughts swirled between the investigation and the tantalizing possibility of a job offer from the senator.

The thought of packing my bags and heading east sent a zip of excitement through me I hadn't felt in ages.

But even that couldn't drown out the other thoughts that whirlpooled inside my still-aching head. With any luck, by the time they settled down, my brain would spit out something that would tell us if Andrew MacLain was telling the truth.

Or if he was a cold-blooded, coldhearted murderer.

"Big crowd out there." Sophie limped into the Terminal office, and luckily I had enough time to close the computer screen so she didn't see my e-mail to Fletcher Croft. "George says we'll probably need a few more quiches for tonight."

"I'll get right on it." I popped out of the chair in front of the computer. "And you . . ." I looked Sophie over and shook my head. "You're pale, you're limping like a peg-legged pirate, and . . ." I gave her another quick once-over. "You're smiling. What are you smiling about?"

She'd had one hand tucked behind her back and when she whipped it out, I saw that she was holding a newspaper.

"Have you seen this?" Sophie asked, then answered, "Well, of course you haven't. You and Declan were out all day, over at the library talking to Andrew MacLain. You haven't seen the news. You haven't seen the paper."

"Seen what?" I plucked the newspaper out of her hand and stepped aside so she could sit down and prop up her leg, still encased in some sort of thingamajig designed to keep her knee safe, before I glanced over the front page. There it was for all the world to see, and in a typeface as big and as bold as any I'd ever seen.

News of Aurore Brisson's theft of Marie Daigneau's novel.

The story continued inside and included a picture of the weeping Aurore, who, when asked, claimed she didn't know what happened, that yes, she remembered finding the manuscript in Marie's home, but after that—or so she said—she blanked, and doesn't remember another thing until the finished book appeared on her doorstep with her picture on the back cover.

"Yeah, right," I grumbled. I kept reading and there were plenty of quotes in the article from Meghan Cohan, plenty of references to the upcoming made-for-cable TV series, and plenty of talk of lawsuits and compensation and prison time for the Parisian plagiarist.

"Three cheers for you," Sophie said when I'd finished reading. "Rocky would be so proud!"

"It will take a long time for the whole thing to get sorted out. In the meantime, when I talked to her, Meghan said she owed me."

"Oh." Sophie's smile melted. "Does that mean you'll go back and work for her?"

I'd thought the same thing myself. And it didn't take me long to decide what I'd do if Meghan asked.

Then again, I had Senator Katherine Stone waiting in the wings.

"No way," I told Sophie, and felt a twinge of guilt when she brightened up instantly. "I've had it with Hollywood. Shallow people, no loyalty. Meghan wouldn't have cared one bit about *Yesterday's Passion* being stolen, not if it didn't mean publicity for the TV series."

"I'm glad." Sophie made a face. "Not about the book being stolen, about you saying you'll never leave."

Only that wasn't what I'd said.

Rather than think about it, I zipped out of the office just as a party of twelve over at table fifteen was finishing up a birthday celebration. They crowded around the birthday girl at one end of the table and asked me to take a picture, and I grabbed the phone someone offered me and obliged before I darted into the kitchen.

"Making quiches!" I told George, and I did, gathering what I needed, making the crusts, and filling them with ingredients that included the last of Rocky's griselles, along with bacon and Swiss cheese, then just because I was feeling like mixing things up a little, I made one quiche with rosemary, apples, and cheddar cheese and reminded myself to pay attention and see if our customers would take the chance and order it.

The entire time I worked, though, my brain kept tapping out a message.

Pictures.

Of course I was thinking about pictures, I told myself; I'd just taken a picture of the birthday party out front, and while it looked like everyone was enjoying their meals and having a good time, that birthday party wasn't especially interesting.

And still, my brain kept floating around and coming back to the same word.

Pictures.

The message—if it was a message and not just the product of the slightly woozy head I swore I didn't have when the doctor discharged me from the hospital that morning— stuck around until long after the quiches were baked and a couple of them served (including a few slices of apple/ cheddar).

Pictures.

"Hey, George!" It wasn't like I expected him to answer, because George being George, he never did, but I called out to him at the same time I unlooped the white apron from around my neck and tossed it on the counter. "Tell Sophie I'll be gone for a couple of minutes."

He might have grunted by way of reply. I can't say for sure. Then again, I was out the door and on my way across the street to the Irish store before he could say much of anything.

IT IS NOT his shop.

At least that's what Declan always says. Bronntanas is a family business and he just manages it. He has an office at the back of the gift shop, where in addition to taking care of the ordering and the inventory, he handles the other family business, which, if what the local gossip says is true, is not always on the up-and-up.

You'd never know it from the gift shop itself. It's small and well lit, as clean as a whistle in the County Mayo air and as well stocked as any Irish store I'd ever seen.

Not that I'd seen all that many Irish stores.

Still, I knew wise merchandising when I saw it, and Declan made sure he had a little bit of everything from Waterford and Galway crystal and Belleek pottery to T-shirts and sweatshirts in various colors (okay, well, in emerald green, anyway) that said things on the fronts of them like *Gaelic Girl* and *Irish to the Bone* and *I Speak Fluent Blarney*.

Just inside the door, I smiled at Paddy the stuffed leprechaun and store mascot, who sat on the counter and who

Declan had loaned to us at the Terminal during the weeks we featured Irish food.

"Welcome to Bronntanas," he called out from the back office. I'd spent a lot of time trying to remember exactly how to say the word which means "gift" in Irish. *BRON-tuh-nuss*. I could never get it quite right, so like everyone else, I simply called the place the Irish store.

"No hurry," I replied. "It's just me."

He was out of the office in an instant. "Hey! How you feeling?"

I assured him I was fine.

"But not looking for the perfect Irish gift, I bet." He crossed his arms over his chest and leaned back against a glass display case that featured kilts and tams and tweed caps. "What's up?"

"I keep thinking about MacLain," I told him. "I keep wondering if he was telling us the truth."

"Tony will get to the bottom of it."

I was sure he would. Still, there was something about the whole thing that didn't sit right with me. Something about—

"Pictures," I said.

"Pictures?" Declan shoved off from the counter and came to stand nearer to me. Maybe if my head weren't in such a whirl, I would have been able to keep my usual distance—physically and emotionally. The way it was, something about his presence—firm and steady—made me inch forward just a tad.

He didn't miss the move and stepped even nearer. He wrapped his arms around me.

"You've had some busy twenty-four hours. Getting whacked, the hospital, questioning MacLain. If you're thinking crazy thoughts—"

"Except I don't think it's crazy." I backed out of his hug, but slowly, so he'd know I wanted to order my thoughts and be able to look into his face when I presented my theory. "I was thinking that lots of people must have taken pictures at last Saturday's Statue of Liberty parade."

He nodded the way people do when they're not exactly sure where the conversation is headed.

"And I'm thinking about what happened at the parade. How Rocky said that the past overwhelmed her and she had to leave."

"Because she finally got a look at her son after all these years."

"Maybe." It was hard to try to stand there and be logical when that gray gaze of his was focused on me. I turned toward the nearest counter and ran my hand through a pile of wonderfully soft woolen plaid scarves. "But remember, before the parade, she was so excited she could barely stand still. She couldn't wait to see MacLain."

"And it got to her. The memories. The past. How wonderful it was that he was a successful and intelligent man and how terrible it was that she'd missed out on all the years with him."

"Maybe," I admitted. "But maybe not. Maybe she was thinking of something else."

He didn't ask what. He didn't have to. With a tip of his head, Declan urged me to explain.

"Remember when we were talking in front of Taco Bell, and then I went to see how Rocky was going to react because Aurore Brisson was just driving by? And Rocky, she didn't react at all?"

He nodded. "I remember."

"Well, I remember that when I got back over to where

Sophie and Rocky were standing, Rocky wasn't even watching the parade. Her eyes were on the grandstand."

"And you think there was something there that made her think about the past?"

"I think if we had pictures, we might be able to say for sure."

I knew it wouldn't take him long to catch on. "Pictures people took during the parade."

"I was thinking we could have a contest. I can have them e-mail the pictures to the Terminal and we'll display them out near the cash register and we'll give some kind of prize—I don't know, a certificate for dinner, maybe—to the person whose picture gets the most votes as the best, or the cutest, or the most unusual."

"And you're hoping that someone might send a picture that shows what Rocky was really watching."

"I know it's a long shot," I admitted. "But it might be worth a try. I'm going to announce the contest on social media and we'll see what we see."

BY THE NEXT morning, what we ended up seeing were dozens of photos e-mailed to us by people who'd attended the parade.

A lot of them were pictures of the little kids in their Statue of Liberty costumes.

Others were of Aurore Brisson, and the e-mails that came with them said things like, "Here she is before the prison stripes," and "Felon alert!"

Still others showed the usual group of campaigning politicians, including Muriel Ross, who, when she arrived at the Terminal for breakfast on Sunday with her husband

and another couple, stopped to admire the picture board we'd put up near the cash register.

"I need to learn to smile with my mouth shut tighter," she confided to me while she pointed at a picture of herself with her mouth open. "Not exactly the best picture I've ever taken."

"You look like you're having a good time. I think that's all people care about."

"And I think you have a beautiful smile." Ben wrapped an arm around her waist and pulled her close. "And besides, a politician without a big mouth isn't worth having in office."

It soothed her and they went to their booth, and Ben waited until his wife was seated next to the window before he sat down at one of the tables that looked out over the railroad tracks just as the first train of the morning rumbled through.

"I never get tired of watching the trains," Ben told me when I took their menus. "I guess I'm just a little kid at heart."

A lot of people felt the same way, and while Ben and Muriel were busy staring out the window, I checked e-mail and found a few more photos waiting for us. I printed them and took them out to hang on the board.

"Nice!" Misti was working the morning shift, and she peered over my shoulder at the board. "Which one is going to be the winner?"

To tell the truth, I hadn't thought about that. I'd been too focused on scanning each picture, hoping against hope that one of them would show Rocky.

None of them did.

I told myself to stop obsessing and got to work. I made

a few quiches to put in the fridge, added to what we had left of the potée champenoise because it would be featured on the Monday lunch menu (I knew our regulars, Phil, Dale, Ruben, and Stan would love it even if it did have a funny French name), and tried my hand at a pot of French onion soup. While I was at it, I called some of the farmers who sold us produce and gathered the ingredients for a big pot of ratatouille.

Yes, I was overcompensating.

Yes, I knew it was because I was feeling guilty about heading to New York the next morning.

No, it didn't mean I would even consider canceling the interview with the senator.

Not for the world.

Three more times that day I checked e-mail, down-loaded photographs, printed them out.

Three more times, I tacked them onto the board out in the lobby and each time, I grumbled a curse.

No sign of Rocky on any one of them.

By the time the dinner crowd had thinned and it was time to close, I was pretty much convinced that my plan was a bust.

"At least we have some great pictures and everyone's enjoyed looking at them." We were standing in front of the picture board, and Sophie put a hand on my shoulder. "It will be hard to pick a winner."

Which meant that in the future, a photo contest like this might be a good way to get our name out and drum up business.

Even if it was a bad way to find the motive for a murder.

Once the last of our customers left, we took care of the usual cleanup and I sent Misti and George home. Sophie insisted that she should stick around and help tally the day's receipts, but I'd seen the way she was favoring her leg. She needed rest, and I needed to finish up the work without her constant interruptions. I had to get back to her place to pack, and I had to be up bright and early the next day for the drive to Cleveland and my flight to New York.

I sent her on her way and settled down in the office.

"Just one more look," I told myself to excuse what had become the day's obsession, and I checked the Terminal's e-mail account again.

There were only two photos. One showed the Hubbard police car with its light bar flashing.

The other was from Muriel Ross.

"I'd forgotten I took pictures last Saturday," her e-mail said. "But after I saw your wonderful display this morning, I thought it might be worth a look. Here's one I took from the grandstand, a different take on the parade, I think."

Attached was a photo shot down Main Street and into the heart of the parade.

It was a different perspective on the parade, all right, and if it wouldn't look too much like we were supporting a candidate and giving Muriel Ross some extra publicity, I'd be tempted to award her the prize we'd promised to give out.

The view from the grandstand included the lines of kids in their cute and hokey Statue of Liberty costumes streaming up the street. It showed the flashing lights of the cop cars, spectators waving from the curb, and even Aurore Brisson, staring in Rocky's direction like she was sure Rocky was going to come pounding across the pavement and go for her throat.

It also showed Rocky.

I'd already printed out the picture, and my hands trembled against the paper as I studied it.

Rocky's mouth was open in a perfect little circle of surprise and even in the picture, I could see that her face was ashen. Her eyes were as round as saucers, her gaze was focused on—

My heart thudded to a stop, then started up again at the sound of breaking glass from out in the restaurant.

"What the—" I leapt out of the chair and pulled open the office door and was greeted by an odd, undulating light out in the lobby near the display of pictures we'd already hung.

Fire!

Sure, I know that at a time like this, a person is supposed to spring into action. But here's the honest truth of it: when faced with something completely unexpected and totally frightening, it's hard to move.

Forget the springing, I had a hard enough time convincing myself that what I was seeing was real.

"Fire." I mumbled the word, but a plume of acrid black smoke and the sudden, blaring sound of the restaurant's smoke alarms snapped me out of my daze.

"Fire!" I screamed. "Fire! The Terminal is on fire!"

Chapter 19

The 911 dispatcher told me to get out of the restaurant and get out fast.

I knew she was right.

Getting out—fast—was the smart thing to do.

Getting out—fast—was the safe thing to do.

Tell that to the voice inside my head that reminded me that the Terminal was all Sophie had, and if she lost it, it would not only ruin her financially, it would break her heart.

For a few panicky seconds after I made the call, I stood there in the office, frozen by fear and indecision, listening for the sounds of sirens, and when they didn't come, I sucked a breath deep into my lungs and held it there, then darted out of the office.

Out in the lobby, I saw the flames ripple and swirl, like a living thing. They shot out a tentacle of black smoke that snaked into the dining room outside the office and came at me like an outstretched hand.

I was mesmerized, horrified at the same time I was fascinated, but when the air in my lungs ran out and I had no choice to suck in a breath, I caught a lungful of smoke. Coughing, I ran into the kitchen.

The air in there was clean and cool, at least for the moment, and I let go a shaky breath and ran for the fire extinguisher we kept near the back door.

We had fire training in culinary school.

It had been a long time since I was in culinary school.

I glanced at the heavy extinguisher in both my hands, trying to remember what to do and what not to do, but when the first wisp of that black, acrid smoke sneaked under the kitchen door, I threw caution to the wind. Armed with the red extinguisher and with a voice screaming at me from inside my head and warning me not to do it, I ran back out into the restaurant.

"WELL, THAT WAS dumb."

Detective Gus Oberlin was the last person I expected to see along with the firefighters who arrived just seconds after I started spraying down the flames inside the Terminal's front door. Something told me he wasn't planning on being on duty that Sunday evening. That would explain why he was dressed in raggedy khaki shorts and a purple polo shirt that tugged over his bulging belly and was stained across the front with what I'd bet any money was the night's dinner. Pepperoni pizza with mushrooms, if I wasn't mistaken. Gus had a toothpick in his teeth, and he slid it from one side of his mouth to the other and bent to look me in the eye where I sat in on the curb across the street from the Terminal, an oxygen mask over my mouth.

"Dumb," he said.

Yeah, like I hadn't figured that out already.

I pulled the mask off my face and was grateful when the cool night air rushed into my lungs. The way I remembered it, when two burly firefighters hauled me out of the Terminal, breathing was the last thing my lungs wanted to do. "If I hadn't started putting out that fire—"

"The fire guys would have done it." Gus has a doughy face, a flat, wide nose, and the personality of a pit bull with a bad case of indigestion. "The dispatcher told you to exit the building, didn't she? Why didn't you exit the building?"

"What are you going to do, ticket me?" My knees shook, but I wasn't about to let that stop me. I dragged myself to my feet and pretended like being trapped in a burning building was all in a day's work. "What are you doing here, anyway?" I asked Gus. "This is a matter for the fire department."

He glanced over his shoulder to where the guys on the fire truck were just rolling up their hoses. The street was two inches deep in pooling water, and in it, I saw the reflection of the Terminal.

Still standing.

I released a shaky breath.

There was bound to be damage to the lobby from the fire, and more damage beyond from the smoke and the water.

But the Terminal was still standing.

By now, word had gone out in Hubbard that there was a fire in Traintown and the entrance to our little enclave was packed with cars and gawking spectators. I saw one

cop allow Mike and John to get by the barricades that had
been erected. Naturally the first thing they did was look
down the street at the Book Nook and when they saw that
it was untouched, they hurried over.

John handed me a to-go cup of coffee and I smiled my
gratitude.

"Sophie's right behind us," Mike said, glancing that way.
"She's a little upset."

I looked toward the mouth of the street, but there were
so many people packed in there, I couldn't find her. "She
shouldn't have driven here," I said.

The lenses of John's wire-rimmed glasses caught the
light and winked at me. "I don't think she did. Declan Fury
is with her."

Declan. Of course. As a business owner in Traintown,
he would have been just as concerned as everyone else
when word of a fire went out.

Only when I saw him barrel past the barricade with
Sophie in tow, he never once glanced at the Irish store.

"Are you okay? You're okay?" He left Sophie in the care
of the firefighter nearest the Terminal and grabbed me by
the shoulders. "She's okay, isn't she?" he asked Gus. Since
he and Gus had never exchanged a pleasant word in all
their long association, I think this was something of a mile-
stone. Declan pulled me into a quick hug and I guess the
fact that I was breathing told him something good because
when he held me at arm's length, he smiled. "You're okay."

"I'm okay," I assured him. "It just happened so fast . . ."
I shivered, and when it slipped off my shoulders, it was the
first I realized someone had thrown a blanket around me.

Declan picked up the blanket and patted it back into
place.

"She might be okay." Gus rolled the toothpick around in his mouth. "But she's dumber than a box of rocks." He studied me and shook his head. "The way I remember it, I always thought you were smart."

He was referring to the murder of the Lance of Justice, a local TV investigative reporter, and how I'd helped him solve the case.

"I am smart," I said, and I would have said more if Sophie didn't limp over.

"Laurel!" She threw her arms around me and gave me a bear hug and again, it was impossible for me to breathe. "I was so worried! We didn't know what we'd find when we got here. And I was so worried!"

Once she let me go, I was able to turn her around so she could see the Terminal. "Everything's okay," I reminded her. "The restaurant is okay."

"The hell with the restaurant!" Sophie burst into tears. "I was worried about you!"

I guess I started to cry, too, because when I swiped my hands across my cheeks, my fingers were gooey with a combination of soot and tears. Declan handed me a handkerchief with a little green shamrock embroidered on it. I gave it to Sophie.

And while I was at it, I thought about what Gus Oberlin had said.

He thought I was smart.

He was right.

The thought hit and I flinched.

"It wasn't an accident," I said.

Gus grinned. "About time you caught on."

Declan frowned. "What are you talking about?"

I kept my gaze on Gus's. "I heard glass break. Right

before I realized there was a fire. Someone threw something into the restaurant."

"Molotov cocktail." Gus spit the word out around his toothpick. "Don't see that kind of thing around here. Poor man's grenade. Isn't that what they called them back in Northern Ireland?" he asked no one in particular even though it was perfectly clear who he was addressing.

Declan clenched his teeth. "My family's never been to Northern Ireland. And even if we had, we wouldn't have been there making Molotov cocktails. And who—" He turned away from Gus, but I could see that it cost him. Declan would have much rather gone toe-to-toe with the cop. "Who would do such a thing?" he asked me. "Who has a beef against the Terminal?"

"Not the Terminal." I knew I was right, knew it in my heart. "The pictures."

Sophie had dried her tears and she clutched Declan's handkerchief in trembling fingers. "Who would want to destroy pictures of the Statue of Liberty parade?"

The same person Rocky was staring at during the parade.

It was such a crazy idea, I didn't say a word. Not then, anyway. I would let it marinate and make a decision about telling someone—or keeping the crazy theory to myself—when I got back from New York.

JUST FOR THE record, I washed my hair three times that night when I got back to Sophie's and again in the morning before I boarded a very early flight to New York, and I swore I could still smell the faintest whiff of smoke. With any luck, no one at the senator's penthouse would notice and mistake the aroma around me for burnt food.

The good news was that I was able to leave the senator's massive and perfectly stocked kitchen for a bit right around ten and run out for the fresh herbs I'd never had a chance to get at Rocky's, what with being hit on the head by the intruder and all. Thank goodness there was a place in Union Square that had all the fresh herbs I needed!

More good news . . . the luncheon went off without a hitch, and according to Senator Katherine Stone, who I spoke with personally for fifteen minutes when she was done eating, it was the best crab soup she'd ever tasted, the steak was cooked to perfection, and the sweet potato meringue pie . . . well, maybe it was wishful thinking, but when she said she hoped to include it at her Thanksgiving table and didn't ask for the recipe, I took it as a sign that I was a shoo-in.

Fingers crossed.

Back in Hubbard before sundown, I was exhausted and as happy as any chef looking for a new job had ever been.

Which doesn't mean I wasn't worried about Sophie and the Terminal.

"So," I asked the minute I stepped inside the door of her tiny bungalow not far from the Terminal. "What did the insurance company say? And the cleaning crew you had in. How did they do today? When can we open again?"

She was in the kitchen with its green Formica countertop and, over the sink, a window that looked out onto a tiny backyard. Across from the sink, there was a table big enough to seat two, and that's where Sophie was seated, drinking a cup of tea and eating a homemade oatmeal cookie. She handed me the cookie platter. I try to avoid sweets, but I was tired and now that I thought about it, hungry, too. I grabbed a cookie and would have plunked right down across from Sophie if her black-and-white cat, Muffin, weren't already there.

"Scram," I told the cat, but in the nicest way, since Sophie adored the creature. The cat and I didn't get along, but Sophie had yet to catch on.

With a sneer, Muffin exited, and I took his place and crunched into my cookie.

"We'll be open by the weekend." Sophie grinned. "It could have been worse. It would have been worse if you didn't spring right into action."

"Instinct."

"Bravery."

"Oh no." I waved what was left of my cookie at her. "Let's not get carried away. I did what anyone would have done."

"Anyone who loves the Terminal."

This, I couldn't even begin to discuss. Not still floating from the euphoria of my interview with the senator.

I took another cookie, poured myself a cup of tea when the water boiled, and was about to change the subject when Sophie beat me to it.

"What did the doctor say?"

It took me a moment to remember the lie I'd built to explain why I'd be gone all day.

"Right as rain!" I said, and gave my skull a tap. "Everything looks good."

"I'm so glad!" The way she said it—with so much enthusiasm and so much sincerity—only made me feel more guilty. Rather than think about it, I finished my cookie. "Let's look through Rocky's newspaper clippings again," I suggested.

Sophie perked right up, and I don't think it had anything

to do with the additional cookie she snagged. "You have an idea," she said.

"I have questions," I admitted. "Like, why would someone want to destroy our photo display?"

She crinkled her nose. "I've been wondering the same thing. And you think . . ."

I told her I wasn't sure and went to get the pile of things we'd rescued from the safe deposit box.

AN HOUR LATER, we'd been through all the materials another two times and we decided we were hungry, and not just for cookies, but for real food. On days the Terminal is open late, Sophie and I usually just grab something there. On weeknights when the restaurant closes early, we bring home to-go containers of whatever the day's special is.

That night, we didn't have the luxury.

I rummaged through the fridge and found enough for a giant salad. She dug through the freezer and came up with a container of fried chicken. I was too hungry to ask how long it had been in there, and too tired to care.

We added baked potatoes that we cooked in the microwave, and within thirty minutes, we had dinner in front of us.

Dinner, and all those newspaper articles.

"So . . ." As we'd looked through Rocky's research materials earlier, I'd divided it into piles, and I pulled one of them closer. "What do you think?"

Rocky poured blue cheese dressing on her salad and offered me the bottle. "I think I don't understand," she admitted. "What do these things have to do with the photo board? And why did someone want to burn the photo board in the first place?"

"I can't say for sure," I admitted, "but I think someone thought there was something in one of those pictures that would implicate him in Rocky's death."

Sophie had just taken a bite of salad, so sucking in a breath of wonder was not the best thing to do. Once she was done swallowing, coughing, and pounding her chest, she looked at me, her eyes wide. "You think the murderer started the fire?"

"I think it's a very real possibility."

"And you think these old newspaper articles are somehow related?"

This I couldn't say, so instead I munched a piece of chicken (maybe I was just hungry or maybe it truly was the best chicken I'd ever tasted) and sifted through the articles. "These are all about Steve Pastori," I said. "A couple of them talk about how he died."

Sophie reached across the table and grabbed the article at the top of the pile. It was written the day after the last bombing, the day after Steve's body was found in the rubble of the burned-out ROTC building.

"What a shame," she said. "What a waste of a wonderful mind and a precious life."

"The article talks about how he used Molotov cocktails to start the other fires," I said. "I guess that's what got me thinking about him, the Molotov cocktails."

Sophie nodded. "I remember hearing about it at the time."

"But don't you think it's odd," I said, "that he'd start those other two fires with Molotov cocktails, but that's not how he started the fire that killed him?"

She wasn't sure what I was getting at and honestly, I couldn't blame her. I wasn't exactly sure, either.

"His body was found in the building," I said, putting down my fork long enough to tap one finger against the picture of the burned building. "He was inside when the fire started, and he got trapped there. The other fires he started from outside, by throwing the Molotov cocktail through the windows and into the buildings."

"Just like someone did at the Terminal." Sophie put down her fork, too, and wrapped herself in a hug. "What do you suppose it means?" she asked.

"I'm not sure," I admitted. "But I have an idea, and I wonder if Tony Russo would go along with it."

Chapter 20

The grand reopening of Sophie's Terminal at the Tracks was set for the following Friday. We decided early on that in honor of Rocky and all those pictures that were destroyed in the fire (they'd been e-mailed to me, of course, and the restaurant computer was just fine so the firebomber made a mistake there!), we'd continue with our French theme.

Our French flag had been in the lobby at the time of the fire, and we had it sent out and cleaned and we hoisted it on our little flagpole up front to show the world that Sophie's restaurant might be a little waterlogged, but no way was it out of business.

I baked quiches and we made tartines and I cooked up a whole bunch of crème brûlée because in my book, there isn't anything more festive or more delicious.

And we invited all of Hubbard to join us in celebrating.

Our doors opened at four, and that's when our guests started to arrive.

Phil, Dale, Stan, and Ruben, our lunch regulars, were there and they brought their wives and an assortment of children and grandchildren.

Gus Oberlin showed and grumbled something about how he had better things to do but since Sophie had phoned him and personally invited him, he couldn't exactly say no. We seated him with Tony Russo (with our apologies to Tony first), thinking that maybe they'd have something in common and something to talk about.

Andrew MacLain showed up, too, which was something of a surprise since it was pretty much my fault that he was still stuck in Hubbard. I guess the fact that he was promised a free dinner somehow made up for the inconvenience.

Just as we expected, Muriel Ross and Ben Newcomb showed, too. Muriel, of course, would never miss an opportunity like this, not when she knew the press would be there to cover the reopening. As usual, Ben was at her side and when he wasn't, he was talking up her best qualities to anyone and everyone who would listen.

Declan's cousins, who played in an Irish band, had learned some French songs for the occasion and they played outside the office, and from the number of dancers out on the floor and the diners with smiles on their faces, I guess they did a pretty good job.

"Congratulations." I was headed out to the lobby to cash out a customer when Declan grabbed my hand. "It's going well."

"It is," I told him, and tipped my head to tell him where I was going and invite him along.

He joined me behind the front counter.

"You still haven't told me why you wanted Tony to be here," he said.

I handed our customer his change. "He's a nice guy."

"He is," Declan conceded. "And just so you know, when he got here this evening, he talked to me. About you."

I turned to face him. "What about me?"

"Oh, just the usual," he said. "He wondered how you were recovering from all the excitement on Sunday night. And he wondered if everything here was shipshape and you were ready for the crowds. Oh, and he asked me if I'd mind if he asked you out."

"On a date?" The words came out like a squeak, but then, they kind of stuck behind the ball of astonishment that blocked my breathing.

Declan's expression was stony. "Yes, on a date. He wanted to know what I thought. He wanted to know if he asked you, would you go?"

Would I?

For a moment, the question felt like it took up all the space in the room. Like it sucked out all the air.

I shook myself to reality. "What did you . . . what did you tell him?" I asked Declan.

"What should I have told him?"

"I asked first."

He conceded with a nod. "I told him that I'm not your keeper, that I can't make decisions for you, that I don't know what you think. I told him I'd ask you. So I'm asking you."

I was glad when a customer walked up and I had to cash her out. It gave me a few moments to think.

When she was gone, I slid a look toward the table where we'd seated Tony and Gus Oberlin.

"Tony's a nice guy," I said.

I don't think it was a product of my imagination; Declan's shoulders actually did droop a bit.

"And he's cute, too," I said, because let's face it, guys don't usually notice that in other guys and I thought it was important to point it out. "He's been great about us helping out with the investigation. I mean, after he got over how he thought Rocky killed herself. He hasn't treated me like I'm dumb or like I'm getting in the way."

Those wide shoulders drooped a little more.

"But . . ."

"But?" Declan's eyes brightened.

Saved by the bell, literally. My cell phone rang.

I checked the caller ID, excused myself, and hurried outside.

"Hi, Fletcher." I held my breath.

"The senator wants to know how soon you can start."

It was unprofessional to let out a whoop of jubilation so I controlled it. But just barely.

"Two weeks?" I suggested.

"That will be . . ." I heard him hit a couple of computer keys. "Actually, she'll be on vacation in three weeks, so four weeks from now would be perfect."

"For me, too," I said without actually looking at a calendar.

"She wants the pie for Thanksgiving," Croft reminded me.

"She'll get it," I told him, but actually, I think he'd already hung up.

For a couple of minutes, I stood on the sidewalk and simply enjoyed the sensations that cascaded through me. Victory! I shuffled my feet against the pavement in a little happy dance.

"Good news?" Declan asked when I pranced back into the restaurant.

I wiped what there might have been of a smile off my face. "Nothing to worry about at the moment."

"Good." He'd cashed out a customer while I was outside and he handed the man his change and slipped out from behind the counter. "Then we can get back to talking about what's really important."

What was really important was if my car would make it to New York. If I was going to New York. I forgot to ask Fletcher Croft if the senator would need me in Newport or D.C., or if she'd be in New York City in four weeks' time, and made a mental note to send him an e-mail as soon as I could.

Then there was my wardrobe.

I glanced down at the black pants I wore along with one of the yellow golf shirts usually reserved for the waitresses. In honor of the grand reopening, I was wearing one that night, too, and I looked at the picture of the Terminal embroidered over my heart.

And my stomach did a funny little turn.

Something that felt very much like guilt shot through me and turned my blood to ice water and I lifted my head and looked at Declan.

"What?" I asked him.

"What?" he replied.

"Why are you staring at me?"

"I wasn't staring. We were having a conversation, remember? About Tony Russo."

"Tony." A new thought flooded my head, temporarily drowning the thousand little details I'd have four weeks to think about. I raced out from behind the cash register and into the restaurant just as Muriel Ross and her husband got their plates of quiche and they picked up their silverware, ready to dig in.

"Oh, I'm so sorry!" I made a face. "There's something floating in your water."

"Is there?" Ben smiled up at me. "I hadn't noticed. It's no big deal. You can have the waitress bring me another glass anytime she has a chance."

I whisked the glass off the table. "It's a very big deal. Believe me. A very big deal, indeed."

TONY RUSSO CALLED early the next day, and not to ask me out.

He told me he was on his way over to Muriel Ross and Ben Newcomb's house, and he didn't ask me to go along, but he didn't say I should stay away, either. I pulled up to the front of the spacious colonial just as Tony got out of his car and Gus Oberlin pulled his car behind mine.

"Really?" Since Gus was officially on duty, he was better dressed than he had been the night of the fire. Which did not mean he looked especially good. Khakis, a white shirt that could have used a serious ironing, a tie decorated with . . . I bent a little nearer for a better look . . . coffee stains and a sprinkling of glazed donut crumbs.

Gus glanced Tony's way. "I can't believe you invited her along."

"I didn't."

Tony didn't need to remind me, so I gave him a casual shrug, like it didn't matter.

But maybe it did.

Because no sooner had we set foot on the wide porch where overflowing pots of yellow mums shared space with fat pumpkins than the front door flew open and Muriel

Ross raced outside. It was early and she was wearing a pink chenille bathrobe that flapped open to reveal pale skinny legs, bony knees, and the hem of a blue nightgown that brushed her calves. Her hair stood up in crazy clumps and without her makeup, she looked older, frail, and as pale as a ghost. Well, except for her eyes. Those were swollen and red and tears streamed down her cheeks.

"Help him! Help him!" Muriel threw herself at Gus Oberlin, her words nearly lost beneath the ragged breaths she took. "Please, please, help him!"

Gus handed her off to me and because I didn't know what else to do, I hung on to Muriel when Gus and Tony raced inside.

Her shoulders heaved. "He didn't mean it," she moaned. "I'm sure . . . I'm sure he didn't mean it, but you see, he didn't know . . . I don't think he knew what else to do."

I didn't have to ask who she was talking about, and I didn't need to ask how serious it was; I heard Gus inside on his phone, calling for an ambulance.

I tightened my hold on Muriel. "What happened?" I asked her.

She hiccuped and choked and shook so badly that I piloted her over to a wicker couch and gently set her down in it. There was a matching white wicker rocker nearby and I pulled it over, sat down, and took her hand.

"Muriel."

Like she'd forgotten I was there, she flinched.

"Muriel, tell me what happened."

She closed her eyes and she didn't open them again until we heard the scream of a siren in the distance.

"Ben . . . !" She made to get up but I kept hold of her hand and kept her in place.

"They're going to help him," I said. "You know they're going to help him. Now, tell me what happened."

As I've found out is so often true when stress and panic and fear threaten to overwhelm a person, she glommed on to the simple question and grasped at the hold on reality it allowed her.

"The phone rang." Her voice was flat. Her eyes were blank. They didn't see me, but saw only those minutes before I'd arrived with Gus and Tony. "Ben's phone rang and he spoke to someone for . . . for just a minute, and then he got out of bed."

She scraped a hand across her cheeks. "I fluffed my pillow and turned over. I didn't think anything of it. Maybe if I did . . . maybe if I would have . . ."

The paramedics arrived and scrambled into the house, and Muriel watched them, each of her breaths shallow and fast.

"When I realized . . . when I saw that he wasn't coming back to bed, I got up and Ben . . ." Her voice snapped along with her composure. "He was packing his things. He was leaving!"

"But he didn't leave." This seemed all too obvious, but I knew if I didn't keep her focused, I was going to lose her. It didn't help when Gus stepped out onto the porch.

He was about to ask something, something painful. I could just about see the words form on his lips, and I stopped him, one hand in the air, and I kept talking.

"Did Ben say where he was going?" I asked Muriel.

She hauled in a shaky breath. "He said he didn't know. He said it didn't matter. He said you . . ." She registered Gus's presence; she looked up at him, then away again, as if just meeting his eyes would cause more anguish than she could handle.

"All he said," Muriel whispered, "was that the police were on their way, that they knew."

By this time, Gus had a small notebook in his beefy hands and he sat down next to Muriel and wrote down everything she said.

I looked to Gus for the go-ahead and he gave it with a nod.

"What did they know?" I asked Muriel.

Her slender shoulders rose and fell. "I asked him what . . . what he was talking about . . . and at first, he wouldn't tell me. He was angry. I'd never seen . . ." She squeezed her eyes shut. "He was never like this. Not ever. Not since we met."

"In Cozumel." I thought mention of happier times might soothe her, and for a few seconds, I'd like to think it did. Her eyes cleared. The tears stopped falling.

"I was on vacation. And so was he."

This time, there was no stopping Gus. "He wasn't vacationing there," he grumbled. "He was working at the Tropicana Hotel next door to the hotel where you stayed, Ms. Ross. He worked there as a bartender."

She shook her head so hard, those clumps of hair shifted and settled in a new position that made it look as if she'd faced a windstorm. "No. I would have known. Surely. He was there as a guest, just like I was. He was a successful man, not wealthy by any means, but well-to-do, surely and—" For the first time, she dared to look Gus in the eye. "Are you telling me my husband lied to me about that, too?"

Neither of us failed to catch the significance of that one final little word.

"It's a possibility."

I was surprised Gus could be that tactful.

Before he said something else and blew it, I took over.

"How much did Ben tell you about his past?" I asked Muriel. "Do you know where he's from?"

"Well, New York, of course." Her shoulders stiffened. "He's from New York."

"And he never said anything about being in Ohio before?" I asked her.

Her mouth puckered. "Why are you asking me these things? We have . . ." She glanced at the house and the two paramedics who rolled a gurney inside and she pressed a hand to her lips. "We have other things to worry about. We have Ben . . . poor Ben!" It wasn't so much a statement as a mournful keening, and my throat clutched.

"Tell us what happened to Ben this morning," I said.

From inside the house, we heard the sound of someone unzipping a body bag.

"I told him he couldn't leave," she said, her voice suddenly as strong and assured as I'd heard it when she talked to the people she hoped would be her constituents. "I told him we had to talk, that he had to explain what was going on. I asked who called and when he said it was . . ." She didn't speak Gus's name, just glanced his way. "I asked Ben what he was afraid of. And that's when he told me . . ."

By this time, I wasn't holding on to Muriel as much as she was hanging on to me for dear life. Her fingers clutched my hand until I was tempted to cry out from the pain. At least until I realized the pain I felt was nothing compared to hers.

"He had been in Ohio before." She hung her head. "He told me that, years ago, he'd gone to school at Ohio State. That's when he also told me his real name. He wasn't Ben Newcomb. He was Steve Pastori."

Gus and I exchanged looks, and really, I wanted to give him the classic *I told you so*, but I knew there would be time for that later. On Friday when I'd talked to both Tony and Gus about my suspicions, Gus had pooh-poohed the entire idea.

Which is why I'd had to resort to collecting Ben's water glass to get his fingerprints.

"You're right." Muriel fell back and pounded one fist against the couch cushions. "You're right. You're right. You're right. He had lied to me. Ben admitted it. He said he'd been hiding out all these years, moving from job to job and place to place, changing his name and his hair color. Hiding. Always hiding. He told me that back when he was in college, he did a stupid thing and he was wanted by the police, and when he got that call this morning . . . he was afraid they'd discovered something. He was worried that they knew too much. He said that's why he had to leave and he didn't want to involve me so he said . . ." Even now, she couldn't believe it. Her breath caught. "He said he couldn't tell me where he was going. I told him he wasn't going anywhere!" she added in a rush of words. "I told him that surely we could work together to get everything cleared up, that nothing could possibly be as bad as he portrayed it to be. But he said . . ." The tears started flowing again and Muriel could barely get the words out. "He said that years ago, he'd bombed buildings. He'd killed people. And that he had to keep it a secret, and that Raquel Arnaud . . ."

"She knew, didn't she?" I asked her.

Muriel nodded. "He said that as soon as he read about her in the local newspaper, he knew there might be trouble. They knew each other back in college, you see, and he was afraid that once she started doing her research for that seminar she was supposed to speak at . . . well, he said he was afraid she'd remember a little too much."

That explained it, then. The note, *Leave the past in the past*. The midnight visits to her house to try to locate her research materials.

I knew that then, Rocky couldn't have had any idea she was dealing with a man who was supposed to be long dead. Not until the day of the parade.

"She called him," Muriel continued. "That Saturday. After the parade. I knew something was wrong after he hung up the phone, but he said it was nothing, and there was no reason for me not to believe him. But this morning, he told me the truth. That the Arnaud woman saw him at the parade and she didn't recognize him." She shook her head. "She didn't recognize his face because it's been a long, long time and we all change, don't we, and Ben, he said he'd had cosmetic surgery to change his looks. You know, when he was on the run from the authorities."

"But Rocky knew him anyway. How?" I wondered.

"She said . . . he told me she said she never would have if she wasn't knee-deep in all that research. She was thinking about the past, and suddenly, there it was, right in front of her. She told Ben it was the way he held his head, the way he laughed. She said she'd never forget those things about him and she didn't think it could possibly be true because Steve was supposed to be dead. But she called Ben anyway. She said she had to."

"Did she threaten him?" Gus asked. "Blackmail, maybe?"

Muriel gave her head another shake. "I didn't know the woman. But I've heard she was kind and thoughtful. I don't know. I don't know. I only know that she told Ben that she had to see him, not to turn him into the authorities, but because he had the right to know that he had a child. They had a child. Together." She looked up at me, her eyes blank.

"Forty-some years ago," Muriel said, "Raquel had Ben's baby. And now that baby is a man and she wanted Ben to know. She said he had a right to know. She wanted him to have that connection, and he . . ." Her shoulders fell and she slumped in the chair. "He went to her house and . . . and you know, we use cyanide, at the furniture factory. He took some and . . . and he put it in her wineglass. He killed her to keep her quiet."

"He told you that?" Gus asked.

Muriel nodded.

"Did he tell you how he managed to fool everyone all these years? For all anyone knew, Steve Pastori died in a bomb blast."

A single tear slipped down her cheek. "He knew they were looking for him. He knew they were close. He paid . . ." She gagged and fought to catch her breath. "I can barely say the words. It's too horrible to consider. He said he paid a homeless man to put on his jacket, some jacket he always wore. Ben said he sent the man into the building. The poor fellow never knew what hit him when Ben tossed the firebomb in there right where the man was standing. There wasn't much left of that poor homeless man, and everyone thought Steve Pastori was dead. And he was dead. All these years. Until Raquel Arnaud brought him back to life again, and he knew he was in danger. That's when he . . . he went into the office. And he keeps a gun in the desk drawer for protection. And he closed the door and—"

The paramedics picked that moment to wheel out the gurney with the body bag on it, and even if she wanted to, Muriel couldn't have said another word. She hugged her arms around herself, rocked back and forth, and sobbed.

Chapter 21

Something tells me it is not normal police procedure to show death scene photos to a civilian. Which is why when I walked into Gus Oberlin's office at the Hubbard police station, I got only the briefest of glimpses of pictures of Ben Newcomb lying on the floor, his arms splayed out and a gun in his hand, before Gus slid the photos under a file folder on his desk.

Not to be deterred, I sat down in the guest chair in front of the gray metal desk. "What's up?" I asked him.

Gus shuffled some papers on his desk, and it didn't fool me for a minute. He was the last person on earth I'd ever accuse of being organized; I knew he was just stalling for time. "Need to get the last of the details down pat," he grumbled. "Thought maybe you could help."

"I'll try," I told him.

Gus tugged at his earlobe. "I just don't get it," he said, and made a face. "How did you figure that Ben Newcomb—"

"Was Steve Pastori?" It was later that same day, Saturday, and my brain had been going around and around about that exact question ever since I saw them cart the body out of Muriel Ross's home. "It does seem weird, doesn't it? Everyone thought Steve was dead."

"Except you."

"No," I told him. "When I heard the story from Sophie . . . when I read those old newspaper articles, I thought Steve was dead, too. Who wouldn't? Then I saw those pictures from the parade."

"Yeah, the pictures." I'd e-mailed them to Gus and he'd printed them out, and these, he wasn't reluctant to share. He pulled out the one of Rocky with her eyes bulging and her mouth hanging open, staring at the grandstand. "Muriel Ross sent this one," he said.

"Exactly." I remembered every detail of the picture, but I scooted forward in my seat, anyway, so I could see the photo again. "That's one of the things that caused Ben . . . er . . . Steve to panic and make his first mistake. Muriel e-mailed the picture, and I'll bet anything that she'll tell us that it wasn't until after she sent it that she told Ben what she'd done."

"She's already told me that," Gus said.

"Well, it makes sense. Ben . . . er . . . Steve . . . oh heck, let's just call him Ben! Muriel thought she'd caught nothing more than a unique perspective on the parade, and she was right. It's a great picture. But Ben saw something else, something he couldn't take the chance of anyone else seeing. He saw the moment Rocky recognized him."

"Which is why he started the fire at the Terminal." Gus sucked on the toothpick propped between his teeth. "Stupid, really. You got these pictures via e-mail. You could have picked them up on any computer, anywhere. He couldn't destroy them."

"I have a feeling he wasn't thinking that clearly. Not when he realized that after more than forty years of dodging the law, his lies were about to come crashing down on him. He took a chance and started the fire and when that didn't work . . ."

"When that didn't work, you dug a little deeper."

If I didn't know any better, I'd think there was actually a note of admiration in Gus's voice. Good thing I knew better.

"I just couldn't see who else would want to keep Rocky quiet about the peace movement," I said. "What difference would it make to anyone after all these years?"

"Except this MacLain fellow—he wanted to keep her quiet."

"He did." I thought of Andrew MacLain and his desperate attempt to keep his adopted mother's secret. "It's sad, but at least before she died, MacLain had a chance to see how much Rocky loved him. At least before she died, she had a chance to see him and see what kind of man he was."

The kind of man who wanted his biological mother to disappear from his life.

The thought made me uncomfortable, and I squirmed in my seat. "Anyway," I said, because thinking about Ben Newcomb was better than listening to the old voices inside my head that wondered about my own family, my own mother. "I sort of did a process of elimination. Who could Rocky have been looking at up there on the grandstand? Why would she care? The fingerprints, that sealed the deal."

"It was a good idea." Like the words tasted bad in his mouth, Gus grunted. "Scooping up that glass that Newcomb used and getting his fingerprints. That's what really proved to us who he was. And he never suspected a thing! So that's that. We solved a nearly fifty-year-old mystery, we solved Ms. Arnaud's murder. As for the suicide . . ."

I'd been dealing with the terrible memories all day. Sitting there with Muriel, feeling the waves of her anguish . . .

It was impossible to get rid of the emotions, but I tried anyway, twitching my shoulders. "Can you imagine what the revelation of who Ben really was would have done to Muriel's political aspirations?"

"Would have done?" Gus tipped his head. "I'm thinking this whole suicide thing isn't going to do her any good."

"But it will," I pointed out. "If Ben had run, well, the news that he was a wanted murderer and that she'd married him might have ruined Muriel. But the fact that he committed suicide, that he was repentant, and that he took his life because of it . . ."

"But we don't know if he was sorry."

I think it was the first time all that day that I smiled. "No, we don't, do we? But I bet anything that's the way Muriel's going to play it up. The wronged wife. The grieving widow. The fact that Ben killed himself as a final act of repentance might actually help her campaign, not hurt it."

The words were barely out of my mouth when I sat up like a shot.

"What's wrong with you?" Gus asked. "What are you thinking?"

What was I thinking?

I wasn't sure, but that didn't stop me from saying, "Let me have a look at those pictures of Ben Newcomb."

* * *

THERE HADN'T BEEN a bigger story in Hubbard in as long
as anyone could remember, and Ben Newcomb's death was
the talk of the Terminal that evening. It was the last night
we planned to celebrate French cuisine and we did it up big,
including crêpes (both sweet for dessert and savory as a
dinner entrée) along with the wonderful French sausage and
white bean casserole called cassoulet. We were slammed
and the dining room buzzed with conversation.

All of it about what was no longer the mystery of the
long-missing Steve Pastori.

Our regulars showed up (two nights in a row!). So did
Carrie from the art gallery across the street, John and Mike
from the bookstore, and even Myra, Bill, and Barb from
Caf-Fiends, though they had to come in shifts because they
couldn't leave their own shop unattended.

I wasn't surprised to see the entire Fury family walk in,
and there were so many of them, they took up every table
in the small dining area right outside the kitchen and the
office. Declan wasn't with them, and since I didn't want to
start up any rumors or spark any speculation, I didn't ask
about him. I did, however, find myself looking across the
street at the Irish store more than a time or two, noticing
that the lights were still on there, thinking that he was
working late, wondering if once he closed up, he'd come
to the Terminal for dinner.

About two minutes after I saw the lights flick off at
Bronntanas (okay, so it was more like two seconds, I admit
it), I realized that my heartbeat had quickened at the same
time my stomach fluttered.

It was the same time I realized something else.

If Declan didn't stop by, I'd miss him.

The thought not only caught me off guard, it smacked me in the solar plexus and left me fighting to catch my breath.

I'd miss Declan that evening.

Just like I'd miss him once I was on Senator Stone's staff and cooking up a storm between Newport, New York, and D.C., using the finest ingredients money could buy, planning parties and fund-raisers and intimate dinners for power brokers with china and silver and flower arrangements in mind.

I stood frozen by the enormity of the thought, and I guess being still, ignoring my surroundings, and listening to the thoughts inside my head were what made another revelation possible—

Once I was gone, I'd miss the Terminal.

I'd miss Sophie, who had no idea why I was standing there like a statue and whizzed by and gave me a smile anyway.

I'd miss the crazy Fury clan and our regulars and even . . .

When a train rumbled by, I automatically clutched the cash register counter.

I'd miss it all, and not just because being there in Hubbard had exposed me to murder and helped me learn that there was a logical side to me that helped solve crimes.

There was more to the town than just that, something that felt so strange and so foreign, I couldn't even begin to describe it except in one simple word.

"Family."

"What's that you said?" Sophie was handing out small

samples of our crêpes to the people waiting for tables, and she grinned at me over her shoulder. "You talking to yourself?"

"I'm . . ." I shook my head, trying to clear it. It didn't work. I knew only one thing would.

I told Sophie I'd be right back, and because there was no place in the restaurant quiet enough, I darted outside and made the call.

I think it's fair to say I caught Fletcher Croft flat-footed.

"What do you mean, you're not taking the job?" he stammered in answer to my announcement.

"I appreciate the offer, I really do. It's just . . ." I glanced up at the French flag that flapped in the evening breeze. "I can't," I told him. "Tell the senator thank you, but I just can't."

I ended the call before I could come to my senses and change my mind, and by that time, a dark sedan had pulled up in front of the Terminal. Gus Oberlin got out.

He tossed his keys and caught them in one hand. "You were right," he said.

I had a perfectly good excuse for not knowing what he was talking about, at least for a few fuzzy-headed moments. I'd just turned down the kind of job offer other chefs can only dream of, the job offer I had desperately wanted just days before. Yet suddenly, none of it seemed to matter. Not as much as feeling deep down inside that I'd done the right thing.

"Right about what?" I asked Gus.

"Oh, come on now!" He tried to sound as if he were exasperated, but Gus couldn't hide the smile that split his doughy face. "Just thought I'd come by and tell you we did some poking around, talked to some friends of the deceased. Ben Newcomb was left-handed, all right."

In a flash, I remembered the way he picked up his fork, and the way he made sure to sit down at the Terminal so that his elbow wouldn't poke into the person seated next to him.

"She was so upset, she never even thought of it," I said.

Gus chuckled. "All she was worried about was how she'd get more sympathy and more votes out of a husband who killed himself than she would if he was a felon who left town. I'm heading over there now to surprise her. You want to come along?"

"Nah." I glanced back toward the Terminal and then, over to the front of the Irish store when Declan stepped outside. "I'm going to stay here. Thanks!"

Gus put two fingers to his forehead and gave me a little salute before he drove away.

"Another cop after you?" Declan asked when he walked up.

"There are no cops after me, not Gus, not anybody."

He carried an Irish store gift bag and he shifted it from one hand to the other. "What about Tony?"

"What about Tony?"

"What are you going to tell him? You know, about going out with him."

I pretended I had to think about it. "What I'm going to tell him is that he's a great guy and I like him. As a friend. Then I'm going to tell him that I'm already spoken for."

Declan's dark brows rose. So did the corners of his mouth. "Someone I know?"

I slipped my arm through his. "I'm pretty sure."

He slipped his other arm around my waist. "Glad to hear it. And now we can celebrate."

Declan led me into the restaurant and into the room where his family was seated. He must have called Sophie and told her he was on his way, because she was there, too, and so were Misti and Inez and George.

"What's up?" I asked him.

Rather than answer, he pulled a bottle of champagne out of the bag he carried and popped the cork. "I have news," he said nice and loud so that everyone could hear him. "I've just been going over some paperwork in regard to Rocky's estate." He reached into the bag and handed me an envelope.

"What is it?" I asked him.

"Open it" was his only answer.

I did and what I found made my jaw drop. "It can't be," I said, looking over the official paper. Rocky couldn't have . . . she didn't . . ."

"She did!" Apparently, Sophie was in on the secret, because she gave me a bear hug.

"She left you this, too." Declan handed me a handwritten note.

Dear Laurel, it said. *Pacifique, it means "peace," and that is what I've found here on my land. Now it is time for me to pass that peace on to someone else, someone I know will love this place as much as I do. I know you are not a farmer! You do not need to be. Perhaps you can putter in the small garden near the barn and grow the herbs for your fabulous cooking. May you have as many beautiful mornings, glorious days, and starlit nights there as I have always had. I give you this place and this peace with all my heart, Laurel. I give you this, a home.*

Recipes

QUICK CASSOULET

Traditional cassoulet recipes call for many more ingredients and much more fussing, but when time is of the essence and you need a hearty meal fast, you can't beat this quick version. To round out the meal, serve with French bread and a green salad.

1 tablespoon vegetable oil
2 carrots, diced
2 stalks celery, diced
1 small onion, diced
2 cloves garlic, chopped
½ pound smoked sausage, sliced
1 (15-ounce) can kidney beans, rinsed and drained

   1 (15-ounce) can cannellini beans, rinsed and
     drained
   1 (14.5-ounce) can diced tomatoes, drained
   2 bay leaves
   1 teaspoon thyme
   ½ teaspoon salt
   ¼ teaspoon ground pepper
   Chopped fresh parsley to sprinkle on each serving if
     you desire

Heat oil in a large skillet. Add carrots, celery, onion, and
garlic. Cook and stir until onion is transparent. Add sausage and cook to brown.

Add beans and tomatoes, season with bay leaves, thyme,
salt, and pepper. Cover and reduce heat to low. Simmer 10
minutes or until veggies are tender.

Remove bay leaves before serving and sprinkle with
chopped fresh parsley.

Serves four.

TARTINES

*Tartines are the ultimate sandwich, and there is
only one secret to creating them . . . use really
good ingredients. You really don't need a recipe
to make fabulous tartines. Just follow this simple
blueprint.*

Use really good, country-style bread. Cut it in thick slices.

Add a spreadable ingredient (butter, tapenade, pesto,
hummus, etc.)—anything that suits your tastes and the
flavors of your other ingredients.

Add whatever else you choose—chicken, cheese, meats, eggs. All these ingredients should be already cooked.

Pop your tartines in the oven or under the broiler long enough to heat through.

Enjoy!

IF YOU ENJOYED *FRENCH FRIED*, TURN THE
PAGE FOR A BITE OF

Irish Stewed

THE FIRST BOOK IN THE ETHNIC EATS SERIES.
CURRENTLY AVAILABLE IN PAPERBACK FROM
BERKLEY PRIME CRIME

"I can explain."

At my side, Sophie Charnowski pressed her small, plump hands together and shifted from one sneaker-clad foot to the other. The nearest streetlight flickered off, then on again, and in its anemic light, I saw perspiration bead on her forehead. "It's like this, you see, Laurel."

"Oh, I see, all right." Good thing I was wearing my Brian Atwood snakeskin ballet flats. In heels, I would have tripped on the pitted sidewalk when I spun away from the building in front of us and the railroad tracks just beyond. When I pinned short, round Sophie with a look, I meant to make her shake in her shoes, and it gave me a rush of satisfaction to realize the ol' daggers from my blue eyes still carried all the punch I intended. Sophie flicked out her tongue to touch her lips, then swallowed hard.

While she was at it, I stabbed one finger toward the train

station and the sign that hung above the door that declared the place SOPHIE'S TERMINAL AT THE TRACKS.

"This isn't what I expected," I said.

Sophie rubbed her hands together. "I know that. Really, I do. I can only imagine how you must feel."

"No." I cut her off before she could say anything else ignorant and insulting. "You can't possibly imagine how I feel. I just drove all the way to Ohio from California. Because you told me—"

"I wanted it to be a surprise." Sophie was a full eight inches shorter than my five foot nine, and as round as I am slender. She had the nerve to look up at me through the shock of silvery bangs that hung over her forehead. Believe me, the hairstyle wasn't a fashion statement. When I picked Sophie up at her small, neat bungalow so we could drive across Hubbard and she could show me the restaurant, I had the distinct feeling I'd just woken her from an after-dinner nap. "I knew once you saw the place—"

"Once I saw the place!" Was that my voice echoing against the old train station and bouncing around the semi-gentrified neighborhood with its bookstore, its coffee shop, its beauty salon, and gift boutiques?

I was way past caring. "Sophie, you told me—"

"That I'm having my knee replaced tomorrow. Yes." She took a funny sort of half step and pulled up short, one hand automatically shooting down to her right knee. She kept it there, a not-so-subtle reminder of the pain she'd told me was her constant companion. "And that I need someone to help out while I'm laid up. Someone to run the restaurant."

"Which isn't the restaurant it's supposed to be."

"Well, really, it is." A grin made her look so darned impish, I almost forgave the lies she'd been feeding me for years.

Almost.

"The Terminal at the Tracks has been a neighborhood gathering place for going on forty years now," she told me, and don't think I didn't notice the way she rushed to get the words out before I could stop her cold. "I always loved it here. We used to stop for breakfast on Sunday mornings after church. And after our Tuesday bowling league, we'd always get a bite to eat here. Only these days . . ." This time when she caressed her knee, she added a long-suffering sigh. "Well, I'm not doing very much bowling these days. But that doesn't change how I feel about this neighborhood. It's got the feel of history to it, don't you think?" Instead of giving me a chance to answer, she drew in a long, deep breath and let it out slowly while she swiveled her gaze from the train station to the tracks behind it and the boarded-up factory beyond.

"When I had the opportunity to buy the Terminal fifteen years ago, I just jumped at it. So there's my name up there on the sign." Sophie made a brisk *ta-da* sort of motion in that direction. "And here I am." She pointed at her own broad bosom. "And now . . ." It was spring and almost nine, which meant it was already dark. That didn't keep me from seeing the rapturous look that brightened Sophie's brown eyes and brought out the dimples in her pudgy cheeks. "And now here you are, too. So you see, everything is just as it's supposed to be."

Really? I was supposed to buy into this philosophical, all's-right-with-the-world horse hockey?

My pulse quickened and my blood pressure would have shot to the ceiling had we been indoors instead of outside in front of the long, low-slung building with a two-story section built in the middle above the main entrance. When that streetlight went off and on again, it winked against the weathered yellow paint and the dark windows of the restaurant.

I hardly noticed the sparkle of the light against the glass.

But then, I was pretty busy seeing red.

I would have leveled Sophie right then and there if she weren't thirty years older than me and limping, to boot. Instead, I followed along when she hobbled to the front door.

"What you did was low, underhanded and dishonest, Sophie," I told her.

"Yes, it was." She didn't sound the least bit penitent. She stuck her key in the front door. "But now that we're here, you'll look around, won't you?"

I should have said no.

I should have put my foot down.

I should have opened my mouth and as so often happens when I do, I should have let what I was thinking pour out of me like the lava that spews from a volcano and incinerates everything in its path.

Why I didn't is as much a mystery now as it was then. I only know that when Sophie pushed open the front door and stepped inside the Terminal at the Tracks, I followed along.

"Welcome." She touched a hand to a light switch and the fixture directly over our heads turned on.

Sophie beamed a smile all around.

I did not share in her enthusiasm. In fact, I took one look around the entryway of the Terminal at the Tracks, and a second, and a third.

That's pretty much when I had to remind myself to snap my mouth shut.

What I could see—at least here in the fifteen-by-fifteen

entryway where customers waited for their tables—was a mishmash of kitschy faux Victorian, everything from teddy bears in puffy-sleeved gowns to posters advertising things like unicycles and mustache wax.

And then there was the lace.

Doilies and rickrack and bunting.

Oh my.

Brand spanking new, it would have been overblown and downright dreadful. With fifteen years of service under its belt, the lace was yellow and bedraggled. The teddy bear propped on the old rolltop desk that also served as a hostess station looked as if it could use an airing, and what had once been a magnificent floor made of wide, hardwood planks was scratched and dull.

"I knew you'd love it as much as I do," Sophie purred.

Fortunately at that moment, a train rolled by, not twenty feet from the back of the restaurant, and the place shook the way LA had in the last earthquake I remembered. My sternum vibrated. My bones rattled.

By the time the train was gone and my body was done with its rockin' and rollin', I pretended I didn't even remember Sophie's last comment.

"There's something special I need to show you." She latched on to the sleeve of the silk shirttail tee I wore with skinny jeans and tugged me toward a glass counter with a cash register set on it.

"Right here." Sophie said, and tapped the glass next to the cash register. That's when her smile fell and her silvery brows knit. "Well, it was here." She chewed her lower lip. "It's always here. I must have left it"—she waved in some indeterminate direction—"in the office. I must have left it in the office when I took the day's receipts in there to file.

You know, on Saturday, the last day the restaurant was open before I had to close." Another puppy dog look. "Because of my knee, you know. And my surgery tomorrow."

Sophie gave the counter another pat. "The receipt spike," she finally explained. "You know, the thin, pointy thing where we stick the receipts—"

"After they're rung up on the register." I'd worked in enough restaurants in my day; I knew exactly what she was talking about.

"This one is special," Sophie confided. "About yay high"—she held her hands ten inches apart—"and made completely of brass. It was Grandpa Majtkowski's. From his bakery shop in Poland. He brought it with him when he came to this country back in 1913. Imagine that, he came with one suitcase, one change of clothes, and less than twenty dollars in his pocket, and he still thought it was important to bring that receipt spike with him. And no wonder! It was all he had of home, all he had of the business he worked so many years to build, and—"

A tap on the front door saved me from any more of the history lesson.

Sophie didn't seem to mind. In fact, when she looked toward the front entrance, she grinned.

"It's Declan!" Quicker than a woman with a sore knee should have been able to move, she scooted over and opened the door. "It's Declan," she said again, and she moved back to allow a man to step into the Terminal.

Let's get something straight here—I had spent the last six years of my life working as a personal chef to Meghan Cohan. Yeah, *that* Meghan Cohan, the Hollywood megastar. I wasn't just used to catering to the culinary whims of the Beautiful People, I was comfortable rubbing elbows with them. When she was working on a film, I traveled with Meghan. All over the world. When she was bored, she'd take me along when she jetted to her place in Maui. Or the one in Tuscany. Or the villa in the south of France. I was in charge of Meghan's diet regimen, and her parties and the late-night soirees that sometimes ended up getting talked about in *Vogue* or *Elle* or *Cosmo*.

Meghan was powerful. She was gorgeous. And she allowed only powerful and gorgeous men into her circle.

I wasn't sure who this Declan guy was, but I knew that one look, and Meghan would have welcomed him with open arms.

Tall.

Dark.

I won't say handsome because let's face it, that's a cliché and Declan's looks put him far beyond platitudes.

His hair was a little too long and tousled just enough that had we been back in LA, I would have suspected he'd just come from some tony salon. He had an angular face defined by a dusting of dark whiskers, and he wore jeans and sneakers and a black leather jacket over a red plaid flannel shirt. Untucked. All of it was casual enough while at the same time it sent the message that whatever else Declan was, he was comfortable in his own skin.

None of which mattered in the least bit.

Not to me, anyway.

No matter how handsome the locals might happen to be, I'd already decided there was no way I was staying.

Declan came inside the Terminal and closed the door behind hm.

"I saw the light on," he said to Sophie, "and no one's usually here this late at night. I just wanted to make sure everything was all right."

"Aren't you just the best neighbor ever!" Sophie twin-
kled like a teenager. "Declan's from the Irish store." She
looked out the window, toward the store, and I saw the
lighted windows of the gift shop that was across the street
and kitty-corner to the restaurant. From here, it was impossible to see exactly what was in the display windows on
either side of the front door, but there was no mistaking
the crisp green colors touched with a smattering of orange,
or the wooden sign that hung above the front door, a gigantic green shamrock.

"Of course, everything's fine. I was just showing off the
place." She closed a hand over the sleeve of his jacket and
piloted him nearer. "Declan Fury, this is Laurel Inwood."

Add a thousand-watt smile to that description of Declan.
And a handshake that was warm and firm enough to send
the message that he was no-nonsense, practical, and far
more sure of himself than 99 percent of the actors (yeah,
even the ones who play tough guys in the movies) Meghan
had introduced me to over the years.

"So, you're finally here." Declan had a baritone voice that
managed to caress even the most ordinary greeting. "I know
your aunt's been looking forward to your arrival."

I'm afraid my smile wasn't nearly as broad as his. Or as
genuine. I refused to look at Sophie when I said, "She's not
really my aunt."

"Oh." Declan pulled his hand back to his side, not as
embarrassed as he was simply curious. "I guess I'm confused because Sophie always refers to you as her niece."

This time, I did take a second to slide Sophie a look. I
wasn't surprised to see something like contrition in her
pursed lips and her downcast eyes.

Which didn't mean I believed it was genuine.

"That makes me wonder why Sophie was talking about me at all."

Contrition be damned! Just like that, Sophie was back to her ol' grinning self. "You know we're all just as proud as punch of everything you've accomplished." She patted my arm. "Laurel's famous," she told Declan, and then, because she apparently saw the sparks shooting from my eyes, she was quick to amend the statement to, "Well, practically famous."

Maybe Declan was also a better actor than most of the ones I'd met out in LA. He pretended not to notice the undercurrent of annoyance and avoidance that flowed back and forth between me and Sophie. In fact, when he turned back to me, it was with a smile sleek enough to send prickles up my spine.

Not that it mattered, I reminded myself.

Since I wasn't staying.

"Well," he said, giving me a quick once-over from toes to top of head and apparently approving of what he saw since his smile stayed firmly in place, "it's nice to know there will be a practically famous chef holding down the fort while her aunt is in the hospital."

He had a short memory.

And he smelled like bay rum and limes.

I shook away the thought and the way the scent always made me think of tropical islands and warm sea breezes.

"Sophie's younger sister, Nina, was my foster mother for four years," I told him. "So you see, Sophie and I, we're really not related."

His smile never wavered. "Except you don't have to share DNA to be family, do you?"

"I'm just showing Laurel around," Sophie said, and she

wound an arm through mine. "You know, because I'll be gone six weeks and someone needs to run the place."

"That doesn't mean that someone is going to be me." I untangled myself from Sophie's grip when I said this, the better to look her in the eye so she knew I meant business.

"We obviously need to talk, me and Laurel," she told Declan. "There might be some rocky road ice cream in the freezer, and I don't know about you, but I think heart-to-heart talks always go better over rocky road."

Declan stepped toward the doorway that led into the main part of the restaurant. The woodwork around it was painted dusty blue, like the trim on the outside of the station, and there were lace curtains in the doorway that were tied back on either side with purple ribbon. He poked a thumb over his shoulder into the darkened room. "If you like, I can take a look around before you settle down for your heart-to-heart."

"No need!" Sophie's warm laugh bounced up to the ceiling fans that swirled overhead. "You know this is a safe neighborhood."

Declan leaned forward just enough to take a peek beyond the entryway and into the pitch-dark restaurant. "Maybe so, but it is late and—"

"And you need to get back to whatever it was you were doing before you took the time to come over here and check on an old lady like me." Sophie led him back to the front door. "A good-lookin' guy like you, you must have better things to do on a warm spring night."

Declan tipped his head, and when he smiled, the air between us sizzled. "Then, good night, ladies."

"Isn't he the dreamiest?" Sophie giggled once he was gone.

Her back was to the door. Otherwise, I wondered if she'd still think he was dreamy when she realized that Declan didn't go across the street to the Irish store. In fact, he walked along the front of the Terminal, turned at the far corner, and headed into the side parking lot.

Once he was out of sight, I turned back to Sophie just in time to see her shuffle her sneakers. "Rocky road?" she offered.

I let go a sigh of pure frustration. "You're not going to bribe me with ice cream, Sophie. I told you, I don't appreciate being lied to. All those years, you came to California to visit and you showed me and Nina—"

"Pictures of the restaurant." She looked up at me through those unruly bangs. "Yes, I know."

"But it wasn't this restaurant."

Sophie's cheeks flushed pink, but I wasn't about to let that keep me from saying my piece.

"You showed us photographs of a lovely place out in the country. Linen tablecloths, soft lighting, a fabulous wine cellar. That's the place I thought I was going to be helping out with while you were recuperating. This place—"

"This place is all I have."

Yes, her comment would have tugged at my heartstrings.

If I had heartstrings.

Unfortunately for Sophie and lucky for me, I didn't.

That didn't mean I was completely insensitive. "I said I'd take you to the hospital tomorrow morning, and I will," I told her.

"And you said you'd be running the restaurant after that."

"It's not going to work."

Her shoulders drooped. "I know. I guess I knew all

along. But still, you're here. Let me show you around." Her limp more pronounced than ever, she walked through that lace-curtained doorway and turned on the lights in the main dining room.

What I saw was pretty much what I expected.

Five, six, seven, eight . . . I counted . . . tables lined up against the far wall next to the windows that looked out over the railroad tracks. None of them covered with linen. Four tables to my left and two doorways, one marked KITCHEN and the other, OFFICE. To my right, six more tables, more lace, more kitsch, and once I skirted the jut-out wall that marked the back of the waiting area, windows that looked out at the street and gave a bird's-eye view of the light that shone on that green shamrock across the way.

And one customer.

I froze and looked at the man lying facedown on one of the tables.

"Uh, Sophie." She was already shuffling back to the kitchen in search of ice cream, and when I called out, Sophie hitch-stepped back the other way. "There's a guy here."

"A guy? That's impossible. That's—"

She got as far as where I stood and she froze, too, looking where I did, at the table against the wall where a man in a brown jacket was slumped, his head on his arm.

And that receipt spike of Grandpa Majtkowski's sticking out of the back of his neck.

"Oh my goodness!" Sophie wailed.

If I didn't act fast, I knew I'd have another problem on my hands, so I pulled over the nearest chair and plunked Sophie down in it before I dared to close in on the man in the brown jacket.

From this angle, there wasn't much to see. In the light of the faux Tiffany chandelier directly above the table, his neck looked as pale as a hooked fish. Well, except for the thin river of blood that originated at the spot where the receipt spike was plunged into his spine.

I dared to put a finger on his neck, but even before I did, I knew I wouldn't find a pulse. His skin was ice and there were tinges of blue behind his ears and on the fingers of the hand that hung loosely at his side.

I fumbled for the phone in my pocket and dialed 911, hoping that when the dispatcher answered, I could make the words form in a mouth that felt suddenly as if it had been packed with sand.

And all I could think was the one thing I knew I wouldn't dare say to Sophie or to the cops—this gave a whole new meaning to the word *terminal*.

Kylie Logan is also the national bestselling author of the League of Literary Ladies Mysteries and the Chili Cook-off Mysteries.